# USER

# USER

## Bruce Benderson

MUSWELL
PRESS

First published in the US by Dutton,
part of the Penguin Group in 1994
This edition published by Muswell Press in 2023

Typeset in Bembo by M Rules
Printed and bound by
CPI Group (UK) Ltd, Croydon CR0 4YY.

A CIP catalogue record for this book is
available from the British Library

ISBN: 9781739638207
eISBN: 9781739638214

Muswell Press
London N6 5HQ
www.muswell-press.co.uk

FOR

Clay, Carlos C., James, Zack, Eddie M., Angel,
Carlos, Tony R., Angel, Cisco, Carlos, Jarratt,
Frenchy, Izod, Freddie, J.R., Sandro C., Sugar
Bear, E.T., Tallulah, Nico, Pasquale, Rubber
Band, Dice, Legs, Murphy, Ed R., Jason, Carlos,
Angel, Lucas, Willie, Hector, Scorpio, Paris,
Hammer Love, Bam Bam, George, Peter, Frank,
Johnnie, Alex, Lionheart, Arsenio, Yvette, Little
Angel, Shady Louie, Mike, Carlos R., Alberto,
Keith, Green Eyes, Dennis, Antonio, Eric,
Joey, Che Che, Chino, Tina, Coco, The Kid,
Cheyenne, Ramon, Dr. Stephen Feld, Samantha,
Hector Xtravaganza, Francisco, Sandy, Consuela
Cosmetic, George A., Stuart, Douglas, Roxanne
Spillane, Pepper, and Beverly.

*My thanks to Ursule Molinaro, Kevin Mulroy, and Matthew Carnicelli for their advice on this manuscript.*

*To Anthony Colon, for his quiet courage and wisdom.*

*My gratitude to Joey P'tail, Kathy, Mayler, and the staff at T.'s.*

He clasped a corpse: a body so cold
that it froze him . . .

—*Là-bas*, J.-K. HUYSMANS

# Introduction

This novel represents a benchmark in my life. Primarily, it was the only way someone like me could become involved in politics. It was, in fact, the "political" gesture I'd always intended to make; the principal backup to my combative disdain for movements, crusades, and the two-party system; a project whose goal was to make the inarticulate members of the lowest economic sector articulate, and to bring the minds and hearts of the poorest into the bookstores of the educated classes. It was, in other words, a determined attempt to force those who thought of the people of the street as nothing but a hassle to be avoided to stop for the first time in their lives and listen to what these people were saying. (It also was a way to assuage my guilt about not voting in the last two elections.)

My "dream" took several years to accomplish. During that time, I certainly enjoyed the "research." From 1985 to 1995, I was spending five nights a week in the still unrenovated Times Square at the hustler and drag bars that proliferated before the big upscaling—or "Disneyfication"—of Times Square. After my first book about these experiences, a collection of short stories entitled *Pretending to Say No*

(Penguin/Plume, 1990), was released, I was often told I was exploiting the people who were my subject matter because their income and education were so far beneath mine. There were even those who couldn't imagine any approach not wholly journalistic and who would assume I'd spent my time in those places with a concealed tape recorder. Others, who could at least envision my participating in that world in a guise other than detached journalist, still wondered if I'd behaved any better than the typical colonizer, who profits from the disenfranchised by packaging what's valuable about them and marketing it to the bourgeoisie.

The truth was that I was wholly invested in the dangerous world of Times Square. I was a denizen—but a denizen with a different pedigree. Beginning in 1985, just as crack was born and had begun to take over the streets of New York, I'd walked head-on into those scenes of chaotic pleasure. I'd shunned neither the drugs nor the sexual opportunities I'd found there as a "john." But unlike my sex-and-drug partners, I often had something to do or somewhere to be the day after a night of drug-fueled sex—a piece of writing expected by a publisher or a freelance job in the world of New York media. I was walking a scary tightrope strung between the underclass world of the street and the middle-class world of work, and I would return to my world just in time to keep from becoming a permanent member of the exiled class. My partners, most of whom hailed from the South Bronx, had nothing but the resources of the street to fall back on.

This difference did not keep me from forming meaningful, sometimes lasting relationships with the people of the street, one of whom, a homeless Puerto Rican boy, I ended up adopting. As can be clearly sensed in my first book, at the beginning I could only portray Times Square as a comedy of manners in which the value systems of a middle-class person looking for pleasure—my main character—clashed, often humorously, with the lifestyles of those who provided that pleasure with their bodies. But for the next book—the one you are about to read—I took the formula further and developed a way to relate to the speech of my street characters and bring their struggles, voices, dreams, conversations, and life stories more and more to the fore. The middle-class characters diminished to supporting roles.

I built the world depicted in this novel not from surveillance tapes, but from the notes I scrawled *in media res*—on napkins, matchbook covers, and on the backs of receipts, which I tossed into an old suitcase each night upon returning from Times Square. Then, extracting the notes made on the run one by one, without any prior plan of order or structure, I built my new cosmology from scratch, fragment by fragment, with the goal of creating a loving, engaged valentine to old Times Square.

This process came to a discouraging halt in the late '90s, when all the bars I frequented were shut down by Mayor Giuliani's administration. Many of the buildings were torn down, and Times Square became a sterile, manufactured, police-monitored evocation of the past with overpriced, mediocre restaurants for families of tourists. My world had ended, and by some miracle, I'd emerged from it without once being arrested or ever becoming totally addicted to drugs; but it felt as if a rug had been pulled out from under my feet. At first, I sought that world elsewhere, which was the reason I took an assignment from an online journal about brothels in Eastern Europe. That project eventually brought me to Romania, a quest that ultimately resulted in a long memoir about my passion for a homeless Romanian rent boy entitled *The Romanian: Story of an Obsession* (Penguin/Tarcher, 2006).

3

Today feels like an optimum moment for the re-release of *User*, because our entire culture is in the throes of a radical transformation. Through the clamor of dissenting voices, I can hear minorities insisting on self-naming and rejecting the definitions of an identity previously foisted upon them by the ruling order. Such changes have affected me by making my central motivation the preservation of the past. My great fear is that the utopic trends we are experiencing may cause some people to succumb to the temptation of rewriting history. Those born after me may never learn that old Times Square once hosted an underclass population that served as the only social space outside their ghetto. Today, my fervent hope is that you'll be as touched and changed by getting to know this now scattered population as I was.

Bruce Benderson
New York City, 2023

# I

Mrs. Buster Huxton III, first name Sofia, an eighty-six-year-old Portuguese, still maintains an elegant triplex over her porno theater on Eighth Avenue. The discovery of her world lies beyond a musty, rubber-backed velvet curtain that must be swept aside upon entering. As the eyes slowly adapt to darkness, sweating walls become visible. You fumble down the aisle, using the sticky top edges of the leather seats as a guide, then slide into a row, your shoe likely to make an imprint in some viscous liquid.

In the second row are men with thinning hair and defeated shoulders, about to watch a dancer, whose name is Apollo, mount the stage in a black posing strap. Lit only by footlights, the room is orangey dark, and the lone silhouettes of the scattered spectators punctuate the gloom. In a moment the music will blast through scratchy speakers; the dancer, a pale-skinned mulatto with a mournful mouth, will leap barefoot onto the stage and lithely slip in and out of a few geometric poses. Then he will drop back onto the stale carpet and zigzag down the aisle to those few stranded men, to ask each under the cover of the blaring music if he might like a private show.

*

*Call me Apollo—that dancer you watched in the shadows and said was mulatto—and you, my date, are somebody in the theater I was lucky or pushy enough to talk into a private show. Thirty's the price I told you, but that will only get me two or three bags of dope this time of night. I only got one foil of crushed-up Dilaudid that I got from a doctor I tricked with. But what about cigarettes and a quart of beer for later?*

*I already know how to play you into coughing up another twenty. At just the moment when I say I don't got enough to get back to Connecticut will be when you feel most off-guard. Right after you've shot your load, in other words. At this moment I imagine you being as high as I am. There is no explanation for this. Maybe it's just being so close to your face. It's that weird feeling of my eyes about to roll back as the Dilaudid races through my veins to begin the lick at my brain.*

In a room below the stage, in the basement, a head keeps bobbing between Apollo's splayed thighs, the taste of rubber blocking out the smell of sweat, mixed with the odor of mildew and cracking vinyl. Up and down the lips and tongue glide, while the bridge of the nose butts dully against him. Each dark, sparkling wave of Dilaudid hitting his brain, reversed by the teasing tongue on body parts.

*This must be cozy as Mrs. Huxton feels in her high-class apartment above the theater. I saw it one time. It's all carpet. There's a silver tea service on the first floor in the sitting room. Polished sparkling furniture in the chandelier light and her lifting the control to that cable television . . . Nothing in this four-story building on Eighth Avenue except the theater and the basement, topped by Mrs. Huxton's three luxury floors. Her middle-aged kids are begging her to sell out and move somewhere safe. But seems keeping up her husband's business, which started as a tiny striptease joint on this very block in the 1930s and can't pull in much now but is worth several million in real estate, became her thing. They told me the evening he finally croaked, and the corpse had to be carried down the stairs past the entrance, they switched the lights on and told guys with their pants down to leave, gave rain checks. It was years before I was even born . . .*

Outside this room, in the dank corridor lit by one bulb, a fat man in pale clothes lurches by the entrance to a dingy lavatory. His sulfur gaze fixes on a dancer in a stretched-out jock strap hoisting a granite leg to the sink to wash off a thick foot, the calf of the other leg bulging in a big knot. In the faint, purplish light, dark hollows of muscle cleave his bending back. He lifts his head to gaze in a dull come-on at the fat man fumbling toward him and parting his lips in a soft popping sound like some marine creature.

Farther away, where the corridor rises in two steps leading to a fire door, crouches a boy shakily trying to light a match. The head of the first match disengages and sparks into the darkness, giving a glimpse of a bristling red crew cut, waxy skin. Then another match flares, revealing an opaline glass stem phosphorescent with smoke, pursing lips, and pinched features. He sucks in his breath as the end of the pipe glows brighter and the match fades.

In the dressing room, in front of a decrepit mirror that is missing bulbs, sits a downy-lipped teenager with large, shiny curls and grimy hands, squinting almost as if in performance in the dim light at the open math book in his lap.

Meanwhile, in the room with the so-called mulatto, the grunts of arousal have become more manifest. The gentleman's hand jerks at the wan penis that sticks from the open zipper of his pants, groanings occur, and an ejaculation hits the black wall. The lips spasm around the half-erect member of the drugged dancer and then loosen. He sits up and clears his throat, then wipes his mouth with the back of his hand; he tucks in his shirt and zips up, buckles his belt, and fishes into his pocket for the thirty dollars he had ready ...

*... My cock shrinking from the peeled bag that I toss on the floor with the others, speaking quick but soft so as not to ruin the mood, going heavy with the lingo of the street that puts the fear in some of you, and putting myself between you and the door, your only means of escape:*

*"You took too long, daddy, I got to take a cab to the station ... man. I got to hit New Haven tonight on that last bus. Come on, I said, now pass me another twenty!"*

*I'll go on and on without budging. The Dilaudid's a drug for cancer patients that kills pain and tranquilizes, but I can get chatty and speedy from its rushes. I know that this must sound very flipped for a john who has come and now wants out of this little room with me blocking the door. But nobody'll probably hear should you call out ... And believe me, in Mrs. Huxton's world scenes like this can turn into a bad dream. Even a big guy who is outraged will think twice before pushing this situation to the max. There might be an argument as you fumble too long in another pocket for more money ... But even if you decide to stand up to me in the tiny room, I won't take my eyes off your face. The Dilaudid gives me a strange kind of courage as you flip back and forth between decisions.*

No one else is there to witness the standoff. The fat man wandering in the hallway and the dancer at the lavatory sink had disappeared together into another stall. At the sounds of agitation, the crack smoker and the curly-haired boy with the math book took the stairs two at a time. But perhaps in a room three floors above, sequestered from Eighth Avenue by concrete grillwork and ventilation ducts, an old woman shifts quaveringly in her sleep.

The so-called live show is over now. A tepid fantasy film colors the screen: the bedroom of a tract house somewhere in Southern California, an acrylic painting of a sunset seascape color-coordinated to the violet bedspread upon which loll two scraggly-haired teenagers whose locked limbs are at odds with the overlay of frantic disco music ...

In the back by the curtained entrance, Casio, an ex-gang member who's been the bouncer in this place ever since he got out of jail the second time, raises a brow over a dark-circled eye at the sound of the dull thuds coming from the private rooms. *What was that crash?* It could be that one of the boys is giving a trick some trouble. And with all the new construction changing the neighborhood, things have become hot; the authorities are waiting for an excuse to come in and shake the place down. By habit, the bouncer pricks up his vigilant, nocturnal ears, unconsciously compresses into an animal crouch ... perches inwardly on the shot of dope that he did earlier to muster what remains of his old machismo.

But maybe the noise was just a seat slapping into position. Or a middle-aged trick stumbling on a stair. He strains to hear. All he can make out is the synthesized disco of the porno film, an occasional sigh or intake of breath. Then again, the unmistakable sound of a body thudding against a thin wall.

He moves toward the stairs but pauses. He's reluctant to go down there before he decides: which of the five kids going out and coming in high and going out again and coming back in is it?

*Carlos is no problem. He's so doped up he don't want no trouble—a papi-crazy faggot who comes off like a barrio homeboy and'll always back down. And white-one-what's-his-face, Red? Even if thirsted out for rockets he'll crumble up the minute he see my face, 'cause of the time I found him doing that queen behind the movie screen for a toke.*

*But the half-breed nigger always talking crap about that Miss Huxton owns this place and inviting him to teas? Wacky enough to go the whole mile! . . . Oreo cookies're like that. I just might end up having to nix his ass.*

He marches grimly down the stairs with a sense of ailing authority. But the trick with the thinning hair has already dodged Apollo after being pushed against the wall by him, has fled the private room and ducked behind the stairwell.

Out of the private room stumbles the stoned dancer, looking for the vanished green. And what conspires next takes place only in Apollo's mind. For only he could explain what happened in the stairwell: how running into the prematurely aged Casio with his glaring eyes and permanent scowl threw him into a rage—back to the South and shorts and a blackberry patch where he'd had the same feeling of being mistrusted for no good reason . . . had picked up a thorny branch lying on the dirt path and started swinging it . . .

Why the bouncer's snide rictus smile filled him with spite at merely being a serf in the empire of Mrs. Huxton . . .

Until Casio's eye exploded under Apollo's scarred fist. The bouncer careened on his heels and fell back, tipped forward again to regain his balance, then fell back off the stairwell for good. His spine struck the floor in a wet

10

smack, and he lay there with his back askew, while the trick crouched in his hiding place in fascination and dread.

Then Casio's eyes rolled up, back, and his mouth dangled wide open. And he couldn't stop hearing his ears ringing. Apollo the attacker ran down the sweltering street, his fist bleeding and pulsing. A dim shiver must have crept along his sweaty spine as he wondered how badly he had hurt Casio. He headed for a haven from revenge—the transvestite lounge just a few blocks up the avenue.

Tina, the drag-queen owner, was slipping her shoulders out of her three-quarter mink, which she wore to offset her expensive green pants suit, despite the summer heat. It fell into the hands of one of her waiters, who hastily locked it in the storeroom downstairs. At the same time, Tina's index finger swept from the center of her siliconed chest to the door, like a sultan in a low-budget movie banishing a subversive subject. Standing near the door was the shirtless and breathless Apollo, who had no I.D. and whose knuckles showed congealed gashes in the orange light.

With glowering eyes, he held his ground until Tina took a step forward. Then he skulked into the street. Tina's pointing hand unfurled into a flattened palm, which daintily patted her extravagant but provincial coiffure.

"Love the little ones," she quipped, "'cause they're real easy to push around."

The embarrassed fugitive was bumped back into the no man's land of Eighth Avenue, his mind seething with the indignity of being kicked out by an authority-figure queen. He headed north with his clotting fist. But the more he ran, the more his anxiety about what had happened diminished ... Soon he let off steam by kicking over a box. It still held the three bottle caps and the pea that he had set up earlier as a betting game to dupe some German tourists. Leaping shirtless through the polluted, copper-colored mists, he became a smaller and smaller dot. For him, the dot of himself was shrinking so fast that it seemed as obscure as one of tonight's tricks. His high dwindled as he dwindled, and he'd need another shot soon. Especially tonight, after what had happened.

As he moved from block to block, he passed other exiles barred from Tina's, such as Angelo, a tall, rotten-toothed adolescent whose speech was permanently slurred by the rigid jaw of constant crack use, and whose bare toes poked from ripped sneakers. Angelo tried to lure him farther west, promising to get him a deal on a hit, but Apollo kept going, past big Cubby, also bare-chested, covered with tattoos that he claimed told the story of his life in stages, like stations of the cross, and who spit out wisecracks about Apollo's butt and alternately pleaded for a dollar.

A shiny limousine caught up with Apollo and seemed to slow down to his pace. In his mind, it must have been Mrs. Huxton's driver, whom she used for her rare outings or for transports of human and other cargo. For him, Mrs. Huxton was the principle of order in all this chaos, the final authority, even beyond Tina and the cops. She stood with the means and the schedules for things. Her high principles even seemed to regulate the ritual of taking dope, a revolving door she watched him go round and round in. If she'd ordained that he be brought in and punished for what had happened, then maybe he'd have to go; but the limo picked up speed again.

The air made his lungs smart. Tonight, the street stank of something worse than the bar or the theater. They had smelled like bug spray and filthy toilets and stale beer, but the street was perfumed by polluted river water or clothing rotting. He gasped for breath and slouched against a trash can.

The trick from the theater—the cocksucker with thinning hair and defeated shoulders—hadn't given him more money after being knocked against the wall but had pushed past him out of the room with a weird smile on his lips. What was worse was that the money Apollo did get must have fallen out of his posing strap when he pulled his pants on after wasting Casio. There was nothing stuffed in the posing strap or in his pants pockets but a folded square of paper with a pinch of the Dilaudid he'd gotten from the doctor, a freaky M.D. who came straight from the emergency room to the theater during breaks from a nearby hospital. This and the Percodan he sometimes picked up from his friend who had AIDS were Apollo's only pharmaceutical sources of downers.

He surveyed the spacious avenue, which made him feel like a sitting duck. Anybody who didn't keep moving on this strip was obviously hooking, dealing, or looking to cop. Bobbing toward him on scrawny legs like a diseased chicken was Gloves (Georgie Golden Gloves, was that his name?), now and then almost losing his balance to shadowboxing. He was the angel-dust head who always carried around a frayed picture of himself losing a Golden Gloves tournament.

Apollo stomped into the middle of the sidewalk, and Georgie collided with him.

"Listen! I got a problem, I gotta get outta here, lemme stay with a couple dollars," Apollo muttered as Georgie fumbled against him.

13

Apollo crashed against him again with more force, throwing his shoulders into it. But Georgie was numb and answered from the fantasy world of angel dust in the voice of Al Pacino's Scarface:

"I took a little on the side, but I never fucked you, Frank."

"Then gimme a stogie," was how Apollo countered the non sequitur.

But Georgie Golden Gloves was already bobbing up the block.

An aftershock of Dilaudid, jammed in some capillary until now, troughed out a wave of high, and Apollo concentrated on riding it. He let the memory of the theater wash away by thinking of this morning's clever evasion of arrest. It had a shiny coating of triumph from this high perspective.

There he was in "Dark Park" in the Bronx at 5:00 A.M. this morning, trying to cop with no I.D., when the cops stopped him, and he was carrying his blade and his works,

*. . . the two white cops saying we don't want 'em, and the P.R. cop saying give 'em to me, I'll take his ass.*

*So they ran up a warrant check on me, but even though the name was right, the D.O.B. (that stands for date of birth, dork) was wrong. What are you, a black or a Hispanic? I got kids, I sobbed. So they just hit me with a D.A.T.—a desk appearance ticket. And let me go. So where does all the good luck come from, you're wondering? People loving you, praying for you . . .*

He crashed off the doctored memory with the realization that he was reciting it to himself as if he were telling it to somebody important. *Getting ready to tell it is all!* he caught himself philosophizing through the high. But then the departed wave of Dilaudid dropped him on his ass again, and pride about the incident deflated. He yawned and peered with fierce vigilance through the copper light of dilapidated Eighth Avenue.

Mercedes was flouncing across the street. The black transvestite, in an outrageous gold lamé outfit, had halted at the curb and yanked up her top to pop out her breasts, grabbing and squeezing them for him. In the shimmering pollution and from a distance, the image took on an idealized quality.

Glancing quickly both ways, she pulled her miniskirt up and panties down, kept her cock pressed between her dark, sinewy legs, and mimed a pussy dance just for him. The astonished passengers of an Oldsmobile stopped at a red light—theatergoers—clicked shut the locks of their car and lurched forward. Apollo delightedly mimed a jerking-off motion to the queen. It was only for a split second that a collapsed version of what had happened maybe two months—a year?—ago flared up in his mind. He'd been her boyfriend then.

*Kind of. But well, then, one night I needed—something— from her purse . . .*

*All right! It was fix money, and when she found out, well . . .*

She'd come looking for him on Ninth Avenue . . . And he'd had the bad luck of being in the act of rapping to another queen when she spotted him . . . *"Mercedes, really, I woulda asked you."*

*"I'll fucking cut you, you son of a bitch!" reaching into her purse.*

*"No, come on now, put that shit away, there's cops around."*

Mercedes's big hand with its inch-long fingernails was whipping the gleaming blade from side to side. First it slashed open his shirt, then made some long cuts across his chest. She kept reaching for his face, but he fended her off, let her cut his forearm instead.

15

Winded, she let the knife drop to her side, her eyes streaming with tears, running the mascara. Her straightened hair had come undone and was plastered by sweat to her face.

It wasn't so much being cut by a queen in public but noticing that one silicone-plumped cheek had fallen slightly below her prominent cheekbone that curled his fingers into a hard fist. It hit the cheek and her mouth, chipped part of a front tooth out . . .

*"Is this guy giving you trouble, little lady?"*

*"Yes, officer, he tried to rape me." Her head was bowed, her hand clasping her bloody mouth. She was sobbing.*

*"Against the wall! Put your arms up!"*

*"Can't you see it's a guy, officer! That's no lady!"*

*"Keep your mouth shut!"*

The cop found his works and a bag right away, so he was sent to Rikers, bleeding like a pig, and waited three months without bail.

The queen was gone. The space where she had appeared across the street was now a dull blot of dirty air, tinged with red neon from the porno marquee above it. With the sensual certainty of still being a little high, Apollo reassured himself he no longer had feelings for her, or anybody else on the street. The thought itself was anesthetic, so he slipped hypnotically into it, probing the dimensions of that lack of feeling.

He remembered a conversation about johns with another hustler from Tina's. The hustler moved his out-turned palm up and down the length of an imaginary wall as if he were lathing it. The wall permanently divided "them" with the money from "us" out here. *They're fake,* he kept repeating about the johns. *They don't exist,* he kept saying. *But us, we're out here, we're down by law . . .*

A sentimental image of the boy—ripped jeans, big ass, blue tank top—flashed into Apollo's stoned head. A white boy who was also hustling and doing dope. And then one night—

*What happened? Oh, yeah. I ended up in bed with my buddy's john. Hee, hee, hee.*

A tiny smirk crossed Apollo's lips. He marveled at his wispishness. He complacently pictured his own naturally lithe body and imagined steamy breath, those hungry caresses.

*I didn't plan to get over on ole buddy like that. But let's face it that the drug acts like a wild aphrodisiac sometimes. People who say that you don't like sex on dope don't know their ass from their elbow. I can really turn a trick out some days when I'm high. So the john kicked him loose. And then moved me in.*

A burst of breaking glass! Apollo and the john leaping out of bed in the middle of the night. The tank top and the ripped jeans! Apollo's old, good buddy (who'd gotten skinny, lost his big ass) had shattered the kitchen window, was crouched by it.

*Yeah, but had I already moved my things into the john's house by then? Yeah, that must be how I lost that jacket . . .*

Apollo's thoughts flipped back once again to the guy's working tongue, his inner thighs tensing and relaxing with wetness, before—crash! . . . *My ole buddy has him facing the refrigerator and is trying to tie him to it. The john's looking at me over the turns of rope with pleading eyes, like why don't I help him? What the fuck am I supposed to do? You don't treat a hustler like that to make him your favorite boy and then dump him for another. "Just don't hurt him," I told my ole buddy. But I had to let him lie in the bed he made . . .*

\*

17

After the john dropped Apollo for not protecting him, Apollo shortchanged the same hustler by buying him a bundle—ten bags of dope—and then cutting it with talc and baby laxative. Then he made a vow to fly solo, which he'd kept to this day. It was an obvious mistake to trust anybody in this world of sudden calamities and quick solutions. As if in confirmation of this idea, he saw Angelo, that crackhead he'd passed earlier, lurching out of the all-night fruit-and-vegetable store across the street with a bag-sheathed quart of beer. A tall, dead-faced guy in a stocking cap stumbled next to him.

Apollo squinted at them through the copper light, which seemed suddenly to have thickened, making everything look distorted, as if through gelatin. The cap had a shimmering white X on it, but it was too hot for a hat. *So this guy is obviously worried about his hair looking nappy.*

Through the rubbery light, Apollo watched Angelo snake a brotherly arm around the guy's shoulder. *But that's the dude Angelo said killed his cousin!*

Apollo momentarily wondered how Angelo could hang with a guy that murdered relatives. Then that thought too began to shimmer like gelatin. *Something about Angelo's cousin doing codeine that night? And Angelo said the guy slipped eye drops in his cousin's drink that put him over the edge. A dude who always wears a big stocking cap that said X.*

He squinted again. The *X*-cap was passing a few bills to Angelo, who palmed them quickly.

*But is that really the one he said's the murderer?*

Either the guy seemed like somebody Angelo imagined had killed his cousin—and he'd probably imagined it when he was high—or the guy really was the killer. But now that Angelo was high he didn't remember it. Or maybe wasn't thinking about it. If you asked him about it now, his eyes would dim, he'd say, "Hey, you know why I know it wasn't him? 'Cause I was with them all that night!" 'Cause the guy with the X-cap was his buddy, kicking in bucks toward another bag of rockets.

Apollo considered bolting across the street and trying to pry one of the bills out of Angelo. But he wondered how the X-cap guy would take it. That's the way things worked out here. One minute you slithered your arm around a shoulder, the next you vowed to off somebody.

*What's a friend anyway but he gives you something? What a fool you are to give that to somebody. And knowing he does it makes you feel please don't deny me 'cause I'm so hungry! It makes you feel low, so you just grab for it, it shows more balls. 'Cause both of 'em are games, pretending I care, pretending I . . . don't care . . .*

Apollo condescendingly watched the unholy couple moving up the block until they too were swallowed by the gelatinous light. His thoughts strayed to the one time he'd admitted having feelings for somebody and had gone to jail for it. It was a man who'd been to college. He supposed the guy had been well-meaning—in a white sort of way. In fact, now—just a year later—they were speaking again, the poor dude was sick with HIV symptoms. It was him Apollo got Percs from now and then.

Back then they'd kept tricking over and over. The guy had even wanted to help Apollo kick dope and get rehabilitated.

*. . . So he buys me bags of dope and feeds 'em to me, trying to cut down the dose little by little. "I'm in love with you," he keeps promising . . .*

Until Apollo believed it was true. But whenever he tried

to act appreciative it was the worst—he got goose flesh. He felt a force field of depression forming around him, pressing in and keeping everything out. It fed on the need for the dope and sucked everything good he had seen in the john out of him . . .

One night in the sex theater Apollo started to get the shakes because he needed more dope. The guy wouldn't pass him any money.

*I guess he was from a spoiled background and didn't have the balls to keep up with my habit and turned into kind of an asshole.*

Words started to shout in Apollo's bursting head. He was sweating and puking.

*Saying you care when you leave me here with diarrhea in the dirty toilet . . .*

Apollo stalked him out of the theater to the street to try to explain things better . . . *"Don't leave me without a penny to my name when I told you plain and clear that I just needed help this very last time . . ."*

. . . traipsed faster after the bright spot of money getting into a cab, pushed past the pain of his cramping legs to catch him before he got that taxi, rage at what had suddenly diminished to a retreating piece of green taking hold of him . . .

The guy was lying on the pavement, and Apollo was kicking him convulsively.

*I didn't really attack my friend, my withdrawal went into spasms.*

Connecting with the guy, joining his pain to him with the toe of his boot . . .

So the man pressed charges, and Apollo went back to jail.

*

Some of the cons in jail had put ads in gay papers, about being lonely and needing a gay they could write to and call collect. After that you were supposed to write about your big dick until the guy cracked. You'd talk about all the things that would happen when you got out, and then hit him up for money and cigarettes.

For some, the person on the outside started to do all kinds of favors. He'd send cigarettes, books, commissary money, call relatives for you. Occasionally, the locked-up one got strung-out, so that the other's generosity took on strange, impossible significations. Sexual identity stretched like a rubber band . . .

It was just Apollo's luck yet again to attract one who wanted more than anything else to be a nice guy. This weird type kept popping up. *"Don't write me sexual letters. Let's be honest with each other."* A series of "spiritual" letters passed between them, discussing third-world liberation and the prison system, which he'd learned about from his first white sugar daddy. The guy complimenting his intelligence. There was sensitive talk about relationships, the meaning of friendship, and dreams Apollo had had.

*"May upon the arrival of this letter, it will find you in the best of health . . ."* Apollo always began each letter, cursing the fact that his perpetual, damning, and desperate need always had to rear its ugly head again. *"I sincerely hope that you . . ." "Please forgive my asking but . . ." "Hope you are well and by the way could you . . ." "I'm sorry we got to know each other under such bad circumstances for me but if you could . . ."*

This time it was worse. When you're alone in your cell after lights out, anguish might settle in. The loneliness seems limitless. You're tempted to think that this guy could . . . Later it will seem absurd.

Nightmares of torture and sadism, witchcraft being

performed on and by him. He felt, as he sat bolt upright in the bunk in the middle of the night, that it was only fair to warn his pen pal with whom he was dealing. *"I've got to admit to you right off the bat that I'm not a very trusting person." "I hate to say it but I'm full of bitterness and rage."* He even told him why he was doing time—for stomping the only guy he'd ever liked outside a sex theater.

But the admissions backfired. "I'll take the chance . . . I can handle it" were the guy's responses. An avalanche of feelings piling up. An intolerable need to believe that the guy really might understand everything. Ferocious hate about the better possibility that he would not. He wrestled with it and pushed it away.

*"Dear Comrade . . ."* But it was too late. The mark had already marked him.

There were sweet moments, his weakest, when he sank into the dream of a friend and protector who was taking care of everything. A kind of Frankenstein patchwork of a buddy-father-brother with a strange, scary erotic aspect. It intoxicated him like the dope. Coming off it was worse. The sense of injustice riddled him, made him feel murderous.

*"This will be our last letter. For both our sakes, I think it better we stop communicating. I'll never be able to make you happy."*

But the guy kept writing. Was he the con artist of the century? It had almost lulled Apollo into what seemed like a passive, infantile state. A desperate, intolerable need leaking with sexuality. It felt like incest. There he was daydreaming about lying in his arms like some kind of woman. He'd turn into jail pussy if he wasn't careful . . .

Then on Christmas came the pair of Nikes he'd been asking for. And with it the letter that set his teeth on edge.

*"This should finally prove to you that I'm really thinking about you in the best possible way."*

What exactly was that supposed to mean? A man who needs shoes on his feet like anyone else having to bow down and suck the dick of the one who provides them? He wrote a grateful-sounding letter, but he had the gnawing sense that every word of it stoked the guy's ego.

A month later the guy came to visit. Apollo was saving the expensive sneakers for when he got out and never thought of wearing them. Not thinking that the guy would not understand the communal nature of prison, he borrowed new sneakers from buddies to dress up for him. Traded a pack of cigarettes for hair gel, got a pressed shirt, and even some stolen cologne. He cleaned his teeth ...

Sitting in the visitors' room surrounded by couples with their tongues in each other's mouth or hands up skirts, a sinking feeling as he tried to imagine what he would do when he got out to please his benefactor—*the guy's hairy arms, his schoolteacherlike clothes.* He pushed it out of his mind, courageously promising himself not to let his benefactor down.

*The guy is staring at my sneakers!*

*"I thought you said you desperately needed sneakers."*

*"I did. I borrowed these from somebody."*

*The guy is giving me a doubtful look!* It made him feel lucky to be locked up, because all he wanted to do was slash up the guy's face and hurl the sneakers into the wounds. Everything he'd suspected had come true in one overwhelming wave.

By accepting the sneakers, he had branded himself a user, coated himself with slime. And all of it had been ordained by the other person, who was always in power.

23

But for the guy it had obviously been no big deal. He kept up the sweetish letters, spelling out high ideals, forging a high-class image.

Apollo's emotions like hot coals put all his strength into playing along, waiting for the chance to strike.

The guy's letters and calls had a plaintive element now, because his father was dying. Apollo mimed the right sentiments.

*I told him I was there for him* . . . Until the guy wrote that his father had finally passed away. Then Apollo went right to work. *"May upon the arrival of this letter, it find you in the best of health . . . I've got to admit what I think of you . . . Sad, lonely gay guy who likes to fantasize that he can control other people . . . felt sorry for you and appreciated what you did for me, I was willing to make some sacrifices for you when I got out—sacrifices, if you know what I mean!"*

Gleefully, but with gritted teeth, he took his punishment as cigarettes, commissary money, books, and promises of lodging stopped abruptly. The rejection was exhilarating, as the reins fell back into his hands. The bitterness reinstated its bulwarks, and life became simple again . . .

Until his time was up. He was back on the streets with no place to live and no sponsor. Within a few days he was combing the sex theater with a needle in his coat pocket. It was almost as if time had stood still.

So still that here he stood: in the spot he had been hundreds of times before, a couple blocks from Tina's bar. No money and a gnawing yen to get high. Eighty-sixed from his only source of money, the sex theater, for wasting that used-up bouncer Casio—who'd fallen half a flight and landed on his back with a wet smack.

# II

A middle-aged guy with a sad, droopy look to his shoulders, thinning hair, came loping up the street, almost as if he were heading for the spot in which Apollo was stuck. The dirty sneakers were appropriate for his Caucasian look.

It took Apollo a couple of seconds to place him, even though they had had sex at the theater less than an hour before. It was the john who'd dodged past him and out of the room after he'd pushed him.

Using the instinct-radar of being high, Apollo tried hard to place the nerd. It was obvious that the guy liked taking the tightrope walk between this world and the namby-pamby world he'd been born into. That's why he was still out here cruising the streets, long after scoring and being threatened. Neither world was probably enough for him, only some war between the two. In a way he reminded Apollo of his HIV-positive buddy with the Percs: the well-meaning one he'd shamefully stomped outside the bar a long time ago. Apollo knew he had an instinct for attracting the do-gooders. But a closer look revealed something different, opposite, about this new guy.

When the guy was just about to pass, Apollo leapt into

the middle of the sidewalk and spread both arms as if greeting a long-lost friend. The man stopped and reared slightly.

"Remember me?" Apollo beamed, fixing eager, lap-dog eyes on the man's startled face. Hidden within Apollo's puppy eyes was the fang of a threat. He was hoping for a chance to play on the guy's fear, or even guilt feelings about their sleazy hit-and-run sex an hour ago.

Just as he'd figured, the man lapsed into a white-bread reaction. Apollo, who had a white mother, congratulated himself on his instinct. The man simply did not have the skills to brush off the street greeting for what it was. After all, he'd just sucked his dick, even if Apollo had gotten a little rowdy afterward. The well-brought-up man felt he owed him a stiff, sheepish handshake. Apollo slapped it with a confident high-five.

The man's eyes swam eerily under Apollo's bold, dead glance. He looked at Apollo's bare chest but was too tongue-tied to question where his shirt was. It was at this moment that Apollo realized again there was something he didn't understand about him. Like most people who ended up here, there was some flaw ...

With windup-toy jerkiness the guy resumed his walking, but Apollo caught up to him and stepped up the conviviality. Unable to break the white-bread streak, the guy made some pleasantries but quickened his pace. Apollo matched him step for step, looking for an opening. He decided to go for broke. He apologized about his behavior in the sex room and launched into some big offers that couldn't be refused. He promised the man he'd show him the kind of time he'd never had. Now that he was stuck in the city for the night, he explained, and couldn't get back to Connecticut— though he didn't blame the guy for it—there'd be plenty of time to make up for too short a session earlier. If the guy

26

wanted, they could even get it on when they woke up in the morning.

A cab had stopped for a light at the corner they were passing, so Apollo boldly yanked the door open. It was somewhat to his surprise that the man climbed in without hesitation and mumbled an address to the driver. The taxi lurched from light to light as Apollo searched for the rhythm of the man's breathing. He let his knee fall casually against the man's thigh and tried to tune his mind toward his occasional mute gaze. Still, he felt something unfathomable, even the weird hunch that they had something in common.

What he didn't know was that two years and two months had passed since this white-collar worker had touched a crack pipe. Self-help had gotten him to a level where he could be without drugs, yet strangely enough still craved atmospheres where they were illegally taken.

Even the most insignificant word or image could start a tantalizing chain of associations going—a synaptic series with a will all its own. "Smoke," "match," "rock," or the sight of a wire hanger like the ones he had used to dig out his stem, certain odors not uncommon in urban settings—all had special meanings. Gashed knuckles and sullen expressions like Apollo's could draw him back to the past as well: the air of a sealed-off room, a young hustler-addict, and occasional voiceovers from a porno tape that had contributed to the heightened atmosphere of crack smoking and sexual chance-taking.

Apollo slouched nonchalantly against the door and sensed the guy's sporadic glances dive-bomb his body like insects. With that detached flow of consciousness of the constantly at risk, he idly wondered what he could be in for. But the man's face in the gloom was charged with thoughts that were unreadable, and, with the wisdom of those who know that almost any decision may be their last, Apollo decided not to worry about it.

With his next nervous glance, the man drank in the two creases showing in the skin over Apollo's brown stomach. He may have had sex with him in the gloomy theater, but now he could get a different perspective on the leanness of that kind of stomach that had nothing to do with the gym. Those creases reminded him of the thrill about to come, in former times, as he rode with some wiry adolescent or other back to his house, his pocket filled with little plastic vials.

Their taxi cruised on past the theater where they'd met, from which a sheet-covered stretcher was now being carried. Though the man was fairly certain that Apollo didn't know he'd seen what had happened in the theater, dread mixed with eerie satisfaction began to trickle through him. He imagined a finger poised on a button that could blow up their world, then promised himself he wouldn't do it . . .

Next to the ambulance in front of the theater, a man in a chauffeur's cap lounged against a gleaming black limousine. He was talking to the fat, greasy theater cashier, who wore an obvious toupee. The chauffeur gawked at the stretcher being hoisted into the ambulance as the cashier undoubtedly held forth about what was supposed to have happened. His four stubby fingers sliced by rings flew up into the light from the garish marquee to make a point.

Apollo ducked below the cab window and eyed his companion warily. The man noticed that in the gloom of the taxi the whites of his big, panicked eyes seemed to glow like two golf balls. The shadows had reduced Apollo's chest to the two pointed black dots of his nipples.

"Wonder what all the ruckus near the theater is?" the man ventured in a neutral tone.

Apollo glanced nervously at the man's battered sneakers. Then his eyes darted to the thinning hair as he shook the question off. "You got to watch out around here, but not with me!"

"You sure?"

"I'm not sitting on my ass all day like these other guys. I'm going to go to junior college. You can search me if you don't believe me."

A cone of light illuminated the man's swank yet sterile, disordered bedroom. Apollo didn't even bother looking around. His face sank into the junkie's lunar passivity and showed no interest in the sparse furnishings, books, or jumble of papers on the table. He imagined a clarified version of his real face floating above it, leaving behind a dimension. This made him feel handsome in a posed sort of way. At this point he had stopped strategizing. All he wanted was to do up the Dilaudid and feel high.

His bare, sinuous arms snaked apart to shove both battered hands beneath his black jeans. The jeans popped open and slid down his hips so he could knead his pubic hair. Then a knife tumbled out of his pocket and clattered to the floor.

"You aren't going to need that here," said the man in a tight voice.

Apollo's large, downturned mouth made a show of resenting not being trusted. He picked up the knife and placed it gently on a table. In sullen defense of himself, he began listing the magazines and TV programs of an educational nature that he chose to read and watch in preference to comics or karate movies—something that distinguished him from all the other hustlers. They were one reason a person needed to carry something to defend himself out there. He told the man about his white, college-educated mother, who was now into New Age. But the man mugged large indifference to the calculated harangue and held out his arms in a conciliatory gesture. Apollo wetted his lips with a little spittle and parted them in a grimace of gratitude for being understood.

Against the man's mouth, Apollo's lips tasted like tobacco. In the man's arms it was as if the body were fading in and out of the approximate picture of itself. The boy's skin smelled cloying yet phosphorescent, like the scent of those moments the man had seen time telescope into a jagged series of arousals and climaxes, coming impossibly close to a perpetual state of orgasmic disintegration . . .

Such continual stimulation, aided at times by an erotic videotape, had been fueled by frequent passes of the pipe between the man and his partner for the night . . . And only when the last rock had melted into smoke did the nightmare of groveling for more life-substance descend upon him with any reality. Then consciousness was compacted into a ghoulish struggle, and each gesture was fraught with imminent failure, as life slipped through his fingers like sand through the hand of a skeleton . . .

"Got any porno with girls too?"

The man firmly shook his head.

Apollo stared dully at the tangle of limbs for a few seconds before pressing Stop.

"What kind of work you do?"

"Research."

"Use me as a guinea pig and you better make sure I get something out of it."

The man had noticed the bilge color intensifying on the surface of Apollo's skin as his eyes clouded with impotent annoyance. Frustration was trickling into those eyes as the drugs drained out of the membranes of his nervous cells. He slumped onto the bed and his cigarette dropped out of his hand. Patiently the man stood up and put it in the ashtray.

"I don't understand why you would pick up guys around where we met," Apollo mumbled from script. "They're all about getting high."

"____"

"Some of these men pick up guys to get high to have sex with. Next you're gonna tell me you get high and that you smoke crack? I don't like to be around that shit."

"Don't worry."

"I mean, I smoke a little reefer or drink a beer. You got a beer?"

"Unh-uh."

"I don't know if you know they got some really wack people working in that theater I work at."

The man threw him a blank, noncommittal look.

"This one guy, the bouncer or what you call it, he's really fucked-up, man, been a junkie for years."

"Oh?"

"Casio? You ever heard of him?"

The man shook his head.

"These other guys got no control. It's okay to get high from time to time, but you got to have discipline."

"Some chemicals don't even respect discipline."

"You sound like one of those N.A. people. Like sometimes I have done dope, but I have never gotten hooked on it."

"Keep doing it and you will."

"I appreciate your concern. Listen, I'm going to do some

dope tonight. Not really dope. It's pharmaceutical Dilaudid. I got a doctor friend gave me some. That doesn't bother you, does it?"

"Well . . ."

"No. Don't worry. The guy's a doctor."

The man's face turned even more poker-blank. "Can I put you in the alley when you overdose on me?"

"A man with your high morals wouldn't do that to me, I know, and besides, it won't happen!"

The mixture in the bottle cap bubbled over the flame of the lighter that Apollo had asked the man to hold. Apollo's unzipped pants had fallen farther off his hips, revealing the swell of his ass cheeks. In one hand he held the bottle cap. In the other he balanced a needle and a wad of cotton.

Apollo moved the cap away from the flame and dropped in the cotton, which soaked up the whitish liquid immediately. Then he inserted the point of the needle into the cotton and slowly drew back the plunger. The point sucked the liquid silently.

Once the spike was in his arm, a little blood gushed out of the punctured vein around the point of the needle; then it mixed with the liquid in the syringe as he drew the plunger back. In small taps he eased the solution back into the vein.

The man's face began to mimic Apollo's pasty glow. For some reason he too had lost his color. Witnessing penetration into the taut striation of muscle under velvety bruised skin must have thrilled him with the possibility of entrance to the pain swirling inside, about to be extinguished in a flash.

The image of a functioning body began to dissolve as Apollo fell out of the cone of light and sank onto the bed, coughing and consciousness flowed out of the large, fluid eyes.

One arm snaked about the man's neck, and he pulled him toward him. He lit a cigarette and inhaled.

"You liked watching that."

"I was afraid you'd O.D."

"Not with that, it's pharmaceutical, I know how much to do."

"Really? Where did you get your training?"

"See, I'm smarter than the others you probably go with."

Emboldened by his high, Apollo made another wild stab at credibility. "I got this friend—well she's kind of a friend—name of Mrs. Huxton, who owns the whole neighborhood we just came from and can see I'm not exactly like the others, so she kind of has me keep an eye on her theater for her—you know, where I work. She wanted to keep me from getting into trouble, see . . . and offered me this apprenticeship with a friend of hers. It's a school."

"What kind of school?"

Apollo fumbled for an answer. "Technician's school."

"What kind of technician?"

"Guard-dog training," he blurted out.

"You train dogs?"

"Sure."

"How do you train them?"

"Well you have to make sure the dog isn't distracted. So you get all in white—dogs don't react to white—and you take the dog in a white room all lit up white. Nothing in the room but you and the dog. Now you're whispering and the dog has to listen, because you're the only stimulus."

"What do you tell the dog?"

"To attack things . . . "

The voice trailed off as the man's eyes moved more hungrily over the body. The pants had slipped all the way down and been kicked to the floor. Apollo fell back in a slump against the wall. His chin was down; his eyes rolled back into his skull, then reappeared as consciousness came and fled. One naked arm rose and floated through the air. Then it lay dangling over the edge of the bed, a raised, shiny purple scar showing on the soft side of the forearm. There were several light, crisscrossed scars on the chest.

Farther up the arm, in shadow, the man could see lightly festered holes, ringed in black at the beginning of tracks that seemed to fade away in their journey along the skin. The boy was sleeping or had fallen into a deep nod, for the breathing seemed incredibly slow and heavy, the soles of the feet curling into faint spasms.

On the TV screen the image of the stretcher and theater and even the gesticulating cashier appeared, so that later the man would wonder whether he had actually seen it on the street or only on television. Then a commentator talking, it seemed, about an attack, a man in critical condition holding on to life by a thread.

The kaleidoscopic light of the TV enveloped Apollo's body as if it were a cloud of incense. It used all its colors to baptize him a "perpetrator," from whom all consideration or empathy was now supposed to be automatically withdrawn. Yet at moments, the man suspected that a sixth sense was making the perpetrator aware of the television or of being watched. He would stir suddenly as if ready to second-guess, flee, or defend himself at the slightest sign.

The tension of harboring him was suddenly excruciating, intolerable. So the man shook him awake.

"Let's play guard dog."

"Huh?"

"What about your education? Who's going to be the dog, you or me?"

Apollo shrugged in perplexity, then began to nod out again, the lids heavy and convex.

*The guy got down on his hands and knees. He opened his mouth and stuck his tongue out. He started licking me all over like he was starving, gobbling my nipples and armpits, licking and kissing my balls and legs and toes while I fell in and out of my nods . . .*

Then anguish opened the man like a ravine. He slapped Apollo awake and told him to get dressed fast, gave him money, and ushered him out. He rinsed out the filthy glass of blood-tinted water with hydrogen peroxide . . . after picking up his cordless phone to call the police to report the whereabouts of the fugitive.

# III

C asio lay in the ambulance, unable to stop hearing the ringing in his ears. It was like rubber striking steel; originally, the early-morning sound of the guard checking for contraband in every pipe of the common room, in a section of the prison known as House of the Dead.

This echo from the Joint was a sound as real as that which a person who has tried everything to stop still hears perpetually—until he finally throws himself under the protection of a head-shrink or hypnotist or drugs. Razor blades, spikes, joints, condoms, or other contraband stuffed inside the hollow of steel, so that when the corrections officer had finally struck that spot with his mallet, it rang out with a duller tone.

That day eleven years ago when the corrections officer had struck his fatal blow against the radiator pipe, the very young Casio had managed to stuff a shank through the steam-valve socket into the radiator. The shank was some strip of metal a member of his crew had been able to lay his hands on, stroking it over and over against fixed metal until it got razor sharp, then wrapping it with cloth and string to make a handle.

It was long enough to go through two thicknesses of guys—or through one guy and half a foot out the other end. Dangerous enough to cause big trouble for the one caught holding or hiding it.

Behind the Wall, new, beautiful fish like wiry-limbed Casio, whose then-angular face had boasted a lush mouth and whose skin was like satin, sometimes sought security by running in a rat pack or posse whose actions they'd try to help "perpetrate." But once you were down with a particular crew, there'd come a vulture who was a member trying to make you out to be his happy-butt or siphoning every cigarette off you.

When this vulture stuck another con over a stupid dis, zooming in on him from behind so the shank slipped between his ribs and came out wet the other side, Casio had the rotten luck of being in the vicinity, and the attacker passed the shank to Casio, telling him to stash it as the C.O.s came charging.

*"And for months now 'cause of that, this ringing shit in my ears driving me fucking nuts, Doc, reminding me how's I got glazed by a brother and took his rap and got tossed into the Box for this vulture for ninety days. It's the same fuckin' sound all the time—when the C.O.s come in and hit everything with this rubber mallet that tells 'em ifs you was holding contraband."*

The Box is Solitary, where the only light comes from the small grate at the top of the wall facing the corridor. And when the light in the corridor is off, it is total blackness. Though he tried to keep his muscles toned with endless calisthenics, there was no way to mark time or the passage of days. His mind began wandering. The ringing sound was something flying in the dark: an insect or bird getting closer and becoming louder. But when he swiped at the blackness, his hand closed on nothing.

At times the sound swelled: into absurd laughter when he ate those *chiba* cookies with Tito and started to trip in class on the white teacher's wack hair; or spinning on his back on a piece of cardboard when the crew used to break. Or it got evil, swooping into replays of past wrongs and imagined revenges. Like the bird or insect, his mind zoomed closer to panoramas of primal scenes.

*That bitch playing virgin on my ass and then shacked up next day with one of my boys. Or that shithead calls himself a father raising his hand to her again . . .*

It was hard to tell whether you were dreaming or not in this blackness as you slipped in and out of consciousness, thinking once that he held his great-grandmother's two front teeth in the palm of his hand, after that time they'd been knocked out by her boyfriend and he'd watched them roll across the pavement like dice . . .

*I had to pick up drunken Abuela, a little bag of bones—like some bird wrapped in her shawl, and go up six flights to lay her on the bed . . .*

Out of Solitary and back on the street, the sound got louder. It was the same ringing; he was out, but the city seemed to keep up jail-thinking. *Once you been up river you find it . . . wherever.* Each nonwhite guy on the subway seemed to have honor to protect. *You got to control where you let your eyes rest.* The eyes of homeboys never met your glance but for a transaction or a challenge. How he moved was being judged with contempt or fear—in other words, respect. One arm stretched behind your back, the palm resting upturned on a buttock, meant "ready to cop." Thumb hooked in front pocket, fingers splayed across thighs, meant "My dick is king" and/or "I got a weapon."

*Don't pull your knees together pussy-style somebody sits down next to you. Let the bastard scrunch up.* The rush of the train accompanying the building rush of insult ... and always, always this shrill ringing in his ears.

Though a dose of heroin would smooth it out sometimes. But because of Casio's enormous stamina for suffering, he shot it only when he could take the ringing not a second longer. Then he went chasing after a bag and did it up with borrowed works, but so infrequently that his habit was spun out over a couple of years before it began to interfere with his routines.

He was still lean and smooth-skinned, with big, liquid, stoned eyes, working the door to Tina's, the transvestite lounge. An old gang member named Sugar Bear had risen to temporary prominence by hooking his giant dick up with Tina, the queen performer. She was half-owner—with strings attached to some old Portuguese lady. The dude had not forgotten Casio but gave him the afternoon post, which paid minimum. It was mostly just a security job, since almost nobody but a few queens came in during the day. Casio could nod out and put himself on automatic.

Nighttime he'd stick around and sneak some drinks at the circular bar or catch the show, always half in Spanish. He liked fielding the sex quips of the queens who worked as hookers, some of whom were not half that bad looking. And then finally, the party for someone's birthday, where there'd be food—a mountain of chili and rice or a sidewalk of lasagna or franks and beans. And here, how you lined up for the food told them who you were. Everybody made a big show about not being that hungry, they were used to better. No one wanted to turn the atmosphere of the club into the Salvation Army. *"Shit, I don't know, I got sick on that kind a stuff once, but I'll try a bite . . . let me have some a that lasagna—no, man, none a that lettuce shit! I don't eat rabbit food . . ."* Grudgingly taking your first chomp on the handout while you boasted about the kind of class food you were used to and your stomach rumbled with anticipation.

Because who was he unless he was hooked up with his own place and own meals? So one day he paid a surprise visit on East 111th to sharp-tongued, diminutive Monica, his son's nineteen-year-old mother. She kept the chain on the door, but he could see she looked good these days: her coffee-colored face framed by comb-studded, bleached-blond hair. Not doing bad at all, she boasted across the chain lock. Getting my beautician's license at night and gonna work part-time in a salon. And as for his getting busted and going to jail one month before the baby was born, I don't blame it on you, I blame it on myself, she answered.

But as she tried to shut the door on him, he forced it and snapped the chain. Brought the bag of reefer and bottle of rum from his hip pocket to the table. He even had an electronic minigame for the kid. Monica's warm eyes widened. "Come out here and say hello to your father!" A cool four-year-old appeared and appraised Casio with hooded eyes, then grabbed for the game like it had just fallen from the sky. *"Where do stuff come from? You just gets it when you gets it."*

Now everybody's happy, so Mom and Pops light up, take a couple shots of Bacardi; Junior wanders away, transfixed by his game. Casio and Monica go into her bedroom to do the Wild Thing. His fingers slip under her lavender sweater and remember her taut body.

*With no bodacious ta-ta's, just little titties, a little Yard Bird body. I always got off on her little butt, a chico-butt I calls it, and nice honey skin. That little twitching birdie lying underneath me ...*

They stayed in bed until the next afternoon, when he had to go back to work at Tina's. Then Casio returned with more weed and ate her *pernil* and avocado and they smoked again and went back to bed. Afterward Monica pulled out her beautician's kit and began to practice a style on his shiny longish hair, rollers and all. Casio had begun talking about the queens, and, stoned as he was, with the rollers in his hair, he found himself doing right-on imitations that made Monica bust a gut. Her nymphlike naked body rolling on the bed in hysterical birdlike laughter, sending some curlers flying to the floor, as Casio with the sheet wrapped around him bumped and ground in a baroque imitation of a queen imitating a woman ... The boy came in to watch with eyes unblinking, his poker mouth giving him a bored, sophisticated look ...

It took a while for Casio's son to really worship him. Casio dubbed him "Baby Pop." And eventually Baby Pop began following him around the apartment all the time, kicking at the closed door when Casio went to the head. Casio put a lock on the bathroom door. At least there he could do some up in peace when he had to stop the ringing in his ears.

By now the boy was five, surprising everyone with his precocious head for math. Casio would walk him through the projects to Central Park on the weekend, taking normal strides on purpose, with the kid huffing and puffing to keep up with him. It gave Casio some satisfaction to see his son's mettle proven—the way a green member of a gang will go through all kinds of shit to keep up with the rest. But on this particular day Casio's brain was stabbed by a memory of a pain in his own side as he tried to keep pace with his own father, the year he was twelve, which was the only year they had spent together.

They were running to a vacant lot trying to get there quick, before dawn, when it would be too late to cop. Running beside him, Casio got a horrible pain in his side. And then his *papi* got there just in time; he copped, the dealers took off, and his father went deeper into the lot behind a burned-out building to do it up, and suddenly began sinking down ... down into the rubble ... because he'd O.D.'d.

Casio pushed the image down. Dwelling on it had nothing to do with surviving. In point of fact, nobody was doing anything else, and, more than food in the mouth and a bed to sleep in, this meant to medicate pain. In his case, with the ringing suddenly there and the phantom hurt in his side, the border between physical pain and mental anguish grew fuzzy. The more medication he took, the more the two merged. The more he needed not to feel bad before he couldn't stand it anymore.

He later swore to a drag queen named Angelita that he honestly never thought things would turn out this way. He wasn't getting high often enough to take responsibility for Monica developing a habit. She knew about his, and sometimes they shared a needle, but most of the time she liked to make love to him when only he was high.

She'd watch him naked and tying up. Then it took a long time for him to get a "dope stick," but when his woody was up, it stayed, all the blood was stuck inside, and he could turn her out for hours while their son slept soundly in the living room. Monica always kept one ear cocked for any gasping, since Baby Pop had developed asthma.

He couldn't put his finger on the time when Monica's cooking stopped and the naked shoot-ups grew more frequent and the house started to go seedy. *But for sure that I'm not gonna take a fall for this one. For one thing, she'd been making drops to support the kid while I was locked up. Associating with dealers, may the truth be known. Her first mistake was Wrong People. Though yeah she was still clean at the beginning. When I come out she was only doing a little bit a mopping, for mascara and stuff from Woolworth's. Seein' that I'm from the old school, I wasn't no way letting her go off on me . . .*

*But then Monica started to park the boy with her father—to come to Tina's instead of to beauty school, hustling free drinks and rubbing shoulders with the queens: When she toots she'd get this squeaky little machine-gun mouth—"Hands off, honey, these* tetas *be real, you can play with the plastic over there." "You dissin' me, bitch? When your man touch 'em I bet he think they feels as real as them little avocados you got." "At least you can take a bite outta 'em, girl, without gettin' a mouthful a silicone," etcetera.*

*When was it, some time or other, when me and her gets locked out of her place for a couple weeks? She who don't never pay the rent on time, so up coming the landlord with a toolbox and changing the lock. Next these friends a hers, these high-class junkies in Brooklyn Heights fixing up a brownstone, tells us, you and the kid can sleep here ifs you bring us a bag a night. Word! Nice black schoolteachers with money from parents to renovate a house carrying on like street junkies! They'd get zombied right in front of the kid, lose all their money, and go to buy loose stogies from the bodega.*

\*

43

By the time Casio and Monica got back inside the apartment, they'd spent a few days in shelters, and one freezing night in the street. It was clear Monica had let go of beautician's school, but Casio made a rule that she had to take back the kid from her parents and start staying home evenings. He'd tie her to the kitchen table and shoot her up before he went to work if he had to. He kept all their money together and portioned out enough for dope and food.

*'Cept for this female is the kind knows how to play men real close to get everything she want. We'd do dope one night, and she's getting up tomorrow and saying she needs bazooka to get through the day. Then sometimes a speedball on the weekends. You don't go back and forth that way without payin' for it. It was gonna do no good cutting her off 'cause she started feeding her father bouncers. Her habits usin' up Daddy's whole account. Stealin' the key to his mailbox to grab the mail from the bank and burning it 'fore he would see. Papi got played by her over and over but came back for more, being she was his only daughter.*

*Then finally that she starts getting too live on me. Real* loca. *All day locked up in the bathroom, staring at her hands. Her arms up in front of her face when I walk in, like I'm going to fuck her up, and saying I was a hypnotist to control her mind. She even got afraid being in the room with our Baby Pop, saying that witchcraft was gonna make him suddenly stop breathing. Went to see a* bruja. *But what's bugged is she wasn't doing too much drugs, really.*

# IV

It was a month later, in that golden age of Times Square's sleaze empire, that a Latin queen named Angelita strolled into Tina's Lounge and eyed the still-young Casio slouched at the entrance, in black from his old days as an outlaw—a black exclamation point of machismo that had drooped into a question mark now that Monica had thrown him out.

She took in his sulky death's head and big vacant eyes and wondered what it would be like to put her tongue between the formerly lush lips, now stretched into a mute speak-no-evil.

As she slinked up to him, he silently took in her body, blooming from hormone injections. She asked him for the key to the ladies' room, and he held it out indulgently. It was still afternoon outside, but in the darkness and orange lights from the bar, her pale, dusky skin took on a matte glow.

Casio had never noticed whom she hustled, and he himself had never been with a drag queen. Yet when she returned with the key in her hand, her thank-you soft-spoken and breathy, it occurred to him that he had nowhere to stay that night, and he caught himself rejoicing at the look sullenly glinting in her black eyes.

Her body came close enough so that her breasts grazed his face. As she stepped away, he let his hand glide gently up her skirt to stroke her buttocks.

That night Casio and Angelita took the PATH train to her Jersey City apartment. He dropped onto her bed as the queen sashayed across a real Oriental rug to a lacquered Chinese screen. Turning on one side, he studied his face and body in her gilt-trimmed mirror, which was turned sideways to give a full view of the bed. He focused on his hollowed-out cheeks and broad forehead, convincing himself that he didn't look half that bad for a guy of twenty-two.

The queen was behind the screen slipping out of her skirt and pantyhose and into a blood-red kimono. Pale as she was, the red kimono made the skin of her downy, frail forearms look olive, and she mentally blessed the new body cream she had boosted from an East Side perfumery because she knew it would make her skin feel silky-soft to the touch. Angelita slowly unraveled her thick chignon and shook out her long black hair. When she strode out, she put the "Quiet Storm" on the radio and swiveled back to him across her prize rug.

His blunt, splayed fingers combed through her hair, making her shiver as she eyed their mirror image: a babe and her shadowy, wiry master—who looked like a pimp— framed by gilded carvings.

It was an image that reminded her of the framed picture on the flowered wallpaper of her sick mother's bedroom in Puerto Rico, when she had been a little boy. There was a woman in a pageboy hairdo, wearing a beret and violet angora sweater, being pushed backward in strict Apache dance formation by a gangster in a pin-striped suit, one eye concealed by a black patch. In imitation of the couple, she and her cousin had choreographed an Apache dance for her bedridden mother, which climaxed in him dragging Angelita across the floor by one of her mother's wigs, as she held it to her seven-year-old head by pulling in the opposite direction.

Suddenly, as if the picture had come to life, Casio was holding her real hair like a shank in his fist. He lowered her head roughly to his crotch and shoved. The violent gesture left a lipstick smear along his fly as she resisted, but then she used her tapered, lacquered fingernails to unbutton his black jeans.

Nothing happened. It didn't go up.

Angelita sat up and sighed. She smoothed her hair in the mirror as her cat wrestled under Casio's callused palm, and he used his forearm to pin it against the bed until it played dead and he could stroke its vulnerable belly.

Her eyes sought the gold-bordered bower of the mirror for an answer and saw that the image had not lost any of its allure. Lean and crouched, Casio still sat on the bed with all the romantic defeat and weary nobility of the degraded macho. And this couldn't mean that he wasn't the man—the pimp, the Apache dancer, the gangster—she'd conceived him to be in the mirror.

The cat, who was female and in heat, had squirmed away from his big hand, and Angelita tried to stand up to feed it. When an arm snaked about her waist and pulled her back to the bed, she gave in willingly, then lay trapped that way and moaning while her mind raced.

The man's hard biceps creased her waist, and she could feel the bones of his lean chest gnawing into her. As he reclined, his breathing was as tense and determined as the breath of a man used to taking his rest in jail. It was best not to think about the motives of men, because the true man never revealed his ultimate strategy. She would now concentrate on waiting like a mirror lake for his will to break through the surface, or until she fell asleep.

And from then, he just stayed there. Under the fur blanket, they'd sleep with the cat on top of them. He'd fondle her breasts and with his lips and teeth nip at her neck and earlobes, sometimes leaving purple marks as a kind of branding. A week later he gave her some of his pay and joked that he'd kill her if he ever caught her hustling.

When Angelita stayed home to sew, some of the other queens came over by train to practice lip-synch routines with her cassette player, while Casio grew restless, drank Olde English, and paced. He boasted about his sexual prowess and told jokes.

*"There was this king a long time ago said he'd give a million to somebody could make his horse laugh. But couldn't nobody until this Puerto Rican comes, says let me behind a curtain with him. All of a sudden, the horse starts to laughing hee-haw. So then a year later the king gets tired of a horse laughing hee-haw all the time, says I'll give a million anybody can make this horse stop laughing and start crying, and the Puerto Rican comes back, says let me behind a curtain with him. All of a sudden, the horse starts to crying.*

*"Okay, here's your million, but tell me for chrissakes how you did it. Well the first time, says the Puerto Rican, I went behind the curtain and whispers in the horse's ear my dick is bigger than yours. And the second time I shows it to him."*

\*

"And what 'bout you, Cas, how you measure up to dat hoss?"

"'Bout the only competition to me round here might be what you got strapped up under that pantyhose, Negrita."

Negrita didn't like him. And privately she began hinting to Angelita that if Casio wouldn't have sex with her, he was holding out—or worse, a faggot. She was a fool to have him in her house and not to demand what was rightfully hers in the relationship.

So Casio tried to imagine sex with Angelita. But how could he think about more than one female at a time? Monica was still on his mind. And anyway, Angie was just a drag queen.

Sometimes her chest felt the worst sense of leaden dread. Her thoughts sorted through the fantasies she had built about true love as she did her makeup at the vanity table and bright mirror for her Wednesday-night shows at Tina's.

Casio lay behind her on the bed. To maintain the fragile formula that kept her female, certain conditions had to be repeatedly fulfilled at all costs, as regularly as the doses of estrogen. But in the mirror she saw the eyes of this husband who was not a husband running up and down her naked back.

She'd gathered her hair loosely at the top of her head, which revealed her shoulders. She intuited his glance grazing the shoulders and being put off by them. But then maybe it moved to the hormonal swellings of her buttocks perched upon the velvet vanity bench with its claw-foot legs and had a different feeling? Lying near the bench on the Persian rug were piles of fashion magazines of the classiest sort, as well as cassettes of the singers she impersonated. Perhaps his eyes were now scanning the cassette covers and imagining the breasts, thighs, and asses of these real women.

She finally agreed that they get a bag for the very first time since he had moved in with her. Angelita didn't get high very often—almost never, in fact. And he'd cut way down. But maybe doing this together one time would create a new atmosphere, and things would happen differently.

He tied her arm up and did her, then himself. Because he'd been off it for a while, the rush overwhelmed him. He couldn't sit up. He fell back onto the pillow, but it was as if his body were levitating.

Angelita stayed sitting up because her body took in the drug differently; she was stoned to the tits, but it just intensified her stillness; she hovered above him like a cumulus cloud, her hand gliding toward his black T-shirt, which floated off under her touch. It was all slow-motion. His arms were dropping over his head, and a sound like a gas jet was in his ears ... open red lips teethed his nipples, stretched taut by his flung arms.

*I putted my cherry suckers on his tits to find out the kind a man he was being and then the tip of my tongue along his blade scar to prove it ...*

The real secret in getting hard was letting her take control. He let her invent the smooth cock that would penetrate as if it were hers. Lips licking from the base of the shaft to nip at its ruffle of foreskin, until it unsheathed gradually along the lean thigh.

*Now if I can slip careful out a this kimono and keep my legs all pressed together.* Then she tipped back with raised knees trembling and an open palm shielding what he must not see while a current of the drug picked him up and he suddenly swooped over her.

The dope decreed no taking or giving, just one body quivering. Casio entered her soft body differently than he had with bonier Monica—sinking deep into a source of energy, while the dope made time for everything in the backs of his thighs, heading toward his cock and balls into more dope spiraling inside of her.

Much later, in the morning, he found it easy to reclaim his cock, to hop out of bed like an athlete and resume the ascendant role. Dark eyes still smoldering, with a touch of irony, Angelita asked him in almost a parody of meekness for a few dollars. Before she went out, while he drank beer and watched a porno tape, she shivered blushingly but triumphantly under his soft, muttered threats as he warned her to keep away from other guys.

"And what you going to do about it?"

Nothing. The longed-for homeostasis had been established. They had to get high every time they had sex. And this time there were no recriminations as to whose fault the growing habit of each was.

The infinite expansions taking hold most nights gave birth to bright pictures more intense than he'd found in Solitary. Angelita's breasts and warm thighs were becoming luminous clouds, the levitating feeling dissolving into an even higher wave of high. Nausea that came during a reach for a pack of cigarettes by the bed was accompanied by bright specks falling through air. Breathing was sand. Then pictures were cut off by dozes on top of her body.

All of a sudden it was the sick urgent morning: a total environment of the kind where dope is making sex into

rubber people who merge into a world without conflict, and
only Angelita's voice becoming more and more insistent . . .

*See, I'm talking to you, Cas, remember that God is good, baby, I
prayed for someone to love, and look, He putted us together. But
you ain't gonna fool Him or nobody to thinking that you treat me
this way. Everybody does know,* papito. *So why you's always
telling I'm your bitch, you gonna teach me a lesson tonight? Lyin'
that you got ahold a me and got me workin' for you and bringin'
in* mucho *money. Where is my girlfriends seeing the act you be
putting on?*

   *I ain't gonna let you dig a hole in my head wid dat same boolshit
no more just to look good. For you I gave up dreamin' of a man
who understands my shoes and dresses costs money. 'Cepting now
I got to go out with the same ratty dress and nothing in my pockets. Tell me how we go about getting some respect in this world
with habits like we got and scroungin' the way we been. We gotta
get more money, and ain't neither of us doin' a thing about it but
playin' ourselves.*

Her words came slashing through his high with a man's
deep-voiced, urgent authority: COME CORRECT, CASIO!
MAKE THE MASTER PLAN WHAT'S NEEDED!

# V

## O'HARA:

*See, way back when ten years ago, even though the drug addicts and scammers had took over, the old Portuguese lady still owned every joint on this block. You could still find people who were what they said they were. You could drink your money's worth at my place: O'Hara's. It stood right over there next to her theater, plain as the gin-tinted noses on my guzzlers' faces. Neither wasn't it breathing foul odors like the joints on the block today. 'Cause it'd been scrubbed with ammonia by my own hands and sparkled like the pasties on one of the old Portuguese lady's naked hootchy-kootchy dancers—when that place catered to men who liked missies.*

*In those days, middays was slow. Only a straggler or two managed to crawl into the bar between 10:00 A.M. and 2:00 P.M.—after the hard-core A.M.-ers had come in to swill down their morning pick-me-ups at seven.*

*And then came that day when the big lady-and-a-half with hair down to her bottom waltzed right in.*

*These were the end of the sweet good-old-days, mind you, before things really took a turn for the worse. Before the Devil claimed this neighborhood but didn't come in person to lay his*

53

claim. He sent his emissary in the form of a lady-and-a-half with seal-sleek skin and lips like rubies to put an end to those days. She walked right through that door over there into my saloon at the stroke of noon and slinked up to the bar. Then she let her head drop on it.

"What's weighin' on you, Missy?" I says. I poured her a stiff one and leaned my elbows on the bar. I'd be lying if I said I didn't give a glance at them two cabbages spilling out of her dress before I went back quick to my business of wiping the mugs. Wary as I was of types like this one, who show off their jugs like prizes at a county show, I still got a shameful kick by eyeing some of the big-boobed trollops of the neighborhood.

"Don't pay me no mind," is what I think she mumbled, "for it ain't you nor nobody can help me now."

"God be with you then," I shot back to her. And true that I'd gone back to my business, still could I not resist one peek at those melons in my mirror. The glance made a flush pass over the big girl's raised face, and she tucked back the cabbages and lowered her round eyes back to the counter.

"I know what you take me for," she complained at my lascivious looking. "But only had you seen me just three months ago in Puerto Rico, you would've had a different opinion of me then."

"Of what might I have been thinkin' if I'd have met you, Miss?"

"But how could you've?" shoots she right back, "it being such a strict order, and them only allowin' visits from relatives."

I'll have to admit, that the remark turned me red as a schoolboy. As a Catholic I could not find the voice to comfort the lady for having lost the cloth and turned into what I saw. So leaving her in the shame that colored both our faces, I went downstairs to curse the world and bring up a case of beer, and then knelt in penitential silence by the cooler, putting away the brew. Still, I could not help wondering how she'd managed to grow so quickly that mane of hair

54

of hers. Neither could I shake the feeling of the lost girl's presence behind me.

"Miss, are you sayin' you've come out from a convent?" I dared not look directly but spoke my words to the mirror.

"Would it weren't true," says she sadly, though I'm sure she phrased it differently, in her own Spanglish. "For if it weren't for my brother's visit I would still be there today."

I was lost in the mean-spirited grip of curiosity now, and filled with pity and doubt at the same time. So coming as close to the large, sad lady as I dared, but keeping the bar between the cabbages and my manhood, I fully coaxed her story out of her.

"You were tellin' me you left the nunnery and followed your brother to America, lass?"

"What choice had I," she tosses back, fixing her eyes straight on mine, "what with me carryin' his baby?"

The rest of her song of woe was more loathsome than the darkest ballad. About a man had made his own sister his whore and brought her to this country like a slave to pay his drug bills. He had her in a death grip that if it weren't for the baby, she would have killed him and then herself.

The girl was sobbing and heaving so helplessly that the cabbages had slipped from their sacks all the way to the brown aureoles. In comfort I reached out a gentle hand to stroke her silky arm, just when an angry bloke burst into the bar. I known it was him right off 'cause the lady screeches and slides off the barstool. She rushes for the door as the cur's big hand reaches out for her and yanks her back by the hair with a snarl.

The lady falls, but he won't let go. And by that hair itself, he drags her from one end of the room to another!

I won't tell what he then started to do, it not being fit to describe. But leave it that I saw more of the lady than any stranger should.

Armed with my shillelagh, which I keep for such emergencies, I shot out from behind the bar. I may be no hero, but I did what any decent man with two arms and two legs needs to have done. "Leave her alone, by God," raising the shillelagh in the air, "or I'll use your skull as a doorjamb!"

Leaving that safe station and not grabbing the revolver I keep at it for such emergencies was my fatal mistake. For before I can bean the scoundrel, he lets go of her—and puts his own gun right up to my skull.

"Don't you make a move, Mick, or I'll blow you to pieces!"

And suddenly our sad sister became full of merry giggles. And sashaying to the cash register without a care in the world, she begins to stuff the bills between those cabbages.

It's not until that moment that I see I'm wearing the crown of the King of Fools. Though I suppose her come-hither act, mane of hair, and phony tale of incest would 'ave laid a trap the same for any red-blooded man. With her as lookout he marched me right downstairs to the safe and relieved me of a few thousand.

Next thing I know I'm lyin' right there where they found me —with this horrible pain between my two ears. The bloke must 'ave beaned me with my own shillelagh.

# VI

The mysterious dark lady disappeared like an apparition. Look as they might, the police could have discovered no closer resemblance to her than a crew-cut, soft-featured boy. He went back to a long-ago name before breasts and hormones.

*Angel.*

Under the clipped hair, the eyebrows were still tweezed, but somehow the eyes had lost their smoldering gleam. In the pocket of his baggy shirt he copped the daily fixes with O'Hara's money and brought them back home to the man who'd held the gun and who now stayed inside, drugged or sick, looking for new veins.

Sex had lost all interest for Angel and his onetime paramour. Casio's mind floated instead back to the days before Monica and his son Baby Pop, to his outlaw days, those all-for-one-and-one-for-all times in the Bronx before he even went to jail. Angel's mind was uprooted from the fantasies that had made him Angelita and that revolved around the mirror. Reverting to the shadow of his original biological self, which had long ceased to be an identity and now became only a shabby alias, he grew emaciated and pale.

One afternoon, without any desire to be near Casio, Angel crept from the bed to the floor and lay beneath the large blowup photos of a queen in her prime. Above him reigned his former self, besequinned and high-heeled, holding a microphone. He rolled up a sleeve and felt among the scar tissue for a vein, but it was no-go.

Across the room, Casio was spread out on the unsheeted mattress, his bent arms and legs flung apart like a swastika. At moments his half-closed lids twitched convulsively while the eyes rolled upward. Suddenly he would come to with a start, and then sink back into his stupor.

The ghost of the propriety of their old relationship made Angel want to be certain that Casio wouldn't be watching. Checking sporadically to be sure that Casio was unaware, he unbuttoned his pants and cupped a blunt penis in his hand. He stretched back a fold of skin lying over a blue vein and delicately inserted the point of the needle. The rush relaxed his back into a curve, and his breasts drooped into loose cones, but he held on to his senses with all his might until he could stuff the member back into his clothing.

Detective Juan Pargero, with his buzz cut and hawk face, was no stranger to cases like this. He knew Times Square inside and out; and his career, first as a beat cop on the street and then as a detective, had involved him in the full spectrum of exchanges between the down-and-out and the not-so. Pargero was a racial mixture and a strange hybrid of tough cookie and sentimental slob, a middle-aged cynic but weirdly goodhearted. A certain fondness for queens had raised some eyebrows in the neighborhood but perhaps gave his investigations a personal touch.

Still, Pargero knew when and where to turn the screw. It had taken an intimidating interrogation of some of the dealers who frequented Tina's and verification with Mrs. Huxton for O'Hara's study of male mug shots to bear fruit. But identification of the female accompanying the gunman had not come to pass.

Weeks later, the search for the gunman led to a rickety two-family house in Jersey City, at the end of a dreary street overlooking the tunnel of the PATH train. Detective Pargero tramped quickly up the creaking staircase with a signed warrant and two overweight policemen to do the grunt work. The cops drew their guns before bursting through the unlocked door, but they stopped in amazement at the sight of the effeminate-looking boy passed out underneath the drag photos. The detective had once watched the lip-synch routines of stunning Angelita at Tina's. Yet the skeletal Latino beneath the posters had journeyed so far from his queenish image that even the detective, who thought himself a connoisseur of female illusion, did not make the connection.

His thoughts were distracted by the heavy slosh of water coming from the bathroom. Inside, the stockier of the two grunts was grumbling about the fact that his uniform was splattered with it. He bent toward the tub and once more yanked at wet wrists, but they slipped through his fingers like eels. The naked body of Casio flopped back into the tub, sending another swell of water onto the floor and forcing the cops to hop backward.

The other cop removed his jacket and rolled up his sleeves to fish in the water for the ankles. His drenched shirt stuck to his stomach, showing the crease of the navel. "I'm surprised the sucker didn't drown," he sneered.

"So maybe we saved his life," answered the other with mock concern.

In the tub, Casio's lids had opened halfway. The thick, dark lashes fluttered effeminately. Casio's fingers twitched once before they fell back into the water, making a tiny splash, followed by a low moan. The voice of the perpetrator won the attention of the detective, who had been gazing at the drag posters with an expression that seemed wistful yet wily, a squeamish yet lewd smile characteristic of some law enforcers.

Creeping to the bathroom door, he stepped over the puddle forming outside and peeked in. His blue eyes proprietorially caressed the flagrant disorder of the squandered body of Casio, lying shamelessly naked and unconscious in the tub.

Detective Pargero was capable of the kind of hard-nosed voyeurism that feeds investigations. However, at moments like this a drop of humanity tinged his voice with soft resignation.

"Get the landlord," he commanded in a whisper.

Not that Pargero liked the looks of the colicky and stony-faced landlord who appeared hesitantly at the threshold. Potbellied and wearing a bathrobe and slippers, he lingered there resentfully until the detective impatiently waved him into the room. When the man saw the flooded floor caused by the cops, his expression blackened. He followed Detective Pargero into the bathroom with lips compressed.

"Who's this?" barked the detective, gesturing with his chin to the naked body in the tub. The cop was holding the head by the hair to keep it from sinking under. The mouth drooped and wheezed. The other cop was fishing in the tub for the plug, but he couldn't find it and began cursing under his breath.

"How should I know?" answered the landlord, averting his face.

"This isn't your tenant?"

"She is." The landlord pointed toward the other room.

*She?* The cop's raw face clouded over only for a second, before he made the connection between the fragile boy out there and the missing voluptuous accomplice. But the realization trod on a weak spot and brought out the fantasist in him. A tight swallow made his Adam's apple bob. "Does this guy"—the detective pointed to the tub—"is he the one that's involved with . . . her?"

"Why you asking me?" said the landlord, looking pointedly at the flooded floor. "I stay out of people's business— unless they cause me a problem."

Breaking off the conversation with a laconic snort, the detective strode authoritatively from the room. Each foot plopped into the puddles. The landlord followed gingerly and hesitated, then crept toward the stairs and disappeared.

The detective had made a decision. Angelita—but only she—would be spared.

When the burly redheaded man and the fireplug blond woman in tight white pants arrived with a stretcher, they made straight for the waxy-skinned boy collapsed beneath the drag posters. But almost betraying a protective instinct, the detective motioned them toward the bathroom.

"Not him—the one in the bathtub. And wake him just enough to verify his name and read him his rights. Don't give him too much, 'cause he'll probably go into withdrawal, right?"

The medics nodded in grim obedience.

"And that would be awful messy," clucked the detective.

When the medics had disappeared inside the bathroom, he walked quietly over to the boy on the floor and nudged him gently with the tip of his shoe. But there was no reaction. .

In the bathroom, the female medic pulled one of the arms out of the water and pressed it firmly against the tub wall, while her partner, wearing rubber gloves, readied the injection of naloxone. Avoiding the reddish, white-ringed hole near the wrist that seemed to be festering, he plunged the needle into the muscle tissue of the forearm near a swarm of scars and bruises. The detective and the two cops peered in from the doorway. This time the detective's face maintained a mask of cold determination.

A barely audible moan came from the submerged form, and it squirmed weakly. The moan increased to a howl as the female medic reddened and struggled to keep a grip on the arm and avoid the sloshing water.

Now the body began to writhe more violently. The male medic backed toward the door, but his partner stuck grimly to her post. Her white blouse was drenched, the form of her bra appearing through it; and one cop nudged the other with a sly smile.

"What the fuck?" Casio's eyes were wide open and red with misery. "What the fuck?"

"Theodoro G. Rodriguez, also known as Casio?" said the detective.

"What the fuck you want a me?"

"You have the right to remain silent. Anything you now say can, and will, be used against you."

Casio struggled against the medic's grasp, while his already wet, pale face streamed with tears and his legs thrashed jerkily. "My legs! I'm dying, you're gonna kill me!" he chanted.

The fatter cop tiptoed in. The water on the floor welled up over the toes of his shoes.

He bent to take Casio's free arm, but it flew into the air, spewing water in his face. The other cop leapt into the bathroom, landing on the flooded floor with a sharp splat as the medic gritted her teeth and tightened her hold on the arm.

Casio was shrieking like a baby. An enormous convulsion arched his back and jerked his head so far back that it disappeared below the surface of the water. The fatter cop grabbed him by the hair and yanked the head above the surface. As Casio gulped for air, the cop and the medic wrenched him forward and yanked his arms behind him to slip on the cuffs.

The body was hoisted from the tub onto the stretcher, and a blanket was thrown over its nakedness. Then the stretcher was eased out the doorway and hoisted laboriously down the stairs, while a singsong moaning spiraled up the staircase and through the open door.

But the detective lingered, staring down at the fragile form that he had pardoned. His face faded in and out of expressions like trick photography: desolate and tender, guilty and knowing, sentimental but resigned.

It was his discreet departing footsteps that finally woke the figure sprawled under the blown-up photos. Angel squinted dazedly at the open doorway and shakily rose to his knees. He peered around the room for Casio. Then he danced to the sheetless mattress and fell out again.

# VII

It was the night he wasted that out-of-it, over-the-hill, sometime-junkie Casio, and soon after the bugged-out trick told him to leave, that Apollo copped some dope with the money he'd earned and jumped the number six train. He was still high and shirtless. And his lucent skin over its compact musculature was stained with dirty rivulets of sweat.

Anyone who wanted to look closely could have seen and studied the tracks, bruises, and punctures that covered his shapely arms, which seemed as perfectly formed, and moved as jerkily, as an automaton's. Paled by fatigue, liver toxins, and the stresses of sex, his ovoid face looked lit and open, yet dazed and numbed.

First he straddled two cars to do up the new bag. A white guy would have said it was like cross-country skiing: balancing the sway with one foot on each car as the train zigzagged around curves while he cooked up in a bottle cap. The vibrations of the train caused the spike to jiggle in his hand, so he quickly found a vein by using the same festered hole. And as the stuff seeped into him, even the sparking steel wheels on their unrepaired track giddied out into a long, smooth rush. Then he went inside one of the cars and stretched out on a seat, feeling relaxed and justified, a hard day of work like anybody.

Against his nodding eyelids, a secret dream resurfaced of the bedroom he had just vacated. He saw the stripes on a sheet and had the sensation of sinking down to it as the guy's breath tinged his nostrils while his nipples hardened.

*Dog training.* But what did that have to do with it all? A cynical delight trickled through him at the thought of the tense, eerily restrained middle-aged man who'd ended up gobbling his toes like a dog. Then laughter chortled out of him and woke him up, causing a glance from a startled passenger, which was itself suddenly cut off by the next dope nod ...

The train clanged along on a powerful dream or fantasy (or had it happened?) of laying on a now nameless trick under TV light a tale about Mrs. Huxton sending him to dog-training school. Then all of a sudden there he was: back in front of her building again.

The theater marquee with its missing letters—OPEN TIL AWN—was still lit. Above it, Mrs. Huxton's windows shut out its light and Eighth Avenue with thick stucco grillwork in the shape of arabesques, like a harem's. Just a little light would filter in during the day, it occurred to him. A view of Eighth Avenue even in the daytime was just not classy enough for her.

Next to the building was her public parking lot, stark in its salmon-colored mercury-vapor light. It was empty at 4:00 A.M. And it occurred to him what a stupid thing it was to do: drifting back to the theater when the cops must be looking for him by now. Anybody could have dropped a dime on him by calling 911. But still his feet remained rooted to her sidewalk, his head thrown back and eyes fixed numbly on her sequestered windows.

*

Slowly but surely, a vulnerable rage was melting some tender core in his narcotized brain. It concerned the fact that the lady would be disappointed in him. How especially painful, since he knew about that soft spot for him in her leathery old heart. What did he have to go through to please her, anyway?

Shuffling like a subterranean, will-less denizen of Mrs. Huxton's squalid realm, he edged into the harshly lit parking lot. He hid in the shadow thrown by her mysterious building. Gulping at the night's rank air, he pressed his naked shoulder against the cool brick, feeling for life in the building. But there was no give-and-take; it wasn't breathing. Inside it was the secret reason for his stupid crime—an illogical rage that had left the bouncer lying on a sweating cement floor. Meanwhile, a dumbass junkie with the high-class name of Apollo who didn't even know where he'd left his shirt cowered animal-like in the next-door parking lot. It was no wonder Mrs. Huxton stayed above in her air-conditioned rooms as he and other nonentities waded through the murky lagoon of her theater. He'd been programmed to let her down; it had been ordained the moment she set eyes on him. So as usual he was just playing a part of some higher power's agenda that didn't give a shit about him.

Mrs. Huxton probably rose early and would soon be opening her closet to dress. Apollo's mind ferreted among the veiled hats and whisperings of taffeta she had preserved there since the forties, for accouterments of a darker, more masculine cast.

The revolver slipped within a stack of lingerie might have a pearl handle, but the blackjack that had always been carried by her husband, Buster, would be blunt, ugly, scarred. Just as uninviting, but arousing because of the respect it elicited, was the leather-covered address book of the payment distributors and intermediaries—all the profiles of all those thugs-cum-chauffeurs she used to palm-grease the politicians or protect her from the smut peddlers.

If only he could be granted an audience with her to explain things, he began thinking. That haughty and slow-moving higher-up in her Colonial-style armchair would offer him a seat and a cup of tea, maybe even a brandy. But he'd be sitting with naked tits and new scabs on his knuckles and a tied tongue, hoping that his sweat-drenched jeans wouldn't leave behind stains on the bone-colored couch upholstery when he stood to be sentenced.

Yet what was the big hurry about standing up, anyway? She hadn't bargained for the fact that he was an ace bullshit artist who could spit out alibis faster than an Uzi could shoot slugs. And maybe they weren't even alibis. A class act like her would have to recognize that he and she were two of a kind. Both of them were trapped in the same sewer by circumstances, yet both saw a myriad of worlds beyond. Both of them were plagued by dummies and deadheads too low class to grasp the heartbreaking insights that he and she shared . . .

The sparkling gray eyes under white hair peppered his plea with her cynicism. Did he really think they were in the same league?

Okay, maybe he *hadn't* had the luck—all right, the smarts—to latch on to the high life like she had. But certainly things had not gotten too cushy for her to see through the grime to his active brain and aching heart. Let's face it: she needed the streets as much as he. And—no offense— but he imagined she'd probably had to make some of the very same compromises when she was his age . . .

In the ticket booth to the theater, the bloated cashier spent this last hour dozing in a bent-forward position. Even on nights of unusual violence like this, his forehead would end up on the ticket counter, the askew hairpiece pressed against the filmy glass.

Apollo's mind was too focused on Mrs. Huxton's unfair judgments to analyze the seduction of being able to sneak past him, back into the theater to turn one more trick.

The musty, rubber-backed curtain caressed his face like the familiar hand of an aged relative as he fell past it. Inside the darkness, he let the thrill of defying the menace of being at the scene of the crime swirl around him and mix with the smell of the sex. It was that unhinged moment when the wildest of plans is a success precisely for its foolhardiness, a moment he had experienced before only during the best of highs.

The seat cushion into which he was sinking sighed with expelled air as a Charlie McCarthy puppet-head rotated toward him. "Want a private show?" Apollo whispered close to the carved wooden ear.

As if the man had been absorbed into his high, they floated toward a door next to the movie screen that led to the other side of it, Apollo's mind still flip-flopping through his defense to Mrs. Huxton. Had she forgotten that up to now he'd been one of the more discreet employees, who never sneaked tricks off the street past the box office like some of the other hustlers did? And maybe she'd like to know about her reliable bouncer, Casio, holding on to cuts from every night's take . . .

*

On the other side of the screen, the porno film was visible in mirror image and as if seen through gauze. There was, he decided, no big necessity for a condom, as he planned to let the guy suck him only for a few, without coming. It would, he knew, take hours to get a woody when he was this high.

The man had unbuckled Apollo's pants and pushed them and the posing strap down. Suddenly Apollo's stoned attention corkscrewed into those spastic rhythms. *The guy's plastered!* He took in the suit in late-for-the-train-to-Westchester dishevelment before shutting it out and forcing him down by the shoulders. He felt the dribbling mouth burrow eagerly into his groin. The hands spidered over his chest and forearms, creating a focus that recrystallized his train of thought.

*The drugs?* Okay, but he was working on that, for her (Mrs. Huxton's) information. It just wasn't that easy after all these years, but someday. Anyway, up until now, like her, he'd never let this Times Square atmosphere come between him and his work.

*Where would even she be without wizards like me who know, when johns stumble into this stinking place, how to reel them in against the odds?*

But her jewel-cut eyes only reflected his low opinion of himself. Hers was the glance of somebody who'd written the whole book, and even the words that were coming out of his mouth.

Apollo pulled back, and his balls slid away from the man's mouth. He stuffed them back into his pants and zipped.

Ruefully, the man stood up to fumble in his pockets for money, and Apollo impatiently grabbed the twenty from his hand. Now it was time for the boldest part of his experiment, and his sense of fate expanded to it. This revisit to the theater had become a kind of reparation for earlier this evening. As he stumbled down the steps to the basement, he half expected to trip against the body of Casio, put back where he'd left it. But instead, he found Casio's fourteen-year-old son, called Baby Pop, sitting at the old makeup table, with its missing light bulbs. The kid was gazing through big uncut curls into the dimmed mirror, his knapsack dangling from the back of the metal chair.

From time to time the kid, whom Apollo found spooky, dipped into the theater and snuck through the shadows in hopes of locating his father and hitting him up for a few bucks. Or he tried to hustle outside the theater. "You seen my Casio?" he asked, as he had many times before, looking at Apollo's face by way of the mirror.

Apollo shook his head. "You know where I can get me a bag right now?"

Still gazing into the mirror, the boy answered with a nod through the obscuring curls. "You don't even got to leave the theater. The Big Man sent Carlos in here to get rid of a bundle. I'll get you one."

Apollo pressed the twenty into the boy's hand. Sending him up there in his place was a good idea, given the fact that they were probably looking for his ass at this point.

"Get me a bag for ten and gimme back eight," he ordered. "Stay with the two dollars."

The boy took the stairs two at a time. Apollo sat in his place at the dressing table but avoided the mirror. For some reason he feared he would see Mrs. Huxton in it. Not looking into the mirror caused their tête-à-tête to fade into the darkness, replaced by an imageless, shimmery gray . . .

*

In what seemed no time at all (was it an hour?), the Baby Pop kid was back. With showy efficiency, he pressed the bag and the change into Apollo's hand.

As Apollo was making the vow to save the stuff until later, he noticed the belt of his old terry-cloth bathrobe lying on the dressing table. Then he saw himself pick up the belt and use it to tie up. He took the bottle cap out of his pocket, filled it with stuff and a little water, and held it over a match.

Why was the rush from this injection steeper than the one earlier? Either he was already too high or the dope was better. He became aware of the boy's hooded eyes watching him unblinkingly, the affect concealed, the way a cat watches a TV screen. Then he was zoomed back to his trial before Mrs. Huxton, the dope inflating her living room to massive, cruelly lit proportions.

The only thing to do was to throw himself at her feet, on the plush, suddenly bristling, carpet, his nose squashed against the squeaky-clean mahogany table leg. For nothing hurt more than being kicked out of this world into nothingness again. There wasn't anything crueler than worrying about how he was going to get high without the lady's help . . .

Mercedes the queen in her improbable costume—a foot-high beehive wig, gold lamé halter with heavy-duty cleavage, black leather miniskirt, stiletto ankle-strap pumps with gold metal heels—stopped short at the parking lot to gawk at nodding Apollo rocking back and forth on bent knees in full sight of traffic.

*After what he perpetrated tonight and here he is nodding out right at the scene of the crime,* was all the transvestite could think. She scrutinized him. The tip of her numbed tongue lightly probed the space where her complete front tooth had been before he broke it a few years back. Her ideas somersaulted on a dainty toke of crack she'd had a few minutes ago. She didn't know why, but every time she saw him, a wash of sentimentality overtook her. Despite everything, words spilled out.

"Parkin' your zonked ass right here of all places on the choppin' block? After you's stupid enough to waste Casio what everybody's talkin' about!"

Apollo's head jerked in astonishment at the sight of the gigantic, mascaraed eyes of the lover from the past not more than two inches from his face.

"I know what I'm doing."

"If you don't do the bird, you're in the meat cooler 'fore you know it."

But shirtless Apollo's eyelids sank, and he teetered again into Mrs. Huxton's world, swaying on bent knees.

*He's clockin' nods with the law out lookin' for him,* reflected Mercedes. *Now ain't that the be-all and end-all of irresponsibility? And he sunk so low into the nod that he won't know he's in the bullpen till the runs set in or he feels a woody up his butt. Well, I'm gonna put on my nurse's cap and feed this sucker some a the devil's dick.*

Mercedes hiked up her miniskirt as she had earlier, but this time it was to pull out a crack stem nestled inside her panties, next to the burn scars caused by stashing it when the cops went by. She took a small plastic bag from her cleavage and pulled out a vial, yanked off the top with her side teeth, and quickly dumped the rock into the stem.

"Suck on this," she hissed nervously, shoving the stem between his lips and holding a flame to the other end. As

Apollo inhaled, a numbing stream of vitality seemed to coat his mucous membranes like molasses. It straightened him up.

It was like being in a barrel going over the falls as the toke melded with the downer of dope and shifted him into smooth fall. Mercedes, looking elongated and Egyptian under her foot-high wig, surged into his plane of consciousness with hyperreality, and he found himself swooning into her fragrant arms.

"Baby, whatever happened to us," he mumbled, nuzzling her breasts and probing for the nipples with his open mouth.

Mercedes rode a lower wave of crack high. She felt the tears rising as she fainted into their mutual myth but was able to pull herself out of it. She yanked his head away from her tits but kept her arms around him.

"Walk now, away from the scene of the crime and into sanctuary."

Apollo moved down the street with her as if he were skating—but no, it was more like a conveyer belt. The murky facades of buildings slid by as he floated on Mercedes's marshmallows, hovering in a royal stillness, a most wonderful high.

"I really should visit my mom, I haven't seen her in a while," he lisped with ingenuous sentimentality.

"Your white momma?" said Mercedes. "Why don't you chill with her till the heat's off." They were approaching the entrance to a subway, and she nudged him toward it. Lying on the railing was a black string T-shirt. Mercedes copped it and pulled it over Apollo's head. "My baby's all dressed to go home now. Make yourself scarce 'fore a rat drops a dime on you." They stood at the top of the stairs, melting into each other. "They can't do me none," said Apollo with jerky bravado. Once again she felt as if she were falling into the old fable; but simultaneously, a drop down from her own high suddenly called for crack in her head. Almost gratefully, she twisted out of the trap of his arms to heed the call.

"You ain't in condition to be wagin' tonight, and no wildcattin', neither."

"What you mean, I know what time it is."

He realized that he was slurring this to nobody in particular, as at some point Mercedes had left (had she ever been there?), and he was stupidly facing one of the barred exit doors next to the turnstile. A blast from the token-booth speaker shot through him.

"Are you buying or crying? Drop a token or get out of here!"

The corrections-facility-sounding voice, mechanized by the speaker, gushed fear through him. Suddenly he began conjecturing what had happened to Casio, from the moment the body was lying on the floor of the theater basement. Even Mercedes had heard about it, though that Baby Pop son obviously hadn't.

Had Casio merely come to and reported Apollo to the cops? Or had he cracked his skull and gone out of this world for good? Apollo remembered the strange crunching sound and the way Casio's eyes rolled up into his skull. "I'm scared they're going to charge me with a one eighty-seven," he said into the air, playing out the fate of a murder charge in his head. The crescendo of the train rush, an unbearable rattling in his ears, cut off any imagined answer and summoned an unusual athleticism. Apollo vaulted over the turnstile and hopped onboard. He knew just what he should do and who would take him in. Only the friend who gave him Percodans, whom he'd once bashed outside the theater, was the one to trust now.

*

The train rattled its way downtown as nausea from the previous dose strained through Apollo. It tightened his esophagus and screwed up his face as he dropped into the nearest seat. Next to him, a large woman, a night worker on her way home to another borough, tightened her grip on the shopping bag in her dark hands. She glared at the shame of his condition but stubbornly remained in the adjoining seat. Her expression convinced him of the continuing injustices toward him, radiating from the wicked entrepreneur Huxton. Simultaneously, the air conditioning in the car tightened his nipples, reminding him that his new shirt was only made of net.

He checked his reflection in the swallowing blackness of the window opposite. To his relief, he found that the shirt set off his muscles and looked good against his skin. The reflection confirmed his narcissistic pleasure in his own body and the excitement some hands found in running over it and consequently buying it dope. In a deep, sensual nod, he began to fantasize the friendly touch of the man who gave him Percodan and whom he was on his way to see.

Apollo let his thoughts play over the mystery of this man, whom he usually took for granted, because it was so much easier that way. He was the only person Apollo knew who broke all the rules in this down-and-out context to which Mrs. Huxton had condemned them all. Some people thought he gave Apollo Percs so he could take advantage of him. But when he gave them, it was because Apollo asked, and that seemed to be the only reason. Others took the guy for an easy mark, but Apollo knew he was more than that. The minute you thought you'd played him, you realized the con hadn't even been necessary.

But there was something else about him, too ... And Apollo's mind only strayed to it when it was feeling most defended by dope: something about the man's sickness, the fact that he had HIV. Because ever since he'd been diagnosed, he seemed to fit into Apollo's world better. This was no mean feat, since he'd been to college—to a fancy Ivy League school, even.

Apollo sat up and winced at the realization. Big disadvantage was the top credential for ending up here. All of them—johns, hustlers, retards, and sick Ph.D.s—were fellow citizens of this Land of the Doomed. And this guy's outsider attitude—wry, ironic, bitter, a little above-it-all—was exactly what brought him and Apollo together again and again.

Apollo's mind strayed back to the months when they'd lived together, until Apollo blew it by stomping on him during withdrawal one day outside the sex theater. And then he had gone to jail as a result and come out and they were cold strangers.

When Mercedes cut him, he went to jail again. The seasons changed; he came out again and was drawn toward the guy like a tack to a magnet.

Two nights ago, the guy had willingly parted with half his supply of Percodan, which his doctor gave him by the hundreds for the pain and numbness in his legs and feet. What was it like to be beat up, to have somebody arrested for it, and then to forgive him a year or so later? At this moment, Apollo's imagination couldn't make the stretch. The closest he could come to what it was like was the time he'd been very high and got caught trying to rob a midtown office by security guards. The guards kept whacking him with their nightsticks. Apollo fell and somersaulted, rolled down the corridor, and stood again, grinning.

But his white friend with AIDS couldn't be hanging around him for the same reason: that dead kick of turning off to life's bashers. Suddenly his friendship with

Apollo—his secret reasons for identification—formed an alibi for the nausea drowning Apollo's body . . .

It was obvious that the friendship felt much too sticky. Whom he sometimes referred to as his only friend appeared in a harsher, nauseating light. His ailing flesh fastened its suckers to Apollo and was tugging at his naked skin.

Apollo irately felt the sensation of being dragged into the heap with the losers. In the safety of an evil high, he considered paying his slick little buddy a visit. House the rest of the Percs? The guy could always go to the emergency room if he needed painkillers, couldn't he? He had AIDS.

But it wouldn't be enough to scoop up the Percodan; if the guy wanted to take care of him, maybe he wouldn't mind if Apollo borrowed a bunch of CDs and the little VCR that only played, not recorded. For when you really thought about it, this gay guy, by the presumption of being different—by choosing to slum, even while sick and in this context where everybody was reduced to the same level—was just playing him. He would probably savor a nice lesson from the sick, mean junkie that pretty-faced Apollo knew he was.

The train jiggled Apollo awake. And in the bright light the image of the guy rotated suddenly. There was an almost grotesque shift, in which the ailing friend became sacrificing and enveloping. Against his will, as the next nod took hold, Apollo was plunged again into the motherly arms and their transcendent familiarity with death.

He was whisked away from the petty plane of street deals and fleeting highs and bitter resentments of the last nod into the smarting ether of real friendship, as painful as it could be.

Mrs. Huxton's world-weary realm of condemnation

withdrew in reverse zoom, an aerial view of the building roofs and water towers of her seedy empire growing ever more distant, as he and his buddy sped into pain like astronauts in a heart-rending free fall.

Out here, there were comets and great wakes of stars that shot through you for loving; it was like coming, but obviously quite sexless, and painful. So above natural laws were they that Percodan, CDs, and the VCR sitting in the apartment were now perfectly okay to take. Even the black lady glaring at him had a right and a reason to feel pain. Life was a tragic banquet free of ownership at which everybody wept and kissed. The woman did a double take as he flashed her a sudden loving smile.

Happy, he hopped off the train at his good buddy's stop, confident that a firm pressure on the doorbell would gain him entrance into his brave utopia. He saw the guy's gentle smile as he tipped the vial of Percodan into his pocket, apologetically borrowed a shirt and socks, and unhooked the VCR. The smile filled him with such gratitude that he wanted to come back as soon as he could with a present: a book the guy wanted to read, flowers, a cake.

But nobody was answering that buzzer. Apollo leaned on it with all his weight. The fleeting realization that it was past 4:00 A.M. only inspired him with contempt for those who were not free enough and big enough to be there when he needed them. So he walked backward from the building and looked up at the darkened windows on the third floor. He opened his mouth and let sound spill out.

"Yo! Yo! Yooooo!"

The street was silent. Then, in the wrong window, a light switched on. He saw a curtain part and furious eyes peek out at him.

78

"Yo, you know my friend? The guy in three A?"

The curtain closed.

The nausea began to well back up. And like last time, it was attached to a feeling. The drama of the friend whom he'd thought of ripping off, who'd then suddenly become a super friend, shrunk. All that had the petty status of a hallucination. It was replaced by a cold sweat in the real air of predawn: the feeling of being a fugitive, the reality of the crime at the theater. He just wasn't high enough to avoid it now.

Everything bore down on him: the cops looking for him, the cold public light from the street lamps, the closed and darkened buildings; his exhausted, stale body.

If he didn't chill out, get some sleep where it was safe, the rock and the hard place moving in on him would crush him. On weary feet he began the nineteen-block walk to his white mother's home, whom he pictured with contempt about ready to rise, climb into sweatpants, and begin chanting for abstract love before eating her vegetarian breakfast. A bubble of energy forced a bitter laugh out of him at the thought of her rent-controlled apartment and her lunar calendar, the jars of grain on a shelf above the stove.

Day was just beginning to break as he tiptoed up the stairs to her roof. As usual, he had no intention of going down to her apartment to see her. On the roof, the air felt fresh and hopeful for the first time.

He stretched out on the tarpaper next to the bag of bread he'd brought up there a few days ago. Inside was a small crust, which he chewed before lying back with his mouth open.

A pigeon winged through the air, dirty and on the loose, curtailed by the world of tar-covered water towers and sparse trees of the stinking city. It looped up and then dove for him. He felt its claws on his face. Its head dipped into his mouth and sucked some chewed bread out of it. Then the bird lifted back into the air.

Mouth fallen open like a baby bird's, with the remainder of the chewed bread in it, soft-skinned Apollo fell into a deep, long-term nod. It relaxed the muscles of his face like a coma and took years off it.

# VIII

"You stinking black bitch, you're a
fake. There's no such thing as a lady
in our world. You either got to be a
bitch or a faggot in drag."

—ICEBERG SLIM, *Pimp*

*This is detective Juan Pargero speaking through your thoughts.
Seems an employee of the Ecstasy Male Theater has been
badly beaten and may be crippled. Turns out it's the same pincush-
ion junkie I arrested for armed robbery of O'Hara's place almost
a decade ago. That time we had to hoist him out of a bathtub, he
was so high.*

*Once more I go undercover. The kind of places I got to go, you
get the goods quick when you blend in with the crowd. The best
snitches about the sucker who attacked Theodoro G. Rodriguez,
a.k.a. Casio, I figured, would be at Tina's. Believe it or not, the
queen is an old pal of mine.*

*We go back. Seem funny to you? Being how she has chosen to represent herself. I mean, her crotch suppressor and all? Then think again. A dick like me runs into all kinds of people. Some are a helluva pain in the butt. But Tina is kosher. She's square with the guys in blue. She knows how one person's hand wipes another's ass. And none of them come up smelling like 4711.*

*I first bumped into Tina undercover as a john on a missing person's case. The brother of a certain V.I.P. had evaporated into thin air two months back. Rumor had it he was a love slave. Some queen was keeping him in vials in a midtown hotel room.*

*His daddy's will was waiting to be distributed, and all that they needed was a signature. The brother wanted him found fast, before the papers did. Somebody contacted Buster Huxton's widow. She said the transvestite bar was a good place to start the investigation.*

*"Looking for female company?"*

*This was way before she owned the place. Just a skinny queen squeezing up to the bar to get in next to me. I could smell Muguet des Bois coming from her armpits. Her bony knees pinned one of my thighs between them. I felt her fingers snake along my pants and slide into my pocket hunting for some green.*

*"I found the family jewels, honey, but no bucks."*

*So I took my wallet out of my breast pocket.*

*"Doubles?" she suggested, testing her luck, and at the word, Ethel Girl, that mop-headed bartender, who might have been a botched transsexual, came running with a bottle of vodka from the B shelf, her lips parted to reveal a rotten-toothed smile.*

*Miss T played the lady, pressing fingers to her mouth while she waited for Ethel Girl to stop pouring and for me to pick up the tab. Then she grabbed her glass and managed to hook her arm through mine. We raised our drinks in a toast, Latin-style: arms linked and eyes glued to each other.*

*A quiver passed through those bare shoulders, jiggling the falsies into action (it would be years before she went the silicone route).*

Her polyester curls bobbed up and down. She poked a finger under my belt to tug me closer. But an alarm must have gone off when she felt my piece through the jacket making a dent in the falsies.

"When a man's carrying it means one of two things. Somebody's looking for him. Or he's looking for somebody."

"All I'm looking for is a little information."

"Why not let your fingers do the walking?" Miss T placed my hand on her buns.

Our research continued upstairs. A week later she'd become my eyes and my ears for everybody that came into that bar.

Ten days later, we had found our man.


Those were the old days, when Tina was just a bit player. Now she owns the whole shebang—second only to Mrs. Huxton in controlling the block. The night the attempted murder happened, an anonymous call came in about a certain Apollo Nelson. The unidentified caller dubbed him the perpetrator, named the theater where the bouncer had been nixed, indicated whereabouts of the suspect somewhat below Fourteenth Street, and gave us dial tone. We put a qui vive on the area, but to no avail.

Mrs. Huxton, being very perturbed about the incident in her establishment, had arranged for her driver to pick me up near my digs in Jersey and drop me in front of Tina's around 4:00 A.M. It was gonna be Sunday morning, and Mom was looking forward to the usual game of gin, but the good woman has adjusted to my operations over the years.

The after-hours crowd had packed the place to busting. Tina was in back counting up the loot from the legit take. A member of the force was parked discreetly outside, keeping the blue laws at arm's length.

She'd already heard about the trouble at the theater and had laid out my first move. So she took her cigarillo out of her mouth and blew me a kiss, poked aside the backroom curtain, and pointed at a black queen in gold lamé with a yard-high beehive.

"Name's Mercedes. Used to go with one of the boys from the theater—fore he broke her jaw and she sliced him up. A junkie, name of Apollo? He's the one you want, if my grapevine honked me right."

"Tina, love o' my life, what would I have done without you these years? If I'd the time, I'd——"

"Shovel the manure for that queen over there, handsome. You're gonna need plenty of it."

And right she was: Mercedes was the proverbial brick shithouse, with nails longer than the switchblade between her luscious chocolate tits. Under her yardstick 'do, her black eyes shone like tacks, ready to nail the first sucker that came along. A sweet smile parted over a broken coconut-sliver of a tooth. Except what was the diva palming? A little plastic squeeze bottle. A homeboy she called Fierce One whispered like the devil into her wig.

I snuck in nearby and pricked up my ears. Seems he was training her for a long con. A milquetoast john in an undertaker's suit was their mark-to-be.

"That's the best way to get the sucker, sweetheart," Fierce One wheedled. "Pour the whole bottle a this in his drink. I boosted it from an eye doctor. After a couple sips he won't remember nothing and starts walking bad. Shitting in his pants before he gets to the corner. You just follow him at a distance, is all."

"Eye drops'll do it?" says the queen.

"Sure will, baby. He'll be hallucinatin'."

"You ain't shitting me, Fierce One? If so, I'd be snappin' mad."

"Baby, read my lips. The Love Bandit don't never lie. I'm into crowd control. Now bus it, 'fore the john leaves."

Her homeboy raised a blunt finger to test the torque on his gold cap. He tapped the queen on the ass toward the john.

She tucked the bottle between her silicone knockers and slinked forward, but it slipped down and fell out of her halter as she walked.

84

I dove for it, and watched her play the john for broke. She moved like an expert, and I had to admire it. He bought them fresh drinks. Then she went for the eye drops and found they were gone.

Five minutes later she was back at the bar. Fierce One had already moved on to one of his other girls. The queen was in a dither, furious about missing the mark.

Up came my line. "Buy you a drink?"

"A couple, if you want."

I paid for the drink and palmed the eye drops. Gave her five dollars for the jukebox, told her to "play our song."

I'm an all-round sport, a good-time guy. All's fair in love and war. Sometimes a man's work takes precedence, so I emptied that bottle of eye drops right into little Miss Mercedes's drink.

She came back and put her two-inch nails around it, stuck her lips to the edge, and took a swig, then ran the tip of her tongue across her top lip, not knowing she was windshield-wiping an optometrist's cocktail.

"Out-of-town?" she asked.

"On it."

"A live wire."

"I got plenty of juice."

"AC or DC?"

"Why?"

"I carry an extension cord, if ya want me to unstrap it."

"I got all the length we'll ever need."

"One prong at a time, baby."

"You got my motor humming."

"Let's go upstairs and git some grease fore it burns out."

Not one to take a man's word, she grabbed hold of my coil for verification. It unwound for her, and we steered it upstairs.

\*

*Watching her hunched on a cheap mattress in the seedy hotel sent a clammy feeling creeping through me. This was no Madonna, but my heart went out. At least the diarrhea was over. The eye drops had had the effect of pulling everything liquid out of her, and they raced her nervous system like an overdose of not-so-good speed.*

*Her problems got worse when I pulled out my badge. She was too weak to stand and too wigged to clam up. Words came pouring out of her like the other stuff had. She jump-cut from one memory to another.*

*"Apollo? . . . Now where that sweet piece been chillin'? Strange fancies, that butch queen. Could never go nowhere without singing to his Mercedes. Ain't that the truth, baby, every day of the week?"*

*She rode the memory of their love affair like it was the Concorde instead of the Coney Island roller coaster it was. But I got to say: she took the swells without a barf bag.*

*"Them days with Apollo! I was runnin' through some crazy money! The nigga's be payin' me stupid dollars! 'Cause I was pullin' 'em in fore they had a doubt. Even so, that nigga had no business dipping in my purse! And catching the sucker on Ninth Avenue conversatin' with another female finished it for me! I'd been faded by the punk too many a time.*

*"So I told him, listen, you know, you got no respect. That why if you don't hand back my loot, I'm gonna cut you. But the dough was already in his veins. And so was the Budweiser. You know, Mister, if you haves a lot of alcohol in you, the blood is thin. It really flows out. So I was sorry I opened him up. The cops come along but my pantyhose saved me. Then I lost my man to Riker's when they found the works on him. Now it's history."*

*She got off the ride to the past quick, a dazed stare at a broken press-on nail. Catching sight of it, she snapped. She put her head in her hands and started bawling. She wailed for Apollo and for lost love. The room was hot, so I unpinned her wig and laid it on the night table. Then I put a finger on her cheek to wipe the tears away.*

"You got heart, Lieutenant."

"Why would a pro like you let a guy like that use you in his Monopoly game?"

"I started early. Everybody made me eat it raw when I should a been on formula."

"Sure, kid. Rough."

"You end up feelin' at home in any bed, 'cause you know you'll never be in any bed you can call home. You got a rag?"

I tossed her my clean handkerchief, and she blew her nose.

"You got no idea where I can find the punk?" I asked her straight out.

"You're askin' me to snitch on my man?"

"You just got finished telling me he was history."

The queen began to bawl again. "But he was no more'n fifteen when I first meets him. Just a nose junkie, and where was he? Oh my me, let's see. Cock blockin', I think? In front a the head downstairs. You know? Reelin' in the Johns comin' to the head before the other hustlers can get to 'em by flippin' out your dick. Turnin' heads that way. The guy that guards the head was clockin' z's and didn't notice no thing! But what was the line he feeds me? Something like, I saw you on a deck of cards. Ha ha.

"Right about then I get interrupted. Some stooge thinks he can get the better of me tellin' me I need gaffer's tape to keep my meat from showin' through the panty line. I can see it, says he. See it, suh? You've sucked it, you no-account! I'm twice the woman you'll ever get, and twice the man you'll ever be!

"The dude's about to bean me when Prince Apollo steps in and drops him. Real fineass sucker back then! Fierce. Say what you'll be sayin' fore anybody can. Kinda educated, like almost white. Although he gots a black daddy. A smile like survival. He was the boy who would a never touched ground, if it wasn't for that habit a his . . . Made him shady. He put it down to the neighborhood and the way things lay. Take some responsibility! says I.

*"And I'm here to see that he does."*

*She couldn't turn off her waterworks. "But seeing that I was the cause of our boy bein' incarcerated . . . Shit that hits the fan there maybe set the stage for what was to come tonight. 'Cause Officer, he come down river again kind a violent. He got that scar on his soul when he was new fish at Riker's, some older boy tryin' to make a female outta him, come-here-I-want-you-to-do-my-laundry, that kind a stuff, and hold-my-dick-for-me-while-I-pee."*

*"Don't ya see? His card was drawn long ago."*

*Mercedes finally stopped crying and honked into the handkerchief. "Okay. You can try the alphabets. His white momma lives there. Over on B and Seventh. Look. My dress's all fucked up. I ain't got no other. How'm I gonna work?"*

*"I'm sorry, baby."*

*"You couldn't help me out, Lieutenant?"*

*"Sure. Come on over to Paramus and my mother'll cook dinner." I handed her my card. "Oh. And maybe she's got a couple designer duds she was looking to get rid of."*

*The queen sobered up immediately. "You think she's my size?"*

*I nodded.*

*"You're cool, Detective."*

*I was only doing my job.*


Pargero's job took him to the computer at the precinct, then toward the building where Apollo's mother lived. To get there, he and his two cops cruised past Mrs. Huxton's block and through the several trillion dollars of real estate that made up their now-deserted midtown precinct, then down the wide avenue still empty in the very early light of morning.

They headed east leisurely, past the 24-hour fast-food stores, with their high-watt fluorescents still fighting the previous night, and turned onto the avenue, where they entered one of the most eclectic neighborhoods in the world, overcharged with races and religions, art students and almost-artists, gay subculturals and squatters, rebellious rockers, adjunct professors, sixties leftovers, window trimmers, illegal aliens, Rastas, welfare families, jazz singers, restaurateurs, numbers takers, pot sellers, permanent outcasts, and transients.

They cruised past ancient bars that had stood in the same spots since the turn of the century, next to silver-painted clubs that had been thrown up yesterday. They passed a mangled, velvet-upholstered chair that someone had tried to spray-paint orange and whose stuffing was scattered all over the sidewalk; they dodged an overturned carton of books and a crutch lying in the street.

They turned down a street from which an unbroken string of building facades was reflected on their window against the hatchet silhouette of Pargero—looking like the figurehead of a ship—its harsh, eclectic, city-made expression fading in and out as images were superimposed on it.

Pargero was thinking about the perpetrator and mulling over the question of race. In the last file dealing with Apollo's previous incarceration, notes still remained about the character-witness appearance of his white mother, as well as the letter she had later written, eloquently but somewhat bizarrely petitioning the Board of Corrections for his early release, using as an excuse the sad fate of his father.

Each of these documents was haunted with the eerie tension of what Pargero sometimes jokingly called miscegenation. And Pargero himself was a product of it. For Pargero's mother was an Anglo, whereas his father had been from Paraguay. And Paraguay had been revealed as that haven for international criminals who ... Suffice it to say that when alibis of mixed race came to the fore, another of the detective's fetishes was stimulated.

His overloaded brain began trying to sort through these thousands of mismatched neighbors, these heaps of lives that defied categorization or surveillance. Normally he would have seen it as just another neighborhood. But as he came closer to the race-scarred mother who had given the testimony and written the letter, he found himself entering some of the buildings in fantasy.

In this part of the city, he had seen countless fauna and numerous habitats, from pierced-nose Caucasian gay boys living tripled up since none could afford to pay the rent singly, to lonely Polish newcomers whose chests had been systematically disfigured during interrogation by the knives of anti-Solidarność police, to university film students in spacious two-bedroom apartments who papered their bathrooms with tin foil and painted each room a different daring fluorescent color. He had entered buildings with all Italian tenants, whose hallways were oil-painted and adorned with the figure of a saint at each landing, and who could be awakened at a moment's notice when irregular noises filtered under their black doors with their peepholes, protected by police locks extending into kitchens with tubs, and windows giving onto air shafts.

He had even encountered a commune of Syrian fundamentalists, who would already be rising to fry the chickpeas for the falafels that would be served at the restaurant on that corner, as well as at the nearby mosque, before each climbed into a limo to drive his twelve-hour shift, as well as an astrologer and satanist Pargero had once seen on a bust, who had painted the century-old floorboards of her kitchen with a six-pointed star, and below whom lived the forgotten black Beat painter who had been the girlfriend of some of the most illustrious abstract expressionists but had put on more than a hundred pounds after years of antidepressants and antipsychotic drugs.

As they neared the next avenue, Pargero remembered the middle-aged Dominican man who had been born in this neighborhood and now lived in its streets and shelters, whom Pargero had discovered in a hallway interlocked in coitus with his deaf-mute lover, also homeless, an empty bottle of Night Train by their side. And all the possible crimes being committed at that moment began to parade through Pargero's mind, drawing from the petty and not so petty busts of his career. Perhaps a white law student in that apartment facing the street was cooking up his second batch of free-base cocaine; or that Israeli exterminator who lived over there had again broken his wife's nose while the children surrounded them in a sobbing circle; or Midwestern squatters in those two adjoining buildings had just crashed out after an evening of mushrooms and garage-band records; or a solitary Vietnam vet was up and cleaning his cache of weapons; or the Ukrainian-speaking homeless woman was now squatting once more in a hallway with a broken door lock where she'd once been caught peeing; or some Austrian accountant had been up all night falsifying papers for a small business; or a black real estate broker was coming home from moonlighting as an elegant uptown call girl, which she'd started to do ever since property values went down.

And now they passed that block and broke into the sunlit avenue, where there was a hyphen of space from the chaotic crush of humanity packed into the buildings, so that Pargero could clear his head before another parade began: the peroxided performance-artist junkie from the South who played with gender, alternatingly ruing his gangly body and savoring the next club date; the bewildered and sullen Swiss dancer who was studying with a New York master and who'd become the girlfriend of a coke dealer; the heavily snoring Puerto Rican super whose son, on summer break from medical school, had been murdered; the Panamanian sex-change and the rehabilitated Irish killer who were living on welfare; the Connecticut gay actor who worked in the cookie shop and once got beaten and robbed by a pickup; the Wisconsin-born missionary who'd lost part of her liver function through a stomach parasite she'd caught working in the city shelters; two black people very sick from HIV and some whites panicking about it whom Pargero had seen in the middle of the night waiting in the emergency room of the nearby hospital.

Until they were so close to Apollo's building that if Apollo had woken up and walked to the edge of the roof, he would have seen the loathsome blue-and-white vehicle pulling up to it. Felt the rush of enzymes in Pargero's brain unable to organize the quirky stew of humanity. Heard the doorbell ringing and the buzzer opening it.

Feared the entrance of the law enforcers, who called no neighborhood home.

# IX

Casio's son Baby Pop lay on a piece of cardboard among the summer homeless at World Trade Center Plaza, his famous and valuable shiny curls poking from a found bandanna.

"You be tellin' me my father is askin' for me?" said the fourteen-year-old. He sat up abruptly on the piece of cardboard and blinked disorientedly, rubbing his eyes with grimy fingers, as if the information had come from a dream.

Angelo, the rotten-toothed crackhead who'd come to find him, ground his big jaw trying to spit out the words.

"Me and Manny, the guy always wears the hat with the big X, was conversating 'bout—"

"But ain't that the dude who nixed your cousin?"

"That's bullshit. My cousin was just takin' too much codeine."

"Yeah?"

"And so Manny says to me, you knowing about that my sister's a nurse's aide over at the hospital on Ninth? Well she's telling to me that they got *Casio* over there!"

"My father?"

"They was getting ready that he was goin' to die!"

"He O.D.'d?"

"No man, some motherfucker wasted him! He was in a coma and shit but he come to and be askin' for you!" Angelo sat down on the cardboard with a sigh and looked at Baby Pop expectantly, like a dog that has performed a trick watches for the biscuit about to be tossed.

"Who?" said Baby Pop. "Who wasted him?"

Angelo shook his head and gave a bewildered shrug. Baby Pop reached into his pocket and took out four quarters, flicking them one by one into Angelo's hand. Immediately the crackhead bought a toke off a nearby smoker, grabbed his blackened stem, and inhaled.

Ten minutes later, Baby Pop had hopped the D train. In his duffel bag he carried a pair of dirty socks, his asthma inhaler, a bible, an algebra book, a Stephen King novel, and a pair of jeans. The socks would be traded for clean ones at the very next opportunity. The bible and the Stephen King book got him through the hours as he sat in a stall in the men's room of Port Authority waiting for it to be late enough to go to sleep at World Trade Center. The algebra book was, in his mind, preparation for college.

Up until his last year in school, which was seventh grade, Baby Pop had proved an astoundingly brilliant student, excelling in math. More than anything he wanted to return to that arena and the adulation that had been poured upon him. But from the time he had run away from the group home—where he'd been placed after being taken from his mother, Monica—he'd had to rely for survival on his lustrous curls, his satiny olive skin, his enormous dark eyes with their curly lashes, his elongated, almost girlish limbs, and his serene, passive charm.

He stripped off his T-shirt to expose another, and then

94

took that one off, so he was down to his tank top. Despite the heat, he'd been wearing three layers on top and four—undershorts, shorts, sweatpants, and pants—below. The layers worked more or less like a walking closet, to which he made additions and subtractions at the homes of tricks.

Circulating through his brain at this moment was a simple thought. It was the impulse to "be there" for his father. The fact that Baby Pop had a father was one of the few palpable proofs that he himself was somebody. This fact needed periodic manifestation, though at other times Baby Pop's perception of Casio was numbed, and Casio seemed like just another street person who worked at the theater that Baby Pop himself sometimes stood outside of when he tried to hustle.

As a hustler, Baby Pop was tops but problematic. His serene detachment pricked some potentially long-term johns with adoration but gave others a sense of inferiority that led to their unloading him. And then, of course, his status as a minor didn't help. His nearly photographic recall of names, addresses, and conversations gave him an edge over others, but his other intellectual powers could also perplex or threaten the typical customer.

The train screeched to a halt, and Baby Pop leapt from his seat and out the door. As he passed a man who had exited another car, he caught the guy eyeing his slender arm muscles. The guy looked like a *bugarrón*—a butch—but Baby Pop looked back. The moment of attention was a sign of good luck for the day. Attracting the male gaze did not make Baby Pop think he was gay. On the contrary, it set off his interest in the asses of both sexes and the possibility of ruling over them.

It was the active role he normally took as a hustler, unless forced, or tempted by large sums, to get fucked. Because of this, he preferred a *loca*, an effeminate party-type who liked clubs and discos, as customer. However, he'd had enough experience to realize that a *loca*'s flightiness and fickleness couldn't be depended upon, and ultimately he was looking for a *casera*, a homebody, to move in with for a while. These types spent their time cooking or making the house look good and usually had a nest egg. But because they were not promiscuous, they were hard to find. They were looking for real husbands and usually saw through you when you played them.

There were other types, including the *bugarrón*—a type who usually ended up wanting to fuck you—who were okay, provided they were white. Blacks and Hispanics might force you, but whites could usually be talked into just a suckfest, and it wasn't embarrassing to go to the movies or dinner with them, because they usually weren't effeminate. But to be avoided at all costs were the *cafres*—the freaks— especially the white ones, because they got high on drugs and could get violent or give you strange diseases.

Baby Pop's hustler skills all dated back to seven years ago— two years after Casio moved out—when Monica began looking for ways of increasing the drug flow into the apartment. Cubby, who was the whiteboy leader of a rat pack of dust-heads and hustlers, had begun visiting with his crew and had become Monica's man. Monica would get zonked on rock and dust and party down with Cubby while Baby Pop looked after his own asthma medication and kept up his schoolwork, leaving the apartment each morning neatly dressed, his homework meticulously packaged in a plastic briefcase, with a glance of cool contempt at the others passed out on the bed and floor.

One night Baby Pop found himself alone with Cubby while the clique and Monica partied down in the bedroom. Cubby began to tell Baby Pop the story of each of the tattoos on his body, which represented landmark occurrences in his life. He would take Baby Pop's finger and trace the blue-and-red outlines of the Executioner, the Bat, or the Devil on his skin stretched taut by muscle. Then he recommended that Baby Pop get a tattoo with a shining light bulb that said "Genius" and told him to strip off his shirt so that he could scratch the light bulb and its rays into his skin with a razor blade and some shoe polish.

Baby Pop stripped off his shirt and Cubby got playful, tickling him as his fingers moved over each part of his skinny chest, belly, and arms, describing how it might hurt to get a tattoo there or there. Then he insisted that Baby Pop's ass was the best place, it being their secret only, and got him to slip out of his pants.

The boy lay facedown on the bed, gritting his teeth but not crying as Cubby traced a light bulb and rays with the edge of the razor blade. He blotted up the blood with a T-shirt, then worked bits of shoe polish into the cut with the tip of the blade. When it was over, Baby Pop stayed naked, on his stomach, until it clotted. But when the cut had congealed, Cubby pinned him to the bed, squeezed two fingers inside him, and entered him.

When Baby Pop reached the hospital, Father Kraus was feeding Casio breakfast. The bouncer had been moved from intensive care to a regular room when his vital signs improved. He lay propped up in bed with his head wrapped in a bandage like a turban.

Father Kraus greeted Baby Pop with a sweetened, dentured smile. The old face floated in Baby Pop's gaze like the easy food and lodging and limp moral advice it had always represented. One of his first memories was watching Father Kraus officiate at the funeral of Casio's old friend Chino.

They'd laid Chino in an open casket spray-painted with the graffiti tag of every member of their already defunct gang. He was wearing all his colors and had two bandannas tied above each knee. His spanking white-and-green Reeboks stood out against the green satin lining of the coffin, since green had been the gang's color.

Five-year-old Baby Pop had held on to the stiff jeans of his father and watched the whole show. The bros had marched past the coffin while Father Kraus prayed, and, as in the days of the pharaohs, each placed in it articles that had been dear to the departed: green-and-white packs of Newports, a hookah and a bag of weed, a steel pipe, a 14-carat gold chain with a devil's tail, and a six-pack of Budweiser.

Now the diminutive gray-haired priest hugged Baby Pop, copping a quick feel like a blushing adolescent, simultaneously clearing his throat and swallowing uncomfortably, before letting Baby Pop approach his dad's bed.

"*Bendición.*"

He bent over his father's sallow face and kissed the forehead lightly, taking in the tube coming from his nose and the IV in his already multipunctured arm. One eye was purple and swollen. "What up?" His eyes moved away when he noticed that one of his father's hands was handcuffed to the bed.

Casio tried to speak, but his lips were dry.

"What happened?" Baby Pop asked the Father.

"An accident," Father Kraus opined daintily. "A boy named Apollo who works at the theater apparently got into a disagreement with your dad—"

*Apollo? So that was the* cabrón! An archaic reflex jerked through Baby Pop so strongly that it bounced his shiny curls. This mental activity was a thing apart from his psychological insights or his superb ability to do math. He pulled his inhaler from the duffel bag and took a couple of tokes. Then he bent over Casio's bed. "You don't have to tell me to waste the *cabrón*, Papi. I'll take care of everything while you heal."

Father Kraus watched this communication primly, with a kind of pained anthropological politeness. Then a doctor strode in. He was a tall man with a thick trunk, a healthy tan, and a shiny bald head.

"Which of you is the nearest of kin?" he boomed cheerily, without bothering to look at either.

Casio stirred and winced. He tried to sit up but fell back onto the bed.

Father Kraus smiled a bit unctuously at the doctor. "The young man," he said, and discreetly left the room.

"And what's your name, young fellow?" said the doctor, without even a cursory glance at the boy.

"Ricardo," Baby Pop answered unblinkingly, trying to tune out the unreal personage in white from another class. "Why they got the handcuff?"

"They found a controlled substance in his pocket," said the doctor with casual heartiness. Then he glanced impatiently behind him at the door. "I want someone to get in contact with if anything happens to your father. Could that be you?"

Baby Pop nodded, wondering at the hair sprouting from the guy's forearm and, with a rush from the inhaler, seeing it as if in magnified closeup.

"Give me your phone number, then."

Baby Pop shrugged and kept staring at the hairs.

The doctor blushed. "Well, just leave us a friend's number."

"What happened?"

"What?"

"He gonna be all right?"

"Do you know what nerve tissue is, son?"

"You ain't got to tell me nothing. I'm gonna go to college."

"Fine. Well, your dad damaged a bit of his spinal cord—" The doctor stopped, having accidentally met Baby Pop's eyes for the first time.

As for Baby Pop, he distrusted such sprouts of hair on a white guy's pale forearm. It reminded him of a *cafre*. A *cafre* was the kind who wanted you to get high or to fist-fuck you or piss on you or something. He really hated white guys with hairy forearms like that.

He squinted up to peer at the too-bright bald head and suddenly remembered the booming voice, as inappropriate in this sickroom as it had been in the bedroom.

*Cafre!* he thought. *It really is him.* The freak was a doctor.

This time the doctor's voice cracked. "So we don't know if your father will be able to walk ... "

Baby Pop stared at the shiny dome with nearly brazen contempt. Was it him? He thought he remembered the man, drunk, offering him some kind of drug. A self-satisfied look smoldered in Baby Pop's large eyes. The doctor was turning beet-red now.

"But with some physical therapy, there's a good chance ..."

Father Kraus had come back in from the hallway, and he too was blushing, having caught the twosome staring with naked recognition into each other's eyes. But Baby Pop's intelligent eyes were about to empty into the blank look of the street hustler, realizing the inevitability of it all.

"Listen," he flatly silenced the doctor, using his eyes to indicate his own naked arm muscle, "you couldn't lend me ten dollars?"

*

100

Later that day, Casio went through a violent reaction from heroin withdrawal. He had been cranked up in bed eating applesauce when convulsions catapulted the tray toward the ceiling. His body released a flood of diarrhea onto the sheets as he jerked in and out of consciousness.

By the time the nurses came running, he had floated out of it, his wrist scraped raw from the handcuff, while he looked like a pale pine carving of himself.

A Jamaican nursing assistant muttered curses under her breath while she sponged him off and changed the sheet. Interns immediately put him on an anticonvulsant and methadone to stave off the mess of abrupt withdrawal.

Methadone maintenance would take the edge off the future. Like an abused animal who finally welcomes the containment of a safe, solitary cage, Casio gave in. By then, Abuela, his little great-granny with her wrinkled, yellowed face, missing teeth, and gnarled fingers, was bending over his bed in ecstatic gratitude. His eyes locked to hers, because he knew she was no stranger to seizures.

She was his maternal great-grandmother and Baby Pop's great-great-grandmother and was in her seventies, but she had acted as his mother when he was a boy, bringing him up when her daughter fled to Puerto Rico and her daughter's daughter died from an overdose. She had laid yucca slices on his forehead when he had a fever, putting a clean glass of water next to a white candle from the botanica near the bed. In those days her room was always moist and warm from the beans cooking on the stove.

The haggard woman bent closer to Casio and announced that she felt no portentous vibrations coming from him. To him she looked like a ghost of a bird now, all skin and bones, but his passive gaze stayed glued to her watery brown eyes. She smoothed the hair away from his perspiring face.

In one bony hand she clasped a small piece of folded white paper, an oration. She tucked the special prayer under his pillow. As she understood it, her great-grandson's body had been full of venomous fluids, the excretions of spirits. The blow he had received had shaken the poisonous spirits into turmoil. To gain exit, they'd caused convulsions.

Whenever Abuela herself had a seizure, it was preceded by a pressure in the head or the chest or a numbness in one of her extremities. Rather than a demon inside her, it was usually a good spirit's foreboding of something negative happening or about to happen. For example, the night Baby Pop had had a bad attack of asthma and had to be rushed to the hospital, Abuela had been in her SRO hotel room blocks away, had felt pains in her chest, and had palpated the area only to be knocked unconscious by a vision of her great-great-grandson lying in a white room surrounded by white flames.

Abuela began putting the room in order as proof of her profound thankfulness for her great-grandson's release from demons. A merciful sense of relief about her great-grandson spun inside her bony chest and issued from her mouth as a humming sound. Apparently, he was now being given a medicine that would keep the bad spirits from reentering. But she was convinced that to keep the entire room in defense against the evil, everything had to be symmetrical. The vase had to be in the very center of the windowsill. She took the comb and brush and mirror and hair oil she had brought for him and arranged them in straight lines on the dresser. In front of them she arranged the beads of a wooden rosary in a perfect oval. This was the kind of order she demanded in her own home. Even change was stacked into neat columns and never put in a place that would unbalance the surface of the table.

She unwrapped the *rellenos de papa* and the little codfish cakes and set them on the swing tray above the bed. She smoothed the sheet at the foot of the bed and sat down on it, beaming at her great-grandson lying in safety with the room in order around him. Even the sight of the handcuff could not dispel the deep sense of peace she felt at seeing Casio released from the spirits.

Casio hardly had time to bring a bite of the food to his mouth before Abuela leapt to her feet and clasped him desperately to her. *Mi corazón. If the boy that did this to my great-grandson has a mother, may she someday feel this terrible pain,* was a thought that suddenly coursed to her lips like brushfire. Against the white sheet, Casio's brown fingers stood out. Her eyes fixed on the extra cartilage covering his knuckles from the many scrapes he'd been in since the time he was a boy. The image of the fighting fingers sent more sobs seeping through her. Why was her flesh and blood being put through these tests? A horrible monster had attacked her great-grandson for no good reason. The villain had almost taken his life, and her flesh and blood might be crippled forever.

Casio kept his free arm around the sobbing woman until the sounds faded into silent heaving. He knew that she almost never left her room. When she did, it was only for a family emergency or because she had not had a drink for a long time. She couldn't stand being so high up on the fifteenth floor and rarely even went near a window. She was afraid that if she did, she might jump. It was Casio who usually brought her groceries, but now he was no good to her. Getting to the hospital must have been a tremendous calvary. Because she feared the elevator, she'd likely walked down the fifteen flights, and then up several more to see him. Now the prospect of getting back would appear with dread before her.

Abuela's heaving became deep breathing. She stood and took a pint of rum from her purse. The swallow went down as if her throat had been numbed. There was no burning, no taste. But the liquid was a kind of resignation seeping through her. She sat back at the foot of the bed and watched her great-grandson eat. She watched as one watches something on another plane—a cloud, a bird, an insect—with detachment and fascination. A blood tie in a strange bed eating. All her fears were absorbed by the stillness of watching, broken by the intervals of swallowed rum.

But why that handcuff? The sight of it suddenly made her powerless as its meaning was driven home. Her great-grandson was going to prison again. This was a place where there were many evil spirits that caused diseases of the body and mind. One new disease that ruined the body even seemed to be invulnerable to counterspells.

Abuela broke down again, slouched at the foot of the bed, strands of hair doused in tears, the pint brought more and more often to her lips. She still could not taste it, but it began to burn her throat, her gullet. Her tears blurred her eyes so that the image of her great-grandson got more and more vague. Through her tears the light haloed objects. It haloed the blur of her grandson's head and the hand he raised, like the light radiating from a hand in a sacred painting. The whiteness of the sheets pierced her eyes. They burned her great-grandson in a purifying fire. Abuela's body was warm with gratitude, resignation.

God would take care of him.

# X

Who dares decide the dose of your
sedative?

—ANTONIN ARTAUD

Apollo's situation is beginning to penetrate his numbed
mind. At the sound of the cops he'd come to and leapt
to another roof. He'd forced a door and run down to the
street.

Foremost in his thoughts is the matter of dope. It'll take
a bundle—ten bags—to chill out of reach of the law for
two or three days. This need shifts his thoughts again to
his AIDS-sick friend. He hops the train back to midtown,
hoping to find him at Tina's before evening. In his head he's
already planning on how to ask him if he can hide out at
his apartment. And if he can't get money for a bundle out
of him, he'll have to settle for his supply of Percs.

*

Tina's opens at noon. Because it's daytime, she's not around, so he gets in the bar without any trouble. He buys a beer and takes a sip. Then he begins to nod out for some length he can't calculate. As soon as he opens his eyes, his friend's pale face is in front of them.

In a plaintive voice that Apollo doesn't himself believe, he convinces the wan-looking man to let him stay at his house and to advance him the money for a bundle. He says it's just to take back with them until the heat is off and he can get himself into detox. The moment the guy says yes, a wave of sentimentality washes over Apollo at the merciful kindness of his helper. His mind flits like a colt to a reminder: his helper has AIDS. His thoughts bump suddenly into the time he beat him up and rear in horrendous shame.

He reverses the vector of his feelings: a customary coolness settles in.

The sick friend becomes a thing, a convenience, that he follows to the cash machine, then sits next to as it takes him, holding money, in a cab to 112th to cop. But maybe saying he is a thing is shortchanging him, since the feeling of security that comes out of sitting next to the money fills Apollo with a warmth coming close to contentment, swollen at times with riffs of infantile gratitude.

After he cops, they ride back to the apartment. Apollo hears himself chatting glibly, even enthusiastically, with his savior. He tries to keep his mind off the first hints of withdrawal and comes up with the usual jokes about queens and lawyers, hypocritical doctors, politicians, or whores, which the guy likes. But beneath it all is Apollo's motivation: the bundle of dope—ten real doses—powerful in his pocket like uranium.

When they get to the apartment, a familiar ritual takes over. Apollo strips down to his briefs, kicking the clothing on the floor next to the bed. In his vision's periphery, his

106

rawboned friend is doing the work of caretaking, bending to scoop up the clothes, hanging up what is salvageable, and tossing the rest into the laundry bag with the dependability of a trusted servant or machine. Then the friend sits down to write in his diary with a fountain pen.

Needle insertion, which represents the netherworld between being about to get high and being high, clefts Apollo's mind to let a shadow-feeling sneak in. It is an image of his friend, who now sits absorbed at his desk, dying in the future, and Apollo losing the best friend he ever had. Although he flinches phobically at the thought, it is also an electric spark that fuels the fantasy of life going on. This is enough proof of being alive to keep pushing the needle and pumping the drug into his bloodstream.

Suffice it to say that shortly afterward, with the needle still hanging from his arm, Apollo finally finds an enormous space opening in his perception of the world. The space is so big that for the first time real characters appear to him with some substantiality. First, of course, he sees his friend who has helped him, in the room, glancing at him from the desk with a defeated, tender look. He rejoices at being in his company and orders the man to sit down on the bed beside him.

Because the drug is making his body feel whole, he suddenly has a strong desire to have that body be made love to. And what better person than the one who has bought him the dope and also has his best interests in mind?

The dope also soothes potential disgust at the gauntness of his friend's body. Instead, lovemaking goes on at a more primal level, in which large fields of intimacy take over the mental screen.

The pleasure of a mouth and hands on a body charged with dope could arguably be worth any pain or complications that are to follow. Time becomes meaningless as a dope-charged body gathers impulses toward a slow climax. He feels the one who had protected him, bought him dope, picked up his clothes, and pressed against his body spinning out the pleasure. Apollo's orgasm comes in slow-motion waves, like the cliché female's. It leaves him hovering in a warm torpor that needs no words or images at all.

The man goes back to writing in his journal. Apollo remains on the bed, and thoughts begin to creep in . . . He's glad they had safe sex. Other real people march across the screen of his mind. To him this is intensely pleasurable, for it's all in 3-D, although he does not realize that this quality is present in the minds of normal people who don't take dope.

He pictures his friend, who is at the desk, still writing. Wonders smilingly how he could possibly have all those thoughts. Then suddenly he sees Casio and realizes that he had very little against him. His mind replays the sight of the bouncer lurching toward him on the stairs and the feel of contacting his eye socket. He sees the body fall, without any fear but with a naked acknowledgment of his responsibility. Then, in clarity, his mind moves to consider his options. He's already heard that the guy almost died from the blow and might be crippled. To Apollo this means he might have to go to jail and wait without bail for an indictment. It would be hell to withdraw in jail, so the point is to get himself to detox as the dope runs out.

The reasoning becomes boring and unnecessary. Instead, he lets his mind play tantalizingly with the image of the queer cop, Pargero, whom Tina's bouncer, Easy, says has been looking for him. The stone-faced guy, his lingering glances at queens, always made Apollo smirk. In a kind of game, Apollo tries to imagine Pargero's erratic trail in track of him—old tricks, drag queens, and Apollo's religious counterculture mother.

Then a weird feeling wins out. In the lovely cradle of the high, he challenges himself to get into Pargero's after-work life. What is it like when Pargero sits down to dinner? Probably with his mom and some queen he's got the hots for? The three of them try on clothes, or gossip about Mrs. Huxton and about the good old days. He can see it right now. Is that what it's like to have a job and lead a life called normal?

Dear Death Diary,

Apollo's my pain pal. In the first place, he confirms all my theories about drug use. At this point in the game, I'm an alienated sonofabitch—always trying to sniff out the hypocrisy of so-called common sense.

Being HIV-positive, I'm lately going through a period where I'm feeling a lot of physical pain. Recently I spent thirty-six hours in one of our city's glorious emergency rooms. I've got an axe to grind with those licensed pill-pushers. It is my opinion that access to ending pain is controlled by a greedy, insensitive bunch.

Why is it that mind-benders become "medicine" only when somebody with an M.D. gives them to you? Seems to me that anybody taking drugs on the street is merely self-medicating. So sorry that they or their suppliers couldn't afford medical school. Which is why I turn over part of my prescription for Percodan for severe peripheral neuropathy to pain pal Apollo. Until anybody with a bigger heart has a better solution for the guy.

Nobody takes drugs just for kicks. Call it, for some, the

psychic pain of poverty if you must. Call it what you will. But a bitter type like me considers Apollo a "qualified professional" when it comes to prescribing for himself.

I, too, dread pain, change—the red stuff going bad in you—and want constant, tangible control of it at my fingertips.


I took Apollo to San Juan a couple of years ago. We stumbled into a seaside ghetto made of tin houses known as La Perla and watched a teenage girl in tears jabbing a needle over and over again into a leg that looked gangrened. I flew into a rage against those who cause the pain in league with those who control the painkillers, who could cure the leg and give them away with scrip if they wanted to. Shortly after, Apollo took me to a shooting gallery on 113th Street to pay for a bundle, and I saw old men who had been in this country all their lives but who still spoke no English walking around with needles still sticking in their jugular veins.

"Why are they doing that?" I asked Apollo.

"Just for the kick of drawing the blood in and out," he answered.

I nodded with some kind of recognition.

Apollo saw the look in my eyes.

Later, when we were in bed, he said, "Don't worry." I knew he'd cop something final for me if I was near the end and decided I couldn't stand it.


Lucky that Apollo left the roof as the cops came up, because I'm sure it was his chanting mother who sent them up to get him. From what the boy tells me, his mother's like that. Principled.

Religious people like her are always judgmental. They refuse to play by the pain rules.

He told me he was sleeping on the roof when he heard the cops' shortwaves come up through the open hallway window. The kid's a gazelle. That's how he lost them and made it up to Tina's to find me. It was afternoon, so he could get in. Tina's not there in the afternoon. Almost nobody goes in Tina's in the afternoon, but, just like he figured, I was there. See, Tina's is the only place I don't get my panic attacks. Cognitive dissonance is so big for me at Tina's that I don't expect anything different. I expect to be misunderstood. So I always feel okay.

During my first few dates from the place, I marveled at phenomena that now have become commonplace for me. There was the kid who pulled a knife from his sock to cut his steak when I took him to an expensive restaurant, raising the eyebrows of the maître d'. The crackhead coated in grime who refused to remove his T-shirt to have sex because he didn't want to mess his hair. Their shenanigans burrowed a hole into my class parameters. Their language interlaced my identity and sent me into a craving tailspin. Call it the dance of death, but it's still better than being hooked up to a catheter.

I like to watch the new hustlers who come in the bar and don't yet know how to act. Popping gum and fuck all a yous, I don't need you, I know what you are. Then somebody, a brother or a cousin that they came in with, takes them aside and explains how it's done.

You see, they say, if the guy thinks you think you're big shit, he's not going to like you. He has to think you're dying to go with him in particular. Some of them can't even go with you if they can't imagine you're not liking it. It's all a psychology.

Next, the new kid goes to a corner and sulks a little. It takes him a while to get it. But before you know it, he is sidling up to you with a big smile on his face.

Ever get to see a master open a fresh pack of Newports you bought for him? He pulls them out and packs them all upside down—except for one, for good luck—then magnanimously extends the first cigarette as a sign of being a cut above desperation.

If he really is a professional, he'll finger the bulge in his pants as he exhales the first puff and portrays himself as not somebody who goes with just anybody, but a man about town with a respect for health and good eating habits, a playful dude who likes to get high on weed now and then with old friends, and a good sport who likes *chocha* but isn't embarrassed to have sex with a clean man.

He might catalog a charmed life full of family, love, luck, "good people," worshipful girlfriends, johns who've made him a regular and a son, money down on clothes, watches, or electronic equipment, and a bright eye on the lucrative professions of the future.

He'll talk about his skills: a Grand Master rapper and Fresh M.C., a scientific weightlifter, and an expert trainer of your favorite sporting dog.

Only Selby's books can measure up to the variety of hawkers, hustlers, pimps, and addicts who frequent Tina's and the streets around it. But the low profiles of the slummers, who finance all the operations and then escape back to their normal lives, are the most unnerving. A nearly illiterate, addicted hustler in this city often spends his time with more entitled, creative, eccentric, or rich people than many celebrities do. Sprinkled among the dope-fiend crew and the queens in Tina's Lounge are a congressman and an ex-bishop, a former boxer who once held a world title, a criminal who is the subject of an Oscar-winning documentary. Oh, and then that prince whose finances created a fashion empire.

Apollo never talked important people or hustler shit to me, which is why we became long-term friends. He merely told me he was a junkie, made it clear that he would only hassle me when things were really bad, and came by from time to time to trick.

Call me identityless. Laugh at me for my silly romanticism about the disenfranchised. Friends did laugh at my goatee, or *chino*, as homeboys call that kind of beard—until it became a fashion for college art students as well.

Even before I was diagnosed with HIV infection and lost all this weight, I had this strange vicarious feeling of solidarity with the outcast types. For me, day-to-day routines always seemed pointless, like endless tasks done only at the injunction of some abstract parent. My apartment was full of all the requisite objects that made it seem as if somebody was living there.

What had stimulated me in my twenties fresh out of college—other cultures, new cities, last exits to someone's heart: the usual fag thrills—had lost their charge long ago. I was at the point where I could no longer fool myself with the initial fascination of the unfamiliar. The rhythms of the day that appear to be so natural and rooted in the path of the sun for everyone else were out of my reach.

Believe it or not, my diagnosis was a reawakening. Having an end seemed to supply me with a beginning. Now the condition of the down-and-out has become a dramatization of all the desperation and defeat that I've been trying to feel. I'm alive through all this street trash.

113

Feeling alive has an allure that can make you the slave to an entire cosmology, which is I guess what happened to me.

Once I left my Weejuns at home and ventured into Tina's, I got funneled into a world of exchanges controlled by a shadowy figure Apollo says is called Mrs. Huxton, who supposedly owns the whole operation. But as close as I've come to her company is a red-haired guy in a black chauffeur's cap who's always parking outside the hustler bar and seems to know all the cops, like that detective who comes in to see Tina from time to time, who Apollo says rubs bellies with queens.

When Apollo and I tricked, I suppose his mind was blown by my once-preppy attire which, because of its unfamiliarity, he interpreted as a potential wig in the closet, since he asked with some fascination, "Why does a real man like you talk like some kind of faggot?"

"I don't," I explained. "It's the way a person with a real education talks."

Apollo didn't start watching the William Buckley show. But he initiated a kind of study of me. In a short time, he was living here.

When he wasn't high, he began ingesting, transforming, discarding my props. The demitasse cups were planted with marijuana seedlings, a real percolator and large mugs appeared in the house, a legless kitchen table from Shaker country that had been leaning against the wall for some months became an ironing board.

He was a regular urban hunter and gatherer, and I was fascinated by his ruthless expropriation of my unreal world. You make everything come alive, I had thought at the time, but I had the missionary arrogance of hoping to reform him.

That was near the beginning of a period when we stopped speaking. In fact, after he beat me up in front of a porno theater, I pressed charges. And he went to jail for a while. But before that came a period when we stuck together.

Like the time I got sick with a terrible attack of shingles. I couldn't stand a sheet on my body, and when I tried to stand up it was worse.

Apollo was babbling under the pleasure of the heroin. This prompted one of his canny monologues on my character: a rare contribution on his part, since he is someone who normally keeps his observations and affects close to his chest.

"You see a bed of nails in front of your eyes, and you feel you won't be anybody unless you lie on it. But you're so scared to be lying on that bed that you ain't going to try it until you can lay yourself out so careful that every inch of your precious body is only pushing a little bit on each nail."

Most would probably not understand that his words made me feel free, promiscuous. I lay there wanting to absorb all the pain. I lay next to my yogi.


I knew Casio way back, too. All right, I tricked with him once or twice. I've never had a thing against him. Too bad he got wasted.

Apollo's asking me for something important.

Okay then, bro, sleep your sleep of the dead at my place, in my arms, before the Enforcers of Pain catch up with us.

*

115

The sick man stood up. The weight of Apollo's body had been enveloping—warming at first, but then the pressure had begun to bother his arm muscle. What's more, he remembered that he had not taken his medication. He rolled away from the gently snoring boy and struggled to his feet. A wave of dizziness made him teeter for a moment, but then he regained his balance.

He looked down at the bruised and scratched body of his fugitive. He thought about the improbability of the plan of getting him to detox, or making the doses he had bought last through the next couple of days. And at detox they kept you waiting as you went into withdrawal. Because it was a hospital, they wouldn't even let you smoke, so you withdrew from both at the same time. Most junkies gave up before they got seen. Even so, he decided to scoop up the other bags and hide them in the microwave. He'd portion them out to Apollo. If Apollo decided to turn the house upside down, he'd never look there.

In the kitchen he took a capsule of AZT from the cabinet and gulped it down with some water cupped in the palm of his hand. He mulled over the next few days for the boy in the other room. From his brief experience as an AIDS activist, he figured there must have been countless effective detox methods that had been lost in the history of medical bureaucracy, special interests, and morality crusades.

The thought ruffled his consciousness and sent him back to the bedroom. He took a book from the shelf and lay back down next to Apollo's drawn-out sleep. He began reading an essay by René Daumal called "A Fundamental Experiment." It told how Daumal sought an exotic remedy for his cold terrors at the thought of the finality of death. Why not work up a certain familiarity with the Grim Reaper, Daumal had reasoned. Make a brief visit to the other shore.

With the help of a handkerchief doused in carbon tetra-chloride, Daumal would sink into unconsciousness, coming close to stopping breathing. Then, as he began to faint and the hand holding the handkerchief dropped away from his nose, he would drift back to life, apathetic to things of this world for days afterward.

A few more moments of reading and he closed the book, gazing at the naked boy next to him again. Despite the needle marks and the liverish pallor, the limbs were still lithe. As he slept, his muscles seemed to draw together like a blunt fist.

*What a laughable irony that I'm half-dead, anemic, clinging to life with expensive drugs; but he's lusty and brown, crying out for reduced sensibility, trying to curtail the life process. That fucking junkie has everything to fear from the future. Yet he is not plagued by fear, like I am. It would be perverse to say I envy him . . .*

*How many times have I watched withdrawal creeping into him like a succubus to take over his body while he's still asleep? A puckering of the skin, as if the hairs were standing on end. An increase in facial twitches—or am I imagining it? Being shut up in this place with him is getting hallucinatory.*

*He dives into a fetal position to hug the pillow: his nose starts to run, chills roll through him like shudders. Has he forgotten that he shot the last bag yesterday? There ain't no more . . .*

*Since I'm trapped in time with him, we all know what the perpetually repeated ending will be. He's changed his mind about getting detoxed "right now." We'll go back up there again in a cab. The cold drizzle will be hell on the numbness in my legs and feet. It'll live in my bones, and I won't be able to keep my teeth from chattering . . .*

\*

117

The cab driver's eyeing this scene in the mirror with increasing dread. Should I consider myself lucky? Look at Apollo, taken over by shaking and cramps. I myself have never felt that bad.

Here we are: the magic corner, and new life at the thought of his death drug just moments away. Out of the cab he leaps on two suddenly strong legs, the meter ticking and ticking . . . Don't want to look at the cab driver still tensely surveilling me in the mirror. I'll look at my eyes cold-fish white in the black window.

Just as sand trickles through an hourglass, the drug is creeping into the space where I'm waiting. Apollo's drug is seeping through the cab and the street and even the air. His wanting the drug gives unity to everything and ties it together. It's like a spirit that inhabits a tree or a forest, informing the reality of all of us who take part in it. Me, Apollo, the cab driver, a junkie passing by. This anima in the drug is no different from magic—is actual magic, it occurs to me.

If I'm really to believe certain nineteenth-century writings, there are easy, effective detoxes thrown out because nobody made a penny from them. To read Freud on cocaine or old reports of cures, you'd think that drugs produced totally different phenomena in both body and mind back then. What if I tried a cure on Apollo described by a turn-of-the-century junkie named James S. Lee, who claimed that you can get off opiates by mixing them with cocaine and seesawing the doses of both. According to him, if you shoot a combination of cocaine and an opiate, decreasing the cocaine over time will have the same effect as increasing the opiate. The trick is to stagger both down slowly, decreasing the cocaine a little more whenever the opiate withdrawal rears its ugly head . . .

Apollo just fell onto the floor of the cab with a thud. The convulsions again. The cab driver is flipping out. But this time I think I can handle it better. I think it has something to do with heavy doses first leaving the body—he's not really O.D.ing. See, he's coming out of it already.

118

*But he's extremely cocooned in the high, and I admit it: how I like holding him in my arms to share in his temporary fantasy that there is nothing to fear as we ride through darkness. Stranded on our small, idyllic, diminishing ice floe, the wet streets sliding by, neither of us noticing time melt away . . .*

*. . . I'm ready for you, Apollo. Fortuitous timing. While you were gaga in front of the TV, I paid a visit to a freshly departed friend from my old activist days and scooped up all the drugs from his night table. Then I made a little street purchase. We've got enough Demerol and enough cocaine to do an old-fashioned cure, if Mr. Lee is right:*

*"Demerol equaling 150 gr morphine distilled and mixed with 60 minims water; cocaine equaling approx. 2 gr mixed with equal amounts (60 minims) water; 4 injections of 9 minims each at 8 A.M., 2 P.M., 8 P.M., and 2 A.M. . . . Watch for symptoms and decrease cocaine proportion accordingly, meanwhile slowly decreasing combined dose of both . . ."*

10:00 A.M. next morning: *Can it be? Withdrawal symptoms already abating. He even reports a light euphoria, wants to get some sleep but can't.*

10:00 A.M. second morning: *Finally, he's sleeping like a baby.*

*Christ, these events are so intense that though I myself am not high, a delirium has set in. I sink against his sleeping body as though into black water. Again that comforting feeling of death seeping out all around me.*

*Instead of just inside.*

119

# XI

Yo, Cubby man. Can I talk to you?

Baby Pops, I'll talk to my sweet bootie any day.

What you be rappin' to me that way, you know I be through with that shit.

I was just fooling around with you, man. How's the studying going?

I'm gonna go to college. Yo, Cubby, you seen Apollo?

Apollo . . . you mean the one gots a finger missing?

No. That be Andre. I'm talking 'bout the light-skinned nigga got the fade haircut.

You mean the faggot with the fade always wears the earring?

No, that be Jose. Apollo.

Oh, yeah, I seen him like maybe yesterday or something.

Where you seen him?

Why?

He wasted my father, man. I just come from the hospital.

Oh yeah? We got to snuff the motherfucker, then. Come on, Baby Pop, let's look for him, I'll go with you.

Don't call me that no more.

Okay, okay, Genius. Let's go see if he's in the stalls, man, maybe the *pendejo* be holed up smoking a doobie.

I don't like to go in the stalls no more, Cubby man.

Why?

'Cause they got the Five-O there.

Shit, Genius, what's a matter, you don't know how to play that scene? You got to *time* it. If it's a good cocksucker I can shoot the first load in two minutes flat.

But what let's say if the trick say he ain't through?

What do you think I do, junior?

Bust his head?

You better believe it.


He ain't here, man. Smells rank in here.

Yeah, but check out the other smell. That fucked-up pair of Reeboks poking under the door of the stall got to be that bootie boy from Jersey. And you see what he's doing right here in the Port?

Smell like scotty.

Sure as the fuzz on his little sister's hole it is . . . Get your ass in gear, faggot! Haul out of that stall before I fuck you up! What I tell you 'bout smokin' crack in here. I'm a friend of the director of Port Authority and he asked me to keep this place clean. Now empty that shit in my hand, or I'll turn your ass in. Gimme the stem, too.


Shit, Cubby, what you do that for?

I'm on a mission, man. The punk had a rock.

You should stay away from that stuff.

C'mon, gimme some bootie in that stall and I'll let you have a blast of it.

Get your hand off a my ass, man. I told you before!

Okay, okay. Hey, where you going?

*Shit, that Cubby motherfucker ain't worth jack shit to find the cabrón hurt my father. I'll go around the corner by Forty-first and see what I can find. Come to think, I ain't checked Tina's. If Apollo the pendejo's in there peddling ass, I could jump him if he comes out by hisself on the corner . . .*

Psst, Easy!

Get away from that bar door, Baby Pop.

Don't call me that, Easy.

You know if Tina was to see it she'd nix you from the whole block.

She here yet?

No, man, but she comin' in a few minutes, at midnight. Get lost now.

I don't know what Tina got against me.

She ain't got nothing against you, man. You're fourteen years old!

Yo, ain't nobody gotta know that, poppa.

Get lost now.

Just let me in for a minute. I promise I won't let nobody buy me a drink.

All right, but disappear before Tina comes or I'm out of a job.

*This place ain't got nothin' but cafres. Like the motherfucking doctor. Looks like they got food in the back. Ain't nobody gonna care if I help myself to a little noodles . . . And I'm gonna eat the lettuce, too. It's got plenty of vitamins, and they're good for you.*

*Nigga ain't here. Word, that don't be Angelita, is it? She don't look half that bad in this light.*

\*

Hi, baby.

Hi, Baby Pop.

Don't call me that. Oh, what the fuck, you can call me that. You know that nigga calls himself Apollo?

Uh-uh.

You know what the dude did to my father?

Hold on, baby, I closed the door on that a long time ago. I ain't vicious about your *papi,* Baby Pop, but they all does know how he brought me down.

Tonight you ain't lookin' so down. You lookin' fine.

Think so, Baby Pop?

Yeah.

You're a sweetheart.

*Mira, muñequita,* you don't know no one name of Apollo?

You mean the one gots the bitch from the projects?

No, no, no! That's Shareem.

Oh.

What you drinking?

Amaretto and milk.

You couldn't put some a it in that empty glass?

Sure.

Thanks. It taste good with these here noodles. So what you been doin' lately?

I won't lie to you. I had my tits redone.

Yeah?

Got me them new water sacks 'stead a the silicone. That shit be dangerous.

You taking care of yourself, girl.

Listen, Baby Pop, don't see me wrong I don't want to hear jack shit 'bout your father. But how I'm seein' it what he did, he strategized to get control a me.

Well, he always be a bootie bandit.

No, I mean control of my mind! Now I'm doin' fine.

You're the finest fineass finance bitch on the block.

I shouldn't boast, but I been pullin' 'em in.

Yeah?

Oh yeah. Come over to my place in Jersey City, it's paradise. I got two CD players, another Oriental carpet, a couple a show dogs . . .

What kind?

Shih Tzu. Listen . . . you know, I loved Casio, but he was dissin' me. He had no respect.

At least he took the whole rap for you when you did the stickup. He could a ratted on you and copped a plea.

They just didn't recognize me, baby. They was looking for a real female.

You always knew how to do your shit.

Yeah, but when they took him in, I was in bad shape. I wasn't even doing drag no more. I went to a program where they key-locked you in for all but a hour a day.

That shit is vicious.

But when I come out, I says to myself, at least the bra's gonna be clean now, at least the dress's gonna be clean. Now I'm workin' here again. You didn't know that?

Unh-uh.

You got to see my routine. I don't do no tired Iris Chacon no more. It's new-wave stuff.

Word. Listen, Angelita, it's cool chillin' wid you, but I got to find this Apollo nigga. You know, somebody could—

Oh, I can't never play you, Baby Pop. Everybody talking 'bout what happened over at the theater. An undercover was in to shake down Mercedes couple nights ago . . . And you know what? I seen the nigger conversatin' on the street with that one in dirty sneakers over there, right after he was supposed to have perpetrated. The one with the droopy shoulders.

*El maricón blanco con la mirada de un loco en los ojos?*

*Si, con los tennis sucios.*

I don't like the looks a him. He look like a user and got a evil look.

Yeah, well, I seen them on the street together. I remember them sneakers. They got into a cab together.

You sure you talkin' about him?

Sure am, baby. Listen, I'm sorry 'bout your pop.

They sayin' maybe he won't walk.

He didn't need that, he already begun to be hurt by the time he ain't got.

Take it light, baby.

Bye, Baby Pop. Gimme a kiss.


*Looking fine for a female her age. Maybe I should try for a piece a that someday. But naw. Word. Dirty sneakers is fisheyeing my* bicho. *My pockets almost empty, and she says she seen him with Apollo. Maybe I can kill two birds with one stone.*


How you doin'?

Steve.

Ricardo.

Hello, Ricardo.

You from Westchester or someplace?

In point of fact, I live in the city.

Listen, if I be bothering you, you just got to tell me.

Not at all.

So maybe I'm gonna sit down here?

I gather that won't lead to any trouble.

I ain't called Trouble. So what you lookin' at me like that for, huh? Maybe you was looking for some fun.

I was just wondering how old you are.

Twenty—I'll be twenty in a couple weeks. But don't tell

125

nobody, I know you got to be twenty-one ... What you lookin' at?

You're so well preserved.

What's that mean?

Some people think it's a compliment.

So where you live, *papi*?

Downtown.

That's the Village, ain't it?

If you like.

How much it cost to get down there and back here with a cab?

Why do you ask?

You mean we would have to take the subway down there?

What do you mean "we"?

You know you can't hide it, you know you like me.

It's true I was looking at you.

I know.

So you think I fancy you.

What that mean? Listen, what do you do during the day?

Write. And I'm a researcher.

A what? You got to work early tomorrow? Don't worry, we gonna come quick, I ain't gonna stay all night.

You're not?

Oh no, *papi,* but I ain't gonna rush it. I like to have a good time. You got any movies?

I'm halfway through a tape I was watching.

What's it called?

*Salo: 120 Days of Sodom.* It's by Pasolini.

I never heard a that one. You mind if I ask you a question? What?

How old are you?

126

How old do you think I am?

You look like thirty.

Flatterer.

Listen, *papi,* you into drugs?

No. You?

Oh no, I don't do that shit. I ain't crazy.

Good.

Want to hear something funny? When I first saw you and shit, I was thinking you was a user.

What made you think that?

Something about the eyes.

I'm drug-free now.

Good for you. So listen, you want to go with me? What you like to do?

I like to improvise.

Huh?

You're not going to tell me you're studying guard-dog training, are you?

Say what?

Just joking.

Wait a minute, man, there's some stuff I don't do.

It won't be a problem. To be realistic, though, the problem might be getting out of here with someone who looks, uh, as young as you.

That ain't no problem, 'cause I'm gonna walk out first past Easy at the door and be waiting for you on the corner.

Right.

*I hope this one ain't a* cafre. *What he wanna do, I wonder? I'm saying he be a user, a old crackhead, I ain't never wrong 'bout that shit. Here he come now. He probably 'round forty. Them sneakers be pitiful, man. Hope he got a pair a socks to give me that I can handle. Like should I ask does he know Apollo before or after he come?*

The encounter with Apollo, and his upright notion of calling the police, meandered like scum on the man's idea flow. He saw the unclean needle piercing one of the holes on the taut, silky skin, caught a flash of nodding eyelids as smooth and swollen as spoons, remembered his greedy excitement when the half-conscious boy moaned under his mouth.

Feigning coolness, he glanced at the new boy at his side. The little hustler's cocky gestures were like alms tossed to an old beggar. He considered slipping the boy twenty for his trouble and asking him to jump out of the cab; but something pulled him on. Maybe it was pride in thinking that he could interpret the gestures and read the mind. Still, he felt himself becoming ill tempered, slipping into a nasty mood.

The boy was talking about his own problems and about his inflated future plans. His bloated bravado snaked through the man's mind and further inflamed his famished emotions. Empathy for the kid's predicament alternated with feelings of contempt. The kick of the potential danger of being with him came in little bursts. But the high needed perpetual reinforcement. The boy had somehow to swoon under his mouth and touch.

*I won't do nothing freaky. And this john going to be real surprised to find out that I don't touch no drugs. I got to live with 'em every day, and even some of the people that I would say I love don't go an hour without that glass dick in their mouth. Yet a man got to deal with that situation whenever it comes along, and for some reason*

*I was put here among the crackheads and dopeheads to make my way in the world.*

*Tonight I got to do right what the nigger done to my father. Got to use my brain to play for time. If it's slam-bang-thank-you-man I ain't going to find out a thing about that Apollo. But being that this guy's got some kind a head on his shoulders, he might want to psychologize me as part of his thrill.*

You got a million books here.

Feel free to take a look at any one you want.

Maybe you'd be surprised if I told you I knew the word *intellectual*.

Why would I be?

Say, what's the square root of one hundred eighty-six?

I don't know offhand.

Thirteen point six three eight one. Now you know something you didn't know before.

You are a smart aleck.

My name ain't Alex. I'm Ricardo and just smart. Maybe I'm out here on the street now, but I'm planning to go to college. You probably thinks I got a pea brain like some of the other punks you find at Tina's. But I can see into your mind pretty good.

What do you see, smartass?

*Off goes them wasted sneakers. What that those look, I better get ready for a very foul odor. But what's this? I don't smell nothing. Ain't that just like a white guy to be wearing the most disgusting kicks and then got feet that don't smell.*

I see you got the bucks to get a new pair of sneakers if you wanted to. But maybe they was your cousin's or something and your cousin died or something—you got an attachment to them.

I just find them comfortable, that's all.

Well, all you got to do is wet 'em and shake 'em in a paper bag with a lot of talc powder. The powder sticks to the kicks and they look good as new.

You know, you seem to do fine without a degree.

Listen, why you keeping all of them books?

What do you mean?

Did you write all of 'em?

Sure, one a day.

Don't make fun a me, *papi!*

Of course I didn't write them all. It takes months to research and write a book—sometimes years.

Then I got a cousin must be a genius.

Why?

How many words on a page?

About two fifty, three fifty.

Well, my cousin she can type fifty words in a minute, which means she can type a page in five, seven minutes.

So?

Which means she could type a whole book in a couple days, and you was telling me it could take you years.

Come on, fella, I said write, not type.

What's the difference? You got an idea in your head. You just type it down.

Tell me something, son, what are you planning to study in college?

Oh, I don't know. I'm gonna be a doctor maybe, or a mathematician or a scientist. You might a noticed when I was giving you square roots out of my head that I'm real good at math. I ain't like the other hustlers.

This conversation is dangerously similar to another one I recently had.

Huh? What's a matter? You don't look so good.

I thought you said you could see into my mind. You tell me. In the meantime, why don't you get comfortable.

You mean take off my clothes that you can start drooling for what you might be getting?

More or less like that.

But first I'm gonna look into your mind a little bit more. You know, some people does say that I'm a mind reader. My great-great-grandmother, she got that talent too.

ESP and all that?

No, it's a real psychology.

Give me an example of your psychological insight.

Well, I can see one thing—you want me to get high.

That sounds more like wishful thinking on your part.

Really? Well, suppose I was to tell you that when I get high, I get really into having sex. What would you say then?

I'd say that I might enjoy it if you got into having sex. Is that a really bad thing to say?

You doubting yourself again. Did I read your mind right?

*Damn if I wasn't right, 'cause the guy looks pale now. Look how he looks toward his pants pocket, like he going to fish out his wallet, all shaky just like if he about to buy the stuff.*

Say if I didn't hit the nail right on the head.

Suppose we said I wouldn't mind finding out about things you like to do.

So why don't you lay some cash on me. I know I can find something down the block.

\*

*He reaching in his pocket, just like I thought, to get a twenty. I'll buy me a bottle from the nigger on the corner, but then maybe he got a surprise coming.*

I'll be back in a few, *papi*.
  You promise?

Hello, *papi*. Like I said, I know my way around the neighborhood.
  What did you get?
  I got me a couple rocks.
  So that's your pleasure.
  I knew you'd like what you saw.
  Aren't you going to light up?
  Well, I'm going to pack the pipe for you, *papi*.
  For me?
  There, that's a nice big rock. Now, you got a lighter?
  Here it is.
  So go ahead.
  I don't smoke.
  Come on, *papi*. You forget who you be talking to. Now you take a blast, and then you can pass it to me.
  I think you're a little confused. I told you, I don't smoke.
  But it ain't no fun doing it alone. Tell you what, you just take one toke, just to keep me company.
  You don't understand. You see, I once did this thing, and now I'm recovered.
  Sure I understand. I understand that just one toke ain't going to change all that.

*I knew he was going to take it the minute he let me go out for it. What he don't know is that I won't touch that stuff.*

132

*I just want to get his mind going so I can pump him about Apollo.*

Satisfied, *papi?* You feel good? Just lay back there, now. That's right, you can put your hand on my leg. Don't be shy now. What you jumping up for?

It really hit me.

Stop walking back and forth. You ain't no animal in a cage.

Go ahead and take your drag.

Unh-uh.

What do you mean, no?

I can't do it this minute. I got to get in the mood. Now I'm gonna ask you something.

What's going on here?

You know somebody named of Apollo?

Did he tell you about being here?

Now calm down now, sit down. Don't get paranoid on me. Ain't nobody sent me here but myself. I just want you to tell me something about him.

Give me that pipe.

You just relax now. You better wait 'cause, like you said, you ain't smoked the stuff in a long time.

I'm just going to take one more drag.

All right, but be careful now ... So where he staying now?

Who?

Apollo.

I don't know any Apollo.

Don't shit me, old man. 'Cause you was seen with him.

Wait a minute, if this is some kind of shakedown ...

Now you know better than that. Relax, here. Go ahead, take another blast. Then we got some talking to do ...

There, sit back down now. Let me rub your back for you ...
Feel good?

I shouldn't have done it, I shouldn't have done it.

Done what, *papi*?

My heart, my heart feels funny.

There ain't not a thing wrong with you.

Listen, I want you to leave here.

I ain't going nowhere till you tell me where I can find
the nigger.

My heart's pounding from having smoked this stuff. You
fed me the stuff, and now you're asking me strange questions. And you, you haven't had any yourself.

Listen to me, you *cafre*. You been associating with a punk
wasted my father!

Your father?

Yeah!

I don't know what you're talking about ... Apollo put
you up to this, didn't he? To get back at me for calling
the cops.

You called the cops on Apollo?

And I can do it again.

Ha ha. You ain't calling no cops when you high like this.
Now tell me, you called the law on Apollo? I hope you did.
That was my father he wasted.

Your father?

Yeah, he wasted him in the theater. But he must a told
you about it, which being why you called the law.

No, no, I don't know a thing about it!

Then why'd you call the law on him?

He was giving me trouble some other way. He ... tried
to rob me.

What you touching yourself for?

I can't help it, I get that way when I get high. I have to

134

have sex or I can't stand the anxiety. Listen, take off your pants, will you?

All right, all right, I know what I came for.

Hurry, hurry.

Take a look at this big one. So, you want it or what? First you got to tell me where Apollo is.

I swear to you I don't know. He left before I called the police. I'm afraid I'm going to get convulsions or something. I'm feeling really strange.

You swear on the head of your mother you don't know where he is?

I swear.

Go ahead, *papi*. Careful! You're biting it.

*This motherfucker is bugging out. I made me a sex freak even freakier. He's beginning to scare me. He gobbling me up like there's no tomorrow. I wanna get out of here.*

All right, already, that's enough! Come on, you got to pay me.

Just a few more minutes!

No! Now gimme forty!

What about the rocks you bought?

Here, you can have all the goddam shit.

Okay, okay. Take the money.

*I ain't even gonna look for hair gel in the bathroom. Much less ask for a pair of socks. This* cafre *likely to lose it altogether and come for me. Look at him twitching on the bed, still playing with his little pootie. I'll lace up my kicks outside!*

As the door clicks shut, he leaps from bed to dresser and spills the white rocks of crack out of their tiny blue bag.

135

The door isn't locked. He lunges for the door and turns the deadbolt and whirls back to the dresser. There really were two more rocks left, weren't there? Everything's going to be okay.

He finds the still-hot stem lying on the bed and tips in one of the rocks, which melts and sticks to the edge. Now it won't matter if his shaking hands accidentally tilt the stem down. The rock still won't fall out. The flame held to the stem is already causing the telltale crackling sound. In a fraction of a second this will be smoke. When the smoke fills the lungs, the surge will come almost instantly. Meanwhile you must carefully put the hot stem down. On the dresser. It's burned the edge of a forefinger already but the hell with it.

This surge feels like it is growing out of control. There is no way to deal with this except to keep pacing back and forth and pray for a de-escalation. This pulse will never stop racing. It's taking forever to locate that videotape with images of flesh-colored legs entwined and a mouth full of penis radiating from the tangle . . . The boy called Ricardo's smooth adolescent legs, how stiff his cock felt.

His heart is vaulting gratefully into those images. So close is he to the TV screen that his nose bumps into it. So constantly and automatically does his hand pull at his limp but sensitive penis that it is more like a nervous tic than masturbation. The constant reference to this penis is giving continuity.

But this part of the tape is suddenly no good at all. The scene lost energy, and that room they're in—it's so depressing. Their legs look cold because the color's too grayed. He can't remember the feel of Ricardo's skin or its temperature.

Instead, he thinks of the boy's father whom he saw hurt. Luckily, the other tape on the shelf is waiting like a lifeboat. Trembling rigidly, he pushes in the new tape and waits for it to rewind to the right part. The floor's caving in and the boy is gone: you're really dying.

This one's better than he'd imagined because he'd never noticed the curve of that guy's hamstrings. Thick sex filling up the room's vacuum and the penis sliding in and out of the ass. Pulling at his own dick, which with the subsiding of crack has begun to stiffen. The guy's upcast, masochistic face and moaning mouth. He really should be fucked harder. Since this has begun to happen he is grateful for it. *Remember Ricardo's thighs splayed and the feel of his balls against my chin?* The sense of completeness is hypnotic. The feeling of climax is building up in his own belly and thighs where before everything was caving in. He's got to lie on the bed and pull his knees to his chest to sustain the flow of energy. But as soon as this is done, he's got to jump to his feet. They've come already, and they're only kissing. *If only some real person would press open lips to mine. I wanted a tender moment with the boy but things had to turn out this way.* He knows the next part of the tape is going to start with a street meeting. Hell will freeze over before they get down to it. Tremblingly he presses Stop/Eject and yanks the tape out.

That other tape has the three-guys part somewhere on it. Exactly where is not certain. *I'll have to fast-forward.* Waiting for this is again a reminder of the vacuum and everything collapsing. Emergency measures to stop this entail a frantic rush to the dresser to tip another rock into the stem, but he had not considered it being the very last rock. There used to be two rocks, but there aren't any more. *Only one. When this one goes into the stem there'll be none left on the dresser.* A giant void swallowing the space of the dresser.

Using a fingernail to split that rock in two is suddenly vaporizing this gruesome inevitability. *Now there'll be two rocks.* But the fragment sticking to his nail mustn't be wasted and must be scraped carefully onto the edge of the stem. He can see the hot stem blister his finger as he does this. Then he puts half the rock in the pipe and positions that whole other half on the dresser. What's left of the rock on the dresser really does have a fullness to it. *Marginally.*

He tries to memorize where that other half is as he swings away from the dresser to light the stem. *There was a bottle of cologne in back of it and a comb at the right.* He's got to make sure that this last rock's not swept to the floor by a clumsy gesture. The smoke from the stem to which the lighter is held is funneling into his lungs more thickly than he'd intended. He feels it fisting through his brain cells to bulge his eyes out of their sockets. I hope I'll go quick when my heart bursts. I hope so. But why no chest pain? Maybe it's the anesthetic effect of the drug.

His rush to the bedroom window to open it reveals that it already is. So he yanks it open even farther. The crack smoke's eaten up the air in here and the air outside is too stale. Maybe if he turns up the air conditioner and stands right next to it the blast will coax his skin, his lung sacs, into staying alive and not dying. The cold blast of air on his sweating skin makes him wince.

Maybe in the bathroom, if he splashed some cold water onto the back of his neck. It's impossible to keep from racing down the hallway, but at the same time it seems forever until he's standing at the sink. There, the feeling has de-escalated with the lowering of the temperature. The coolness of evaporating water on his neck. *In the mirror I look like I'll be okay.*

But he certainly deserves a little pleasure now, after the kid trying to intimidate him, half withholding sex. That tape's been running on Fast-Forward. There's a good chance it's run past the right section. When he runs to the bedroom and presses Play it's not at the part he wanted. *It isn't. This part comes after the three-guys part.* The tape's been fast-forwarding forever. He presses Rewind, then presses Play. *Now the tape's in the middle of the scene.* He feels superstitious about starting here. It's wasting the buildup, which could also be arousing. Then what will happen when there is nothing left? He forces himself to rewind and counts three seconds. Surely this has to be where to start.

The point at which he pressed Play is infused with perfection: right as they are taking their pants off but not before they've started to suck each other's dicks. *Their dicks in each other's mouths might last for an eternity and be like the taste of the young boy's dick in mine.* Everybody's heart's still beating, and everybody has escaped time. *The slick comfort of those balls in my mouth.* As the orgasm is rippling through him, he is beginning to realize that there will be an end to what is happening.

Warm come on his knuckles. But all his muscles are relaxed for the moment, and he feels completely normal. *Except for this heart that won't stop racing and this dull pounding in my head.* Lying on the bed might rest his heart but blood rushing to his head feels worse. This come's drying uncomfortably damp and cold on his knuckles. But the porno is still there, pumping and hot. They're on and in each other now. *Too exhausted to stand but maybe if I keep stroking my dick while he plunges his cock into the blond's ass.* But then he pictures the other half of rock.

He'd forgotten about it. He rolls off the bed and fights

dizziness to reach the dresser. He knows the rock is on the dresser, but he can't locate it. The best system is to lock your eyes to the dresser and scan every inch. *It couldn't take that long. The dresser top's not really that big.*

What he's spotted may be just a tiny piece of plaster fallen from the ceiling. He tastes it and it is, melting in his mouth like the powdery gypsum it is.

But there it is, right next to the comb. *Was the last rock really that small?* He raises it to his face to sniff the faint chemical odor. God, it will never get him up to the same level. The best solution would be to unbend a wire hanger and use it to scrape the sides of the stem to bring the lefto-ver, caked crack to the tip.

*But all the hangers in the closet are plastic. Wait a minute, the dry cleaning,* still covered with a plastic bag. He rips it from the closet and yanks off the bag, tries to pull out one of the hangers but the shirt's buttoned around it. Shakily, he man-ages to unfasten the top two buttons. Then by squashing the hanger he can slip it out and the clothing falls to the floor.

He untwists the top of the hanger and uses it to scrape the stem. Pushes the thin fragments, like flakes of soap, to the tip. Pushes the screen toward the other end of the stem. The flakes will fall out unless he keeps the stem tilted upward. He puts in the last rock of crack as well. In order not to tip the stem while lighting it, he has to tilt his head way back and hold the lighter above it. He almost falls over. But once it gets crackling it'll stick to the stem without falling out. He can lower his head and draw a big one.

*I misjudged again.* The charge of smoke is so thick that he's totally invaded. He lets the hot pipe tumble out of his hand and runs in terror toward the bathroom. There'll be no more reprieves this time. His body, the room, the air, are

140

a pumping, escalating column of high. Sweating, sticklike fingers running through his hair in anguish. In the mirror his eyes are polished stones and pinholed pupils. *It could be that the convulsions will start anytime within the next few seconds.* He looks at the high-tech bathroom clock.

He turns on the tap and splashes cold water on his face. His skin jumps out to the feeling, proving that he is still alive. *Real for a second.* Except for that horrible feeling of having all your muscles in a vise while they try to throb uncontrollably.

Pacing in the hallway to avoid behaving spasmodically. If the right number of seconds pass it will mean that the danger of dying has de-escalated. *Of course, there's always some chance of a delayed reaction.* He paces back and forth. Looking for something. Life, or an ending.

At the VCR, another endless time passes before the tape pops out. This other one, which he is already clutching in his hand, is hetero. *A big cock fucking the pussy.* The novelty and anatomical fit will pull him back into the life force. *She's just about to finish sucking him now.* And because she's small, she can leap up onto his cupped hands intended to make a seat and wrap her legs around his thighs while he fucks her standing up.

This was no disappointment because in helping that cock enter her pussy he is filled with enormous vitality and assurance. *Was a dick ever so hard before?* He couldn't fuck that pussy without the buddy dick, so maybe if he licks it as it slides in and out things will keep growing to a climax. In fact, this orgasm, though the second in the last few minutes, takes over his whole body and proves the reserve of life that is left in it so he can collapse onto the bed like a winded colt onto grass.

Too bad that the dull pounding in his head, the slicing

of breath, sight, dissects the flow of life into uncertain jerk-ings. *Is this the most horrible feeling in the world?* Because the beats are out of synch, death lies between each one. Like a great weight on his face and chest, and the feeling draining out of his legs. Reaching over the bed, he feels along the carpet for the stem he had dropped. Soon a finger touches the rounded edge of the glass.

He picks it up and looks at it. It's blackened, but there are a few opalescent streaks of crack coating it. He sits up and reaches for the lighter, which he'd tossed near the pillow. A small amount of smoke is formed but not enough for a full drag.

His eyes scan the floor. There is just a chance that when Ricardo first loaded the pipe a fragment fell out. *If you look hard, you'll see many tiny whitish chunks on the floor.* Plaster, gravel from outside, a tiny piece of paper tilted into the right light, who knows? On his hands and knees with his eyes a couple of inches from the carpet, he searches the nap, tasting a chunk now and then. Dull, unclean tastes. *That horrible gulf opening.* Is there enough time to jump into his clothes and stuff bills into his pocket?


It was bugged out, thinks Baby Pop. He'd stridden down the stairs of the john's apartment building feeling like he owned the world, exultant about the success of his mission. He had some information worth crowing about to his father. One of the johns had already called the law on Apollo the *cabrón*. He, Ricardo, and only he, was the proud bearer of that exclusive story. Now that was taking care of family. And he'd gotten paid, too, because he'd had the smarts to carry out two plans at once using subtle psychology.

But all of a sudden, the feeling changed. It was still too

early to go to the hospital, and his spirits wilted. That was what was bugged out—how you could feel up one minute and down the next. He didn't really feature having to find a place to chill out this time of night. It was already 4:30, and in less than an hour it would be light. If he fell out now, he wouldn't get much sleep once it was dawn.

Baby Pop headed aimlessly past the black dealer on the corner, who figured he was back for more rockets, but who quit calling out, "What's a matter, man? You lyin' to me if you say you didn't get off on my stuff," when Baby Pop told him he was just looking for a place to crash out. The guy pointed toward the park, and Baby Pop found a bench partly hidden by the broken bough of a tree. Obviously, whoever had used the bench before him had snapped it on purpose, so it would hang down for shelter and privacy. He squeezed underneath. The leaves felt damp on his skin. He took the forty he had gotten from the john out of his pocket and folded it into a small wad. Then he eased it past his waistband and tucked it under his balls.

He lurches down the stairs, his shirt buttoned wrong, no belt, his sockless feet pounding down the backs of the sneakers he slipped halfway into. The luminous dark blue that hits him as he yanks open the door is like colliding with a flatiron, leveling his hopes. *It'll be day in a minute. Every dealer in the neighborhood will be going home by now.* And the effort of taking a breath says that when he finally collapses onto the sidewalk, his back arching in convulsions, it will happen while the street is still deserted.

There is no other choice, however, but to push forward. Past the closed, grilled shops that reflect his askew image, one panel of the shirt hanging out of his waistband, large droplets of sweat on his balding head.

The black guy on the corner who looks like a dealer, new hightops and parka open to reveal a naked chest, has just passed something to a waif-like black girl and is heading east at a trot in his oversized jeans. He risks coronary arrest in running after him and by some miracle catches up.

"I'm out," says the dealer. "And you don't look so good. Better go on back, my friend. Might have a heart attack or something at your age."

The judgment thuds against his psyche without stopping the rekindled thirst for crack. He spots a thin figure on the next corner in the dawn light: the black girl he saw copping from the dealer. She doesn't look afraid of his speeded-up footsteps and what must be a wild, fixed look in his eyes.

*Her eyes are hard and gleaming, too!* Her hand's trembling under the thin sleeve of her blouse. Her face is shockingly refined and emaciated from crack.

"Just looking for a toke," he says breathlessly.

A filigree of electrified hair falls loose as she motions toward a stairwell leading to a cellar.

"Just bought some. I slam-dunked the whole thing into my pipe. You got ten?"

He presses the money into her hand. He sticks as close as possible to her as she moves toward the stairwell. When they're crouched in it, she offers the first blast from a real crack pipe, bowl and all, and holds a lighter to it.

Her long, thin legs crease her calf-length slacks. For the first time he notices the bump in her stomach and realizes that she is pregnant. The smoke is filling his lungs once again and begins revving up his exhausted system. Midstream she yanks the pipe away from his lips and puts it to her own. She inhales as long as she can with the lighter

144

still held to it. She's on her feet and up the stairs, as if she thinks he'll grab the pipe from her hand. She leaves him sitting on the iron step, the crack pushing and insisting, but his body system failing.

Until he gets up, puts one foot in front of another to reach the top of the stairs ... takes one heavy, rigid step after another along the street, passing a woman and her two young children. Shunning their curiosity and their dread.

The automaton keeps moving with eyes hard as marbles, his abdomen a cramping vacuum that seems to want to suck his whole soul into it. His apartment building is many more blocks away than he had thought. But the duty to survive pulls him onward—a contract made long ago.

He's a good, grim soldier—*hep two three four*—marching obediently toward the big crack lack.

The closing of Baby Pop's eyes brought the customary pictures. In this fatigued state, eye closing often worked like instant dreaming. What he had thought of with his eyes open as real thoughts or feelings now peeled away like a veil, revealing images that began to dance across the screen of his mind. Sometimes he thought about them merely as entertainment, his own private picture show, but other times they were disturbing demons that would not go away.

This time a memory of a nearly forgotten trick surfaced as if it had a life of its own. The man's kick was bland and weird. He had Baby Pop sit in an armchair and close his eyes. This was scary, because with his eyes closed the guy could try anything. Then he began telling Baby Pop to imagine leading the life he was describing. The life was one like you saw on television. There were brothers and sisters and a mother and father and a small basketball court in the back yard. When he got home from summer camp his loving parents bought him his first car. Then there was this girl he met at college and, according to this man, they were supposed to marry. They moved into a nice house with a garden in the front yard.

When the guy finished the story, he told Baby Pop to open his eyes and come and lie down on the bed. Baby Pop wondered what kind of action would come next and got ready to ask for a condom for the sex. But instead, the guy pulled him close and held him in his arms. He began to cry and held Baby Pop tighter. His tears got all over Baby Pop's neck. The guy began to stroke his hair. In order to do something to earn the money, Baby Pop comforted him. He patted his back and told him everything would be all right. After a few minutes he said he had to go and the guy got up, dried his eyes, and gave him some money.

Now why was he thinking of that? In answer, he saw an unwanted image of the *cafre* he had had to deal with tonight. Like a tape rewinding, he began to review their encounter backwards. First he remembered the guy's vacuum-cleaner mouth on his dick, then the guy's freaky panic when he finally got him high, and finally the cool conversation before. That cool conversation about books began to make him angry. It suddenly occurred to Baby Pop that the guy thought he was a dork when he asked the questions about writing. This suspicion led to another: the guy was lying. He probably knew exactly where Apollo was.

If that was true, he deserved to die. What had seemed like a coup of genius before was painfully diminished by this suspicion. Anger at the guy boiled up in his mind. If he ever saw him again, he'd kill him.

*

The murder of the guy became the next feature playing on the underside of the boy's eyelids. He saw himself back in the bedroom holding a hammer to the guy's balding head. Blow after blow reduced the scalp to a bloody pulp. Among the shards of bones lay the blood-spattered books the guy said he had written, which Baby Pop had ripped from their shelves, shredded, and scattered on the floor.

Now that he was being questioned by the police about it, he suddenly became a center of TV attention. This was thrilling, and he decided to take it for everything he could get. He told vivid tales to the police and then to TV about his journey of vengeance, and about a shadow world of drugs, cross-dressing, and sex revolving around certain theaters and bars. He gave a string of aliases as his name, ranging from "Baby Pop" to "Genius," but never his real name, to protect the ancestors of his family. He showed the reporters tattoos in places they were forbidden to photograph and described in graphic detail how and in what situations they were scraped into his young flesh. He said, in fact, anything that could explain the downward spiral that had made him a fourteen-year-old murderer, using his brain power to pull as many corrupters, culprits, and abusers as he could muster into his defense.

Finally, he was brought before the chief prosecutor, and it was his turn to show the world how rotten every single player in it was.

*Ricardo Rodriguez, also known as Baby Pop? asked the prosecutor.*
*I seen you before.*
*You have?*
*Yeah, I seen you chilling at Tina's.*
*I don't think you could have seen me at a transvestite bar, son.*

*But what would you yourself have been doing "chilling" in that vicinity?*

*Looking for the* cabrón *hurt my dad.*

*And who do you claim as your father, boy?*

*They calls him Casio.*

*And what do they call the* cabrón?

*Nigger name of Apollo.*

*What made you think you might find this individual at this transvestite bar?*

*Because, counselor, he is a prostitute.*

*And how do you know that to be true?*

*'Cause I seen the sucker with a man's dick in his mouth.*

*Where would you have seen such a thing?*

*Behind the smelly curtain of that theater on the Avenue where he got down on his knees and sucked off a whole roomful of guys without bothering with no condom.*

*What were you doing in that theater?*

*My father works there.*

*Doesn't your father know that that's an adult theater and no place for minors like you?*

*Ain't him who decides who come in and who don't up there. It's a cold, old Portuguese lady never shows her face, from what I heard tell.*

*And who told you that?*

*Everybody does know it.*

*Why don't you tell me what happened tonight, son. Start from the beginning.*

*Well, seeing that they got my father in the hospital, Angelo was telling me to go see him.*

*Who's Angelo?*

*A crackhead. So's I went to this hospital where was the priest molested me when I was no more than this high.*

*You're accusing this priest of molesting you, son? That's a serious charge. Do you really want to say that?*

148

*Yeah.*

*What's his name?*

*Father Kraus.*

*I'm writing this down, you know.*

*You want me to write it down for you? You know I can write.*

*I'm sure you can.*

*So anyway, there I find my father, who used to always be high all the time when I was a little boy, all fucked up in the hospital bed.*

*What hospital was this?*

*Over on Ninth. And he's telling to me that this half-nigger name of Apollo wasted him for no good reason.*

*And then?*

*What do you mean, and then? I figured I had to do what any son got to do. Nix his ass.*

*That's all well and good, son. But the man you killed is not Apollo.*

*You think I don't know that? That's the problem with you people, thinking that you know everything and that I don't know my ass from my elbow.*

*Then tell me why you attacked that man, son?*

*That drug addict was trying for my ass.*

*Hold on, kid. You're saying the man tried to rape you?*

*Okay.*

*What do you mean, okay?*

*Then okay. That's what I'm saying. This is hard for me to say, counselor. I'm sure you understand.*

*All right, backtrack a little for me. First of all, where were you living at the time?*

*I lives in Port Authority.*

*You mean you sleep there?*

*I sleep at World Trade Center. But I study at Port Authority.*

*What do you study?*

*Math. And I read my Stephen King book, too.*

149

*So you're a fan of his? Me too.*

*Well ain't that something.*

*Now, this guy you say tried to rape you. Did this man invite you to his apartment?*

*Yeah.*

*Well, why did you go?*

*You see, I was looking for the* cabrón *hurt my father. And Angelita says the user in the dirty sneakers was a good place to start.*

*Who's Angelita?*

*She be a queen that got them new water sacs now, used to go with my father. You ain't gonna tell me that you don't know who Angelita is.*

———

*So Angelita says to me—*

*Where did you see this Angelita?*

*In Tina's. You know, where they got the queens hustling for loot and a bunch of hustlers, too, trying to get the loot together for a bottle a scotty or a shot.*

*So what was Angelita doing in there?*

*What was she doing in there, counselor? Probably hoping to net one of them rich politicians or businessmen comes in from time to time. You might know their names better than I do.*

*Oh really, and what gives you that idea?*

*So Angelita points out this white man and says she saw him with Apollo on the night the shit went down. He was like a what-you-call-it.*

*A witness?*

*Yeah, a witness.*

*Well, what did he tell you about this Apollo?*

*That he was the one dropped my father and sent him to the hospital.*

*He told you that?*

*Yeah!*

*Now back up again. So Angelita points out this man and claims he was with Apollo on the night of the crime?*

*That's right.*

*And then what happened?*

*I went right up and asked him where was he hiding the criminal. What did he say?*

*He pretended like, what was I talking about? But I could see, nervous as he was, that he was hiding something.*

*Why didn't you call us at 911 if you had information that would help your dad?*

*'Cause, counselor, about a year ago one of your cars picked me up for loitering and the cop pulled up to a dead-end street and made me do all kinds of shit with him.*

*Watch it, boy, you don't know what you're playing with.*

*It don't matter, counselor, I ain't got nothing to lose.*

*Let's stick to what happened that night. You were saying—*

*How come you stopped writing, counselor, did your pen run out of ink?*

*I got things much more dangerous than a pen to work with that you wouldn't want to know about.*

*I bet I do already.*

*Let me tell you something. How you talk now is going to gravely influence what happens later. So just keep talking. You get your jollies now, because you're going to have to pay for it later.*

*I'm only telling the truth, counselor.*

*You seriously think the world cares about your truths? If they did, you wouldn't have been in this situation in the first place.*

*Yeah, well I care. I ain't the world. I care about protecting my family even if nobody else do, and that's what got me into this fucking mess.*

*Ha.*

*What you laughing at, counselor?*

*Did you know your mother has been in?*

*No. Why can't I see her?*

*Well, she didn't really come looking for you. We found her, family man. You see, she was still using your name to collect a child-support check every month.*

————

*Now that's family for you, isn't it.*

*Fuck your mother, counselor.*

*I'm going to overlook that.*

*But you dudes been overlooking too much, seems to me. How come you ain't caught the Apollo nigger?*

*This isn't the case we're concerned with now. Our suspect is you.*

*I wanna talk to the TV again.*

*You won't talk to anybody else until you sign this confession.*

*Pass it here, I'll sign it.*

The fantasy of signing the confession reinstated the knightly mission. The sacrifice was big enough to set him glowing again, like he'd felt when he'd left the john's house. Baby Pop sat up, pushed away the bough, and began walking with new energy. What he was capable of had to be shared with his father and with Abuela. It could raise their spirits a lot.

He jumped the train and then walked briskly toward the visitors' entrance of the hospital. In another moment he would find out his father was no longer there. During the reverie on the park bench, while Baby Pop became a notorious, outspoken murderer in the name of the father, Casio had been unceremoniously transferred to the infirmary at Riker's Island. Abuela, who'd been camping out in the hospital room, had been sent packing.

# XII

*Perdón madre mía*

—Prison Tattoo


*A*ngelita my little angel,
    *May that this letter I hope finding you in the best of health and spirits. Your Casio be thinking of you even if you think he is a rotten bastard who ruined your whole life and never did you nothing but get you hooked on the needle. But that's in the past, baby, and let's let bygones be bygones. Maybe now when my name come up you don't every time say "I don't want to know about him."*

    *Let me on this occasion now that I be paying once again for any shit I caused you say one thing. Out of all the females that I ever got down with you were the one I did respect. That's why I took the rap for you when we pulled that stickup, Little Angel. If you could find it in your heart*

153

to forgive old Casio, maybe that you won't tear this letter up and will listen what I got to say.

It been two months since they shipped me to Riker's. I don't walk so good. I can just hop a few steps on two crutches. Some of the nerves are fucked up in my spine, so they got me in the clinic in protective custody. Most a the other people here got AIDS. I ain't had one visitor save my boy Baby Pop who managed to get out here on the bus a week ago. He told me that Abuela my beautiful little great-grandmother left this world murdered to death by a bum on the sidewalk since she lost her room. That's something I cannot forgive myself, for not being there to take care of granny. When I was around she always had her SRO room.

Angelita Baby I cannot tell you what it's like lying here day after day and watching the AIDS cases die and then to hear news like that about Abuela and I can do nothing about. Making matters worse that they never caught Apollo the cabrón did this to me. If it wasn't for him, I would a been out there to help her. I suppose it was stupid the way I came at him fast on the stairway. I'll admit it's 'cause I never liked niggers. Well one good thing about me is that is changing. Here in jail this time I am getting my education and learning that all us oppressed people got to stick together. Still the lousy jive-ass never had no right coming at me in the theater. So ifs you should see him out there, don't forget what he done to your Casio. And maybe call the Five-O on him? Or better still if you could find a way to get one of our friends to take him down. I'm counting on you, baby.

As for the case who served me right in the hospital, that was none other than Detective Pargero. You know the number. This case must have it in for me lifetime 'cause *according to him he's the one yanked me out that tub in Jersey City so many years ago. That's what he was saying with an evil look in his eyes when he popped me this time. He's a perverted motherfucker who can't leave the queens alone and everybody knows it. What with all the time on my hands, I lie here all daydreaming about him slipping in the mud someday and getting his badge dirty.*

*Now I will not hide the fact that Baby Pop had an earful to lay on me about you, muñequita. Seem that you got so much going for you now that you don't even have to leave your house to get paid. From what I hear you come a long way from when you was keeping a change of clothes in your bag and working the truck routes in your garters. (Now don't get pissed at me but I knew about that shit all along.) They say you got some big-time sponsors to pay your rent. The line on the street is that you about to go all the way with the surgery cause you got enough loot.*

*Listen to me, baby. Whatever you want for yourself is what I want, but I always found you fine just the way you are. You always knew how to keep what I shouldn't be seeing out of sight, so why go through all that pain and trouble, justs so you can call yourself a real woman? If you think I'm getting too familiar, just remember all them nights when you felt me inside you. But let's just leave it at whatever you do I'm behind you. (Ha ha.)*

*I hope you believe me. 'Cause now I got to ask you one thing and hoping you will find it in your heart not to say no. As you probably know, all they found on me was a couple bags and some works. If it wasn't for my past record and a couple warrants for turnstile jumping they would a dropped the whole thing. So I only got another four to five months here is all. Then I get out.*

*Problem is, I still don't get around so well. I ain't got*

155

much feeling in my legs. If Abuela was alive and still had her room I could chill for a while until physical therapy and shit get me back on my feet. But I already told you what happened to her. All I'm asking of you if you got it in your heart is could I crash with you a couple of months until I get myself together. I'll be getting welfare and so can turn the check over to you.

Baby, if any of the shit that ever went down between us means something to you, I know you won't let me down this one last time. Maybe you could come out here on the bus so that we could at least talk about it? If you did I would never forget your kindness should you be bringing with you a couple packs of Newports or a little money for the commissary?

Don't let me lie by not saying my other reason for asking to see you. Every time I think of that beautiful ass of yours I can't keep from getting hard. Matter of fact, right now it is so stiff and big that I don't know what to do with it. (Believe me, the legs got fucked up but what be hanging between them is still in working order.) Oh baby, I can just feel you taking it all the way down.

It's in my hand now and crying out for you. Hope I can wait to shoot my load until we can be together. It's so hot and stiff that it's a sign you ain't forgot all about the sweet good times. I know you can feel these vibrations and that I'll be creaming in your pretty little ass soon.

Peace,
your lover,
Cas (Theodoro)

Hey, Monica Baby, What's up? Same ole same?
Maybe you wondering to yourself which motherfucker

*writing to me from jail this time. It's only your old
husband, Casio. Yeah, a blast from the past. May that this
letter I hope finding you in the best of health.*

*As for me, things finally turned around this time.
Everything's cool! I got no real problems! I'm doing fine! I
got my mind together and when I come out I decided to be
somebody. Don't get me wrong. I ain't talking that played-
out bullshit about having fat cables on your neck and dead
presidents\* in your pocket, but realistic shit. To study some
kind a trade, get it together.*

*So how come you ain't been to see me not once, frosty
bitch? You really should be ashamed of yourself! You
probably find this hard to believe but when a man is in
here for a little while and the time don't past you start to
thinking bout family. Now I know you must be thinking: it
was Casio fucked up the family and my mind when we was
doing drugs all the time. Well squash that. You got to take
some responsibility.*

*Oh and woman, I got another bone to pick with you.
Baby Pop who was up to visit telling me he ain't seen you
since hell freezed over! What kind of shit is that, frosting
your own flesh and blood? You his mother, remember?*

*Oh yeah and listen to me,* mamita, *I know you must
be feeling bad as me about the way that Abuela went out.
But we can be glad in our heart she at peace now and
together with all the other angels. If you ain't too busy you
might want to go over to my aunt's up in the Bronx and
see if you could get me a lock a hair they saved from her
coffin? I ain't asking you to visit me 'cause I know now
you got your own life and shit. Just to put it in the mail? If
you could do me that favor you could tell yourself you done*

---

\* dollar bills

*a good deed for somebody. 'Cause believe it or not, you are the only female that I ever did respect.*

*Otherwise from that, same ole same ole. Oh yeah, there was one time about six Sundays ago when things was a little cool. My pal Shorty got this fat female comes to see him. She got so much blubber that she could put a pint a Bacardi under one tit and they didn't find nothing in the rolls when they frisked her at security. Then we all sat in the visitors' room with her and him. And she snuck the shit out and poured it under the table in a Coca-Cola can so we could take turns sucking on it. I know that don't much sound like much to you but for us in here it was the MAIN EVENT.*

*I'm gonna let you go now 'cause I know you are probably living crazy large with some Herb treating you like a queen. So you can't be wasting time reading letters from old husbands. I'm only asking one more thing, that is could you send me a picture of your legs in them black garters and stockings that I used to like? Or maybe just the titties bare. Don't worry about other cons getting hold of it. I won't let nobody see it, baby. (Promise.) And you ain't gotta show the face in the picture.*

*Peace and Love,*
*from,*
*Your Cas*

# XIII

A pollo, nude, waking up. Through the blinds early-autumn sun striates his rising chest and silkscreens his bare belly. No goose bumps or facial twitches. Just a placid face. Relaxed muscles.

He rolls onto his stomach and deepens the curve of his lower back to rear up in a stretch. Dry forehead. No cramping. The heavy-lidded eyes pop open. He swings onto his side and lets out a healthy yawn.

A touch of ruddiness in the walnut pigment of his skin has replaced the pallor. Extra weight has added volume to the calves and thighs to dramatize the taper of his sturdy legs. This new weight is a thin, soft coating over the old, lean definition. Padding over glass, wrapped in the smooth weave of skin.

It is shocking how he now looks his age. A teenager about to enter his twenties. A sheen of black curls that sets off the bloom of skin color. On the otherwise hairless body a faint line of blunt black hairs running from his navel to his thicket of pubic hair. A stiff morning penis half covered by a sheet. Hairless legs. Paler-colored soles of feet, arches high enough to scoop them into shadow.

He's everybody's early morning—that girl's jock boyfriend, that businessman's healthy son, or somebody's hardworking teenage father. Which is to say: unavailable.

Availability went away with the dope he kicked. Now he's turned into somebody staying in a sick friend's apartment. Lying low because the cops are looking for him but feeling healthy. He has to admit he has nothing else to offer the world.

All the colors have appeared in the world and all the shapes are three-dimensional. What to do with all this new stuff? It takes a long time to start having feelings about it. Some of it humbles him by showing him what a fool he was. Parts of it look so awful he can see why he never wanted to see them.

His HIV-positive friend is seated at the nearby desk scribbling in his journal. Just as Apollo's memory cannot recreate the feeling of being high, he can't conceive the memory of having had sex with the man. He feels gratitude for the sad, sweet, sick, human entity. That's all.

It has become obvious to Apollo that he has never had a sex life. He started taking dope too early to fix one onto other people. He still has a sex urge, but for the first time has to admit it has nothing to do with anybody else.

How to explain this rebirth into the ordinary? It's as unmagical as flesh and blood. Life has become a real morning with sunlight that you wake up to. You're supposed to make a comment about how the weather is turning and how fall is coming and then know what you intend to do with the rest of the day. A day without getting high can stretch on endlessly.

Should he turn himself in as soon as possible and try to make a plea bargain? Should he sign up for a residential drug-treatment program and have them plead his case on the grounds of rehabilitation? Should he say fuck it and get a job and hope they forget about him?

According to his mentor, scribbling away at his desk, these are the tenor of morning decisions that many who are not high often face. But Apollo prefers to spend just a little more time in shadow. A strip of darkness from the blinds is in a perfect position to block the light from his eyes. He shuts them tight and tries to remember . . .

Remember that movie you saw but forgot the ending of? That's what everything that happened before seems like now. There were aimless comings and goings and excuses for not showing up places. You invented things to accomplish on the street. There were power figures like Mrs. Huxton, who held all the good cards in her hand.

Did he ever meet her? All the stories about a rich old lady living above the theater who owned everything. If he ever really did come face-to-face with such a person, it now seems more like a dream.

An old body living in luxury floats above the odors of the theater . . . Then a dream about that fantasy becoming a reason to make up stories . . . a reason to keep taking dope . . . The stories building into a narrative unfolding . . .

You become an actor in it, and your lines flow effortlessly from your mouth. The only unbearable times are when you feel the reason for the story ending. That's called betrayal and is the occasion for more dope. There really was an old lady living up there, wasn't there?

The sick man's fountain pen keeps scribbling. He's trying to deal with the pulsing quandary stretched out behind him in all its luxurious fleshiness on the bed. Now that he's brought Apollo back to life they are "dead on each other"—as the street lingo goes. Meaning there's no sexuality between them. Or, more broadly, no way for them to make use of each other.

What's left has a particularly non-streetish flavor. Milk of human kindness. It's a little hard for this man with just a little life left to admit to himself that he's been making love to dope. It's not easy being Dr. Frankenstein, who succeeded in creating a real entity only to lose control of him. AIDS-sick angst gave birth to a child with perfect limbs and his own will to live. As soon as Apollo became truly desirable, everything about him cut off the flow of desire. But isn't that what friendship is all about?

Dear Dying Diary,

Your pain may live on but mine will be finished by sacrifice. I've got to give though my pen's running dry. It obviously takes sacrifice to convert a zombie into a survivor. But to be a saint, there has to be something gravely wrong with you. If I hadn't gotten sick, I probably would have spent my entire life crossing the street to avoid people like Apollo.

The ancient rules of the game say I will receive no earthly benefit from this. Apollo is probably so life-oriented now that he would balk at the idea of helping me get something for the final exit. When he was a junkie, he would have run out to get a few bags of heroin and let me overdose—if I got to them before he did.

My legacy to the world will be the creation of one more person in favor of self-preservation.

So be it.


Apollo listening. He's tuned the TV to a morning talk show and watches an interviewer ask somebody a question. He notices the movement of the interviewee's eyes and a change in facial musculature that proves the person is listening. He marvels at it. Then he hears the interviewee give an answer based on careful consideration. He marvels again.

His sick friend is speaking now. Apollo can actually hear him. Saying he feels too weak to go out to buy a quart of fresh-squeezed orange juice. Apollo reacts to what's being said. The ebb and flow of Apollo's brain chemicals in reaction to stimuli fill Apollo's buddy with a mournful awe. Feeling Apollo listening is like peering through a microscope and viewing for the first time the cytoplasm of a microorganism flowing. In the wake of this queasy flow are issues from which the two used to be exempt.

What TV program do you want to watch? Is that really the kind of taste you have? Did you really agree with that talk-show host? Do you believe in God? Would you really vote for that president? What did you really think of my unconventional behavior? You mean you never identified with me as an outsider?

The image unattainable—an image of the future—becomes animated. The living boy has stood in reaction to the request for orange juice and is putting on his underwear and pants. Unreal event: Apollo helping out his friend.

At the doorway Apollo hugs his benefactor in brotherly tenderness, pelvis carefully retracted. The man goes back to his journal to jot down a few more lines.

Dear Dead Diary,

Morning brought proof of Apollo's devotion. He went out to get orange juice for me. You, on the other hand, have sapped all the ink out of me you're going to get. One more bloodletting should do it. It's about the irony of the cure I took.

I chased my own sickness like a dog chases its tail and

turned the sickness into health to break the circle and
die alone ...

Make something of yourself. After all, you can't be depend-
ent on your sick friend forever.

After getting the orange juice, Apollo changes into clean
slacks and turns the ironing of a shirt into a detailed ritual.
Hits the streets and inhales the sensation. It's only mid-
morning. *I'm a young, healthy guy looking for work. New kicks,
and my feet don't smell. Anything will do for now. But the future?
Computers, or maybe the nursing profession.*

In the crisp fall sun, people hustle past on their way to
appointments. A guy with a briefcase lunges toward a phone
booth to make a call. It might all be a cliché, but before it
was in shadow. Now the new lighting makes him part of
the scene.

Right on cue, the Help Wanted sign appears in the
Burger King window. He strides in hyperconscious of
the change in atmosphere. His newly sensitive receptors
smell work—the oppressive, grease-filled air—and feel of
squelched immigrants skulking behind the counter and
farther back, in the kitchen. He concentrates on certain
muscles in his wrist to imagine himself as a hamburger
flipper. But the Pakistani manager who hands him the
application seems eerily cut off from his potential.

There's always, of course, the garment district. Jaunting
by foot to midtown with the fantasy of being an eager
young father with mouths to feed waiting at home. In the
shadowy depths of stalled trucks, he can see the black and
Latino faces: some blank with fatigue or boredom, others
stilled into clotted rage. They watch him without welcoming eyes as he walks by. He's more competition. Or
somebody else you must worry about trusting. Or another

mess with the same depressing life story. He keeps walking west and north.

The old neighborhood makes his heart beat faster. Eighth Avenue, Tina's, the sex theater under bright sunlight. Intuition tells him he was never here—like thumbing through somebody else's photo album. It's not just that the buildings are crumbling in a way he never noticed and that the sidewalk is littered with debris. It's not the stale odor or scaling hands and glazed eyes of the crack ghosts. It's not the half-dressed speed-freak drag queen with smeared mascara and punctured forearms in front of a walkup hotel or the up-all-night junkie dazedly staring at a candy bar in a Korean market. It's the sense of the pettiness of it all. A backwater village. Stupid little bars where no one with any big money comes. Big plans that play over and over like a short tape loop.

Back down toward Port Authority he runs into Cubby, a boosted leather jacket open over his bare chest to show off his tattoo series. Cubby, with his devils and executioner, pirate, Smurf, and crucifixes, who had seemed big and bad and absolutely formidable, now seems small, failing, and poignantly inconsequential.

They still go through the high-five and the bear hug as an eerie feeling spreads through Apollo. The guy's tattooed arms are like tentacles with ineffective suckers. Apollo lets them slide off him, but the slime they leave has a catalytic tingle, imparts the hidden urges of the old environment.

Of course Cubby has noticed Apollo's new color, extra weight, and clear eyes and asks a million questions. Apollo is vague, full of shrugs and upturned hands. He plays dumb about knowing that people are looking for him. Where's he been? Chilling out at his mother's to get straight. As a matter of fact, he's looking for a job now.

A chance for a hookup sparks Cubby's gray, thwarted-looking eyes. He just happens to know about a job, and maybe Apollo's interested. It seems that Tina's after-hours were nixed by the cops and in retaliation she's opened a strictly after-hours club way over on Eleventh Avenue, for the wild side of the trade. Cubby's been slapping paint on the walls all morning. It's opening tonight after 4:00 A.M. The cops are paid off; and when it starts to get light you got to get buzzed in, so they need a bouncer.

Apollo's impulses lock like antibodies onto Cubby's offer. This is not the feeling of the Burger King or garment district. *I got a job!* is an immediate, exultant thought. Secret relief at not having to adapt to an alien atmosphere. Cubby agrees to hook him up. All he's got to do is show up around 3:00 A.M. and do Cubby a good one someday in the future.

Time—organization—becomes his next hurdle. What to do for the next sixteen hours or so, until work starts? The only answer is to wait it out at McDonald's by slugging back coffee. He doesn't want to discuss this job with his sick friend just yet.

An after-hours job is a good solution for a gig when you're hiding out from the law. It's off the books. They won't bust you unless they decide to bust the whole operation. The atmosphere will be full of all the old posse, but he's planning on handling it drug-free, which he can already see is going to be a bizarre experience.

They slap hands again. Then, in afterthought, Apollo explains that he wants to be known by a new name now. He thinks for a minute, remembers his new sober state, and says: "Perk."

"You mean, like 'Percodan'?" asks Cubby.

"No," says Apollo. "Like 'Perky.' I told you, I'm straight now."

166

# XIV

Lookin' like the number-one gangster hit pay dirt! What's up, Mercedes.

You been locked up, Apollo, ain't you? 'Cause you damn sure been gettin' three squares a day.

I just been lying low for a while.

With some Herb has a full refrigerator, no doubt.

I got a job, Mercedes!

Ain't we gettin' legit. Who you workin' for?

Tina. I'm the bouncer, here.

Here? You still a boofer?*

I ain't with that.

My man been freed! But he come back to hell just to get a regular paycheck, which is kind a peculiar. 'Bout ten minutes this place gonna be crawling with skin poppers and bazooka suckers.

Well you can't come in, Mercedes. Tina says don't let nobody in high.

Is that so? Ruby Rehab telling me? Lasts times I saw you, you was talking to the subway turnstile.

---

* addict

I don't remember that.

No surprise. You was so zonked you could a made love to the third rail and felt nothing.

I said you can't come in.

You five-dollar trick! I been frontin' for you from get-go! If it wasn' for me that night some snitch likely to call the Man on you! Now I'm stepping into this place, and you gotta deal with it!

Apollo watched her in astonishment. At the door to the bar, she'd showed up weaving in her heels, her platinum wig turned salmon in the streetlight. Her trembling body had made her silver chain-mail dress glitter against her black skin.

When he'd tried to keep her out, rage had contorted her features, like it had when she'd knifed him. Then she'd raised her chain-mail pocketbook and whacked him in the face. With great force she shoved by him.

"Okay, this time only," he called after her. The queen wasn't listening. She'd already trotted into the ladies' room for a blast and would re-emerge even more wound up, more ferocious.

In his unhigh state, he couldn't place the jerky, wiry, belligerent black man in a dress as the syrupy, serpentine queen with whom he used to make love. All he could focus on was the largeness of the fingers sporting clawlike nails and the hard muscle tone.

The impression was drowned out by the great wave of after-hours crowd that began pouring past him. Alert as never before, Apollo cased each and suppressed a sinking feeling. This was not the same crowd that went to Tina's Lounge near Eighth, but a deeper level of exiles. It was full of underage homeboys from New Jersey in oversized clothes and gold chains, petty dealers in nylon parkas and new kicks, and wasted alcoholic johns: trickle-downs from the other bars, now closing, mixed with some of their exhausted staff.

With a new cerebral anxiety that had always been blocked by dope, he was beginning to realize what this job would call for. He'd have to bend or unbend the rules of the game to fit each situation. Anybody had a right to come in high as long as pushiness was balanced against being no real threat. Talks about procedures were so much bullshit. You used them to strike bargains. It was only if Tina came down with a specific sanction that you enforced it to the letter. On the other hand, if he wimped as bouncer in front of comers who thought he held the cards, he'd lose the upper hand pronto.

It dawned on Apollo for the first time—and he couldn't understand why it hadn't before—that he was surrounded by four walls and a ceiling to get high in, after the streets thinned and everywhere else was closed. What might have looked festive to those coming off the all-night streets was denatured in his sober eyes to a moldy bar with a slapped-on coat of paint, some limp paper streamers, and the smell of urinal-deodorizer cake.

With icy wryness he took in the punks with gold teeth and big poorboy caps, looking all mature manhood and lined features, but probably eighteen or under. Skinny bodies made to look big by loose clothing—an old jail trick. Tongue tips that flicked over pursed lips, which he knew was the classic coke tic. One of them, cue in hand, backed away from the pool table into the arms of a sinewy blonde in a pink dress. Look closely: his date was an adolescent drag queen.

In the corner a young mealy-faced gay boy was working

a pickled john who had trouble balancing on the barstool. The boy masturbated him through his leisure pants. He let the guy tongue-kiss him and then asked for a couple of bucks for the "powder room." The guy coughed them up, and the kid disappeared quickly into the head, obviously to buy a beam from a crack pipe. He returned more animated and resumed his job on the old beer-guts.

The images worked on Apollo the way street people work on their marks. They pull you in and grow ugly enough to make you freak a little. Then they try to make you give up everything you have.

A completely pumped Cubby was wedging Apollo against the door frame. His racing pulse vibrated Apollo's breast-bone. The wet heat of his bare skin and his foul odor seeped out of him and began to penetrate Apollo's skin. "I came through for you, Perk," he spat through a crack rictus, "didn't I?" All he wanted was to round out a ten to get high, and he felt Apollo owed him something. "Just six bucks to get me a fried chickens?" he kept whining.

"Away from the fucking door, Cub! You know Tina wants me casing people through the peephole as it gets light!"

Cubby's jaw raised churlishly, and his pinholes glinted menace. He damn well knew that Apollo would already be taking bribes from the few white johns stupid enough to fall for it. He'd be telling them there was a door charge. But Apollo knew how uncool it was to give in to pressure for payoff so early in the game.

The crackhead spun into the street but whirled to face him. "Nigger, I be back in a few, and better you be thinking 'bout me!" He zigzagged east, windmilling threatening arms, past the squadron of homeless camped under the overhang in their cardboard boxes. When he smashed one box with his fist, the woman inside shrieked, "White faggot!" Apollo watched through the peephole of the now-closed door. He saw Cubby taunting the cardboard village, advancing and retreating as the woman flung bottles from her box.

To inaugurate her new club, Miss Tina had decided to make a rare appearance out of female drag. She'd been in the room that held the safe all evening getting her male look together. At the intro to "It's Not Unusual," the crowd was startled into silence as she appeared, her red-lined black opera cape swooping in a great stiff arc behind her, so that homeboys and queens had to lean backward to avoid losing an eyebrow. Under it she wore a loose Tom Jones shirt over bound tits, tuxedo pants, and a cummerbund. She waved a big fake-rhinestone-studded mike in one hand.

The effect was primitive, a great show of dominance, and on either side, Apollo saw drained, drugged faces flinching or straining for her approval: ex-favorites who'd become street people again, essential business associates, drag-queen girlfriends.

He'd seen the fawners hoping to get in Tina's good graces a hundred thousand times before. But what he'd never noticed was Tina's computer-precise assessment of them, glinting sassy acknowledgment at the ones who'd played it fair or the ones who were crucial enough that it didn't matter, sweeping past the others like they were worms.

Worm appeal was the main control factor here. And the wretched often stayed that way to make the powerful all the more so. That the necks of the desperate damned strained like baby birds' was an asset. Usually, they'd made a fatal mistake in the past. They'd broken the rules of this justice system. They'd endangered Tina's business by robbing a paying customer, blabbed secrets, or gotten into an ugly fight.

Hungrily, these scorned beings banned from Tina's other establishment focused their eyes on the spotlight and their second chance. To Apollo, Tina's crucial power was even more obvious in tonight's image as a man—the lined, middle-aged face; thinned businessman's lips; and shrewd, paternal eyes.

No one flinched at the convincingly macho lip-synching of the Tom Jones song. After all, the pope also wore skirts, but did anybody doubt his ability to muster male powers? Then "Woman, Woman, (Have You Got Cheatin' on Your Mind)" came on. Tina lightened up as she parodied its lyrics by scanning the crowd like a schoolteacher looking for pranksters. And a few of the newly redeemed blushed, lowering their eyes in shame.

When the number ended, the mostly coked-up crowd burst into manic applause. At that moment, Apollo noticed the craggy-faced guy near the stage. He looked like a cop, and Apollo's heart skipped a beat. It could have been Pargero, although Apollo couldn't be sure. He'd never caught a glimpse of him when he wasn't high. To the stoned, cops' faces never materialized until the moment of the bust. They were just a fuzzy image upon which to project your fears and furies. Then, when it was too late, they zoomed in, so that every pore was imprinted on your brain cells. Apollo couldn't be sure if this dream image from his past life was the fey cop or not. Or even if he'd imagined such a creature as one of Mrs. Huxton's fantasy henchmen.

The crisscrossings from bathroom to bar grew to a fever pitch. Gesturing arms flew and tongues wagged at ten times their normal speed. There were outbursts of laughter and then tempers snapped. Rigid-faced users with eyes fixed as coins trembled tensely in corners. Queens on a mission exaggerated their protestations of love or revenge to dealer-boyfriends who held the stuff.

Most disconcerting was the number of outcasts. Some of them hadn't been allowed in any bar in the neighborhood for months. Even Angelo, whose crack career had built him a home in the cardboard village, was there, with his X-cap buddy. But tonight, Angelo's bloodshot eyes were bugged out on a crack rush that fixed the X-cap in a deadly stare.

The X-cap raised his arms with the palms upturned as if to shruggingly ask what Angelo wanted of him. Apollo strained his ears toward the danger spot to pick up escalating snatches of gurgled conversation:

"You was wit' him dat night, man . . ."

"What you saying? I was'n even in the vicinity! . . ."

"I'm telling you, man, if I was to find you was the one nixed my cousin . . ."

Suddenly the image blurred, as when two stilled cats with puffed-out fur combine into one snarling ball. The two men hit the floor in a stranglehold.

An erratic wave of action broke throughout the room as some pushed backward and knocked into others, who cursed and got ready to fight. So stoned were they that they had not realized the reason for the sudden movements. The youngest homeboys shoved through the crowd toward the action. They hoped to display their courage by refereeing the altercation. But when they reached it, they hesitated, waiting to see if any weapons would surface from Angelo or the other.

Apollo knew who had to stop the fight, but he too waited for a blade or razor to appear. Then he tightened his buttocks to stiffen his walk and advanced. The X's cap had been pulled off to reveal processed hair standing straight up in stiff sections. One of Angelo's hands was halfway in the mouth of the X-cap, whose jaw he was attempting to dislocate before his fingers were bitten off. Angelo's cheekbone and nose gushed blood as he struggled for his grip.

Apollo froze as Tina appeared in male-to-female transition, wearing her tuxedo pants but with her naked tits unbound. Her Tom Jones ponytail suddenly looked like that of a Connecticut matron, and her irate face was lucent with thick greasepaint. She lunged forward and used the sharp toe of her high heel to kick at the squirming mass until it unlocked. Then she turned toward Apollo and bellowed, "Eighty-six X!"

The X stood up shakily and covered his stiff hair with the cap. Then he swung back toward Angelo and glared. Angelo lunged, but Apollo stepped between them and grabbed the X's arm. Two homeboys restrained Angelo, cooing into his ear like trainers at a boxing match.

"You! Sit down over there!" ordered Tina, pointing to a stool in the back. The two boys led Angelo, whose nose and cheek still gushed blood, to the stool. The X said, "Wasn't me who started it, and I ain't leaving."

But Tina removed one shoe and stood cockeyed on the other. She held it by the tip with the heel pointed toward the X's eye, the finger of her other hand indicating the door.

Stupidly the X lumbered toward her, but Apollo bent and enlaced his waist. He swung him around and propelled him toward the door. The X crashed against it, and the peephole cover dented his forehead. It made a shallow impression that began to dribble blood. As he walked backward in a daze and brought his palm to his head to touch the cut, Apollo swung open the door and shoved

174

him into the street, then slammed the door shut again and quickly bolted it.

Tina bent to put her shoe back on, then stood and folded her arms to cover her naked breasts. She regarded all her gawking customers imperiously and gestured with her chin to Angelo bleeding in the corner. "Clean him up!" she ordered. With a scornful look of nonchalance, she marched back into the room with the safe to complete her image transition.

In the toilet, Apollo pressed dampened paper towels to Angelo's bleeding face and breathed the air that was just as thick with crack smoke as he'd imagined. The atmosphere of the toilet was classic after-hours, and it occurred to him that the elation of late-night violence freshly over had often been celebrated with some form of get-high. The tiny, empty blue plastic bags scattered in the urinal, the lighter lying on the floor, and the rolls of toilet paper padlocked on a metal bar against thieves brought everything back. Even the smell of Angelo's blood on wet tan paper towels was an intoxication to which Apollo briefly succumbed.

These images and odors were deeper reminders of the old world than running into any drug buddies could have been. He'd been pressed into some hollow all evening to avoid the seduction of the world he'd been hired to manage. It was as painful as going to a funny movie determined in advance not to laugh or watching a video of a former main squeeze having sex with somebody else.

In such situations everything seemed flat and grotesque at best. Meaninglessness surrounded him, and dying pressed in through the cracks. The feeling had been like walking on a carpet of eyeballs or wall-to-wall corpses. Now this stronger inhalation of death's perfume fired a sudden jolt through him—as when an insect treads upon the sensory hairs of a supposedly inanimate Venus's-flytrap pod. He had to use every cell in his body to stop the hormonal reaction that was about to take place.

Rays of sun crept in around the peephole cover with the smear of congealed blood. A new mood strangled the left-overs in the bar. The butcher paper shutting the window from the outside glowed sallow-brown, like cooked liver. Angelo was dozing in a corner, and the cuts on his face had formed soft globs of scab. Two or three homeboys and a queen were still doing cocaine filibusters—telling jokes or repeating sexual innuendoes. An oily blue haze of cigarette and crack smoke tinged the air above their necks.

Apollo, whom lack of sleep had turned into a robot, lurched around the room, picking up beer bottles, while Tina went through the night's earnings. Cubby had been back and milked a ten-spot out of Apollo. It was almost time to board up the place and go back home with what he had left from tonight's take: twenty-five bucks from Tina, another ten from the white suckers at the door. But first, as instructed, he was to open the door and scope out the block. Tina had indicated that although the Man may have been tolerating the after-hours operation for reasons of his own, he would not appreciate leftovers making morning trouble.

The door swinging open revealed a greasy sidewalk and a grimy street boy, whose razor shoulders poked from a stretched-out red sweatshirt. His oversized jeans were caked with dirt, and his white sneakers discolored by tar.

All that burned in the pinched face were two brown eyes, peeking in passionate rage through the matted curls. They were eyes that seemed to get their energy from some place other than the ravaged-looking body.

"Apollo, *cabrón*," charged the boy.

"My name's Perk," answered Apollo.

"I don't care what you calls yourself now, 'cause it's you wasted my father!"

The boy extracted a large hunting knife from the folds of his pants and stumbled forward. Apollo took one step aside and the hurtling boy fell on his face at the entrance. The knife clattered onto the floor. It struck the leg of a barstool.

*Only one thing a man got left is honor. Which is to say, you got to do right by everyone used to cherish you. Honor is what makes the man. Which makes me ask myself how I could ever be giving in to this here Apollo.*

*And for ten bucks yet. Lasts thing I'm remembering is hitting the doorstep and hoping to myself that the knife's not up under me. And when I come to, I thought I was in the interrogation room at the police precinct instead of at Tina's. All I could see was this old Irish face hanging over me asking questions quick. Like what happened to you and why you look so bad and ain't you ate and so forth. It's 'cause I never seen Tina without her makeup and in the light. To me, she was looking like she was Tina's brother if he was a cop.*

*All right, it ain't no excuse I tell myself! I know. I shouldn't a taken the ten dollars and told Apollo we was square with each other. But nobody understands what's happening to me since I found out I'm HIV-positive. I don't know how it happened and shit. The guy at the hospital where they used to have my father sat me down after I comes to him. I can't keep nothing in my stomach 'cause it leaks out a me. He says, this is something you should a taken care of, but it ain't a death sentence. We got pills, and maybe you'll be taking in food better in no time.*

*At a moment like this there is no telling what is going to spill out of your mouth. He must a heard a lot of bullshit dealing with people getting the news. But when I says, if I got the AIDS it's that fucking* cafre *of a doctor you got working here gave it to me! his mouth really drops open wide.*

*I'm gonna put that to rest now. According to this hospital dude, however you got it you would never know 'cause it could a been something happened years back. Well then. It must be that fucking Cubby who was the first and only took my ass. Yet the dude can go on and kill his own self. He is such a crackhead he don't need my help taking him off.*

*Maybe it's the feeling that no matter what I do to deal I always get smoked from get-go. Inside, my fantasies about my future are stupid large, but out here the leaves are always falling off the trees. The thought was weighing me down when I headed for the after-hours after Cubby tells me they got Apollo working there. Take care of the bastard for me too, he says, before he went to go ho hoppin'.\**

*When I got to the door I start to feel dizzy and like my stomach was dropping out of its bottom. I'm not the kind of man to let his body get control of him. I'm more like a Ninja master. But I never had this kind of feeling. When I lunges for the nigger with my blade everything turns black. And the next thing I know Tina's asking me them questions.*

*What's the only thing I could say to her? Her bouncer is an attempted murderer is what is the plain fucking truth. So she shut the door and comes up close to the table wheres I am lying. She put a hand on my forehead to hush me down.*

*You know, don't you, that I'm the Queen of the Street, and if a citizen ain't done me no wrong comes to me in trouble, I am always ready to hold out a helping hand. Before you go shootin' your mouth off about my doorman Perk, why you don't tell me why you looking so bad.*

*I got the AIDS, I told her.*

---

\* robbing prostitutes

*Now nobody must know this, but I think I let go on the water-works. What am I gonna do? I sobbed. I ain't going to be able to hustle in this condition, 'cause nobody will want me. Tina stepped back from me, and I heard her mumble, Stay with me for a while is what you're gonna do. Until you get back on your feet.*

*I thought I was hallucinatin' when she said that.*

*Tina's got this big house to herself in Brooklyn. Every hustler on the block is always trying to get a foot in the door. They go in that door as the main man and come back to the block sporting thick gold cables on their neck. They got pockets full of money and drugs and all kinds of new gear.*

*When they come back out Tina's door for good, like all of 'em do, they are the scum of the earth. They can't get in her lounge no more and sometimes they got wicked habits. That's why it was bugged out Tina deciding to put me through the revolving door looking and feeling like I was. I didn't know if I could a done it.*

*You got the wrong idea, says she. I said you can stay with me till you get back on your feet. Nobody wants your body chez moi so squash that idea. It was then I flashed on that maybe I got her wrong all these years. What I thought was evil mean was really just her knowing how things got to stay in proportion. She knows when to be cold and get things done, but also when to be good people.*

*So much to say, but that didn't change my mission and how that cabrón was still standing on two legs out there. Maybe Tina was frontin' for him and thought this was going to get me off his ass. I'm sorry, I says to her, but Apollo, or Perk, or whatever you wants to call him, wasted my father.*

*You think I could run this joint without makin' deals with the Man? says she soft. I know all about Apollo being wanted. But I got no reason to drop a dime on him, 'cause I need me a bouncer too careful to be wandering off into street trouble while he's working the door. You see, round about November when elections come along and I already made my bucks, they are then going to shut us down*

179

*anyways. In the meantime, that nigger out there will stay right where the law want him. When they close this place down, he's going with it. It's all fixed up already. It's a done deal.*

*That's what Tina is, you see. The word for it is* organized. *There be some kind of sweet part to every one of her deals making that it don't matter how bitter they taste on the outside. The only trouble, I knew the nigger would never believe me strolling out there without a word. All that I got left is my honor. I ain't complaining about Tina taking the* cabrón *down for me, but I got to find a way to show him that nobody can mess with Ricardo.*

*So I told Tina would she go out there and let him know how she talked me into a settlement? That he got to come in here and satisfy me before I let him off the hook?*

*So Tina went out to get him, but she closed the door. I could hear the nigger making a fuss with her until my mind began to get floated and my breath short. I took out the asthma inhaler and had a toke. I began to wonder about my stash and whether I should try to pick it up before Tina brought me to her place.*

*About a month ago I moved into Grand Central, you see. If you go down some stairs and then you go down this hall that looks like it's closed, you come to more stairs. And then you pass through another door and everything's all black, you have to feel your way down some stairs, and you are on old railroad tracks. Then you can go down, and then down agains, and even agains, where it is pitch black, except for a light now and then where they fix the trains. But what it is is a train* graveyard. *You can feel your way across miles and miles of them tracks till you come to old silver trains that look like what me and Abuela used to ride to see my father Casio upstate in jail. Sometimes there'll be somebody else living in one of them trains, but sometimes you won't see nothing but a rat or two as you pick your way along.*

*And then you come to my place, where I been living since the weather changed. My train that I got hooked up with a radio and even a bed by unscrewing two of the seats and tying them together. I got a quilt and a pillow too. And I got my math book and my bible and my Stephen King book that you can read by the light I grabbed from the electricity of a live rail.*

*It's so black in there that you ain't got no idea what's happening anywhere else. That air is so black that you could drink it. And when the light's unhooked that black comes pouring back in like syrup. You get the feeling that that train never went nowhere and ain't going nowhere never. It's just stuck in the blackness like a cockroach in Bosco. But it ain't a bad feeling 'cause all of it belongs to you. There ain't nothing else, just you and all that black night.*

*It was then, when I be thinking this, the door opens and in walks the nigger Apollo. So I used all my strength to hop up and get ready should he step up to me and act like an asshole. But instead he says to me, I'm awful sorry about what happened with your dad and shit, but the whole thing was an accident. Tina was watching us from behind. And then he holds out ten dollars and says I hope this donation will take care of everything between you and me and fix you up fine.*

Apollo was so exhausted that pictures of the night's strenuous conflicts still stagnated on his vision. When he entered the apartment in this condition, he was sorry to find his sick friend awake and white-faced in bed. There was panic in his gaping eyes, as if the ground had been swept from under his feet. His voice sounded strident and frantic. *Where have you been?* he wanted to know right away. *Working!* Apollo shouted triumphantly. To make his point, he took out the twenty-five bucks and let them rain down on the bed. But the friend swept them to the floor, and before he knew it, they were arguing.

The friend cited all kinds of "recovery" lingo about the

danger of old crowds that Apollo didn't even know he had in his vocabulary. He said he wanted Apollo to work, but not in that environment. He put a bony hand on Apollo's forearm and clutched it like a drowning man. *I'm afraid to lose you,* he kept saying. *I'm afraid you'll get sucked back in.*

Apollo kept pointing at the money and making a big show of it. He portrayed his plans for future independence with the measly sum. He claimed he could now kick in for the rent while he saved to get a place of his own.

But in the glassy gleams coming from his sick friend's troubled, slightly protruding eyes, he could read a jumble of messages. It occurred to him that it might even be his becoming successful, passing beyond the old crowd—and way beyond his friend—that his friend most feared.

Sleep deprivation strangles Apollo's own eyeballs. Now he sees a vision of Baby Pop, outlined against the morning light as he swung open the door. The image is lying translucent on his sick friend's drawn face. He hadn't made the connection before. The kid must have AIDS.

He sinks onto the bed and waves his friend away. No matter what he does, ghosts come back to accuse him. With or without dope, he is still a perpetrator. How he wants a shot, a toke, a drink—anything!

Weakened and sullen, the friend gives up and retreats in shaky silence to the other room. On the underside of Apollo's lids ghosts of Tina's first after-hours night continue to snake. Snarls and brittle laughter, smashed bottles, threats, and shameless pleading hammer his ears.

Out of this kaleidoscope a dream begins to form. For the first time since he used to get high, her face reappears. Mrs. Huxton, with a new hairdo, sits a few floors above the squirming mess of Tina's After-hours, as little interested in

the details of what goes on below as someone with a blooming garden thinks about the sex lives of its earthworms.

Leading downward from her is a spiral that ends at
the street. Mrs. Huxton picks up the phone and demands
Pargero, who's just gotten back from Tina's After-hours.
*He's at the end of the funnel, she is saying. Bring a bucket with a
lid to pick him up as he pops out.*

But perhaps Pargero is asking for a little more time.
Maybe he and his mom will be entertaining tonight.

*No, Mom, break out another one. I think that one's just a little
too staid . . . Now there's a number for you: the bust's got scarlet
tulle with papier-mache cherries, and the sleeve cuffs are trimmed
with sequins. Will it go with her complexion? Well, to be perfectly
honest, we're talking about a dark-skinned girl here, sweetheart.
Name's Mercedes. But don't get me wrong. She's one of the lookers
on Mrs. Huxton's block. Still has plenty of gas left in her. Where'd
I meet her? During a routine investigation.*

*Don't start getting on me about the old days again, Mom.
You're better off here in New Jersey, with what's happened to the
old stomping grounds. I know you haven't been in the city in years.
But you wouldn't recognize the scene anymore. Devil knows why
Mrs. Huxton hangs on to that property.*

*Put that stuff on the chair and give yourself a break, darlin',
before the little lady arrives. Whenever I get you pulling out the
burlesque stuff, you think you're a young flame again. You know
you shouldn't push yourself at your age. You've been cooking all
day, and you shouldn't have put yourself to that much trouble.*

*Where'd I meet this one? I told you, just in the course of some
routine work! You know I don't like to talk about the business
when I'm off, Mom. No, no, as a matter of fact, this one won't be
a murder charge. Assault only. The victim pulled through. Who?
Works in the theater right underneath Mrs. Huxton.*

*No, no, the victim's no lady! That's all I'm telling you about the case, because I don't want to set those wheels spinning.*

*Yeah, I know where the perpetrator is, and we can thank Tina for that, but now that the victim's pulled through, the case has shifted. I had to put him in the hoosegow. That's all the material for your scrapbook now. Why don't you pull out a pack of cards and we'll play a hand of gin rummy?*

*All right, well, there was one interesting twist—the perpetrator's got an unusual momma. Interesting in the way that you wouldn't expect, him being a denizen and all. She's white. A religious nut. I guess you'd say she's a hippie.*

*No, not exactly that kind of hippie. Got some kind of altar in her home for some kind of chanting. And she tried to serve me peppermint tea when I went up there. Course I didn't drink it. What brought a thought like that into your mind?*

*The father's black. The mom used to be high-class. She's a lawyer's daughter. Says neither she nor her kid have seen his father in years. He's some kind of derelict now, though she says he once had some talent. Her eyes filled up with tears, she didn't want to talk about it.*

*You got me wrong again, Mom! I'm not trying to put down her mixed marriage. You're always confusing these cases with your own regrets. If you think I'm ashamed of Dad, then you're getting batty in your old age. I know your mother was against it. Don't tell me again how hard he tried to do right by us. But this mother and her marriage . . . If you'd read the letter she wrote to the Board of Corrections like I did, I bet your hair would stand on end.*

*I was so moved I went up to Mrs. Huxton's to thrash out this one. Better believe she asked about you. She's mummy-ancient, but that mind is still sharp as a tack. Remembers you and how you used to pull 'em in with the feather dance. Misses the old days, too.*

*What's she still doing there? That's one of the seven mysteries. She's the holdout on that block that's put the whole city to shame.*

That must give her some sense of pride in her sunset years. Keeps the scene going as if by magic, the way it's thinned out by drugs and disease.

I know she's got a feel for the working kids, Mom, same as always, but that don't explain it. If you saw 'em now it would knock your garters off. Like I said, it isn't what it used to be when you were dancing and Mr. Huxton was alive.

Well, your guess is as good as mine. Does it 'cause she has to, if you ask me. What I'm saying is that she needs them as much as they need her. That's the best-kept secret in history. They go in and out of her clutches, and to them she seems fair and square.

Oh, I don't know, Mom. Start dealing those cards and get your mind off the past. Of course I know where you came from when she took you in. Of course I know the old man left us without a penny. I'm not trying to dish the lady.

Now cut the tears, beauty. You can't change what's already past. Huxton is doing fine. She'll probably outlive the both of us. What amazes me is the sense of timing the old broad's got. She's got a feel for the exact moment a prospect will turn bad, and bingo! They're out on the street. A boot from her is a sentence to Burnsville, but the minute they get themselves together they're suddenly in her good graces again.

Okay. But family is definitely not the word for it! Don't you think you see the old lady through rose-colored glasses? All the kids know she might need to throw them away in a minute—they just can't blame her for it. It's never supposed to be her fault; it's theirs.

Of course I know that she's got to make a living. That's what holds her and the kids together. She's successful at what they wish they could do. Call it shark love.

I'll prove to you how slippery the old girl can be. The reason I went to see her was to know should I try to work a drop-charges on the victim. He was caught with some drugs when they took him in to the docs. Now he's crippled. He's been her bouncer for years, but *since she's thinking of moving anyway she brushed the whole thing off. The guy is in jail now 'cause Huxton wouldn't stick her neck out for him. But as far as she's concerned, he's gone with the wind.*

*Yeah, she wants to move. Can you believe it? She's got gentrification plans, too. Wants to spruce up the business and upscale the clientele, so she's planning on remodeling the place that used to belong to O'Hara.*

*What do you mean, you worry about the future, Ma? Nobody can bring the good old days back, but the old girl's sitting on a billion! You mean you worry about the kids, once Mrs. Huxton's gone? Well, you got a point there. But you're doing your best to pitch in.*

*And just between you and me, neither Huxton nor Tina will come out of this mess without their millions. Why, at this very moment Tina's raking it in at a new after-hours place. That's all you're going to hear. Deal those cards now. But first lay out the dress all pretty on that chair. The little lady should be here at any moment.*

Apollo twisted onto his stomach and pressed the pillow to his face. He needed to get a handle on things. Night would turn into day and day into vice versa just as it had in the old times. The realization felt comforting as he drifted awake and then back into sleep.

It's Allhallows eve, but the after-hours has been ruined by a nearly freezing rain. Outside in the big drops, the laws of night cling to the street, indivisible as mud. They chill the bones of the exiled and cut through their highs. At Tina's After-hours the crowd has stabilized. The stabbings have happened, and the eighty-sixes are written in stone. Wearing an orange hat with a jack-'o-lantern face, sullen

Perk sits crouched at the door, holding a witch's broom instead of his blackjack. The coffee spiking through him has peaked his eyebrows and compressed his lips. The scars of old tracks on his bulging arms complement the scowling expression for full ghoul effect. Catching his own reflection in the bar mirror doesn't help his mood. He can't believe the hunched and edgy, scowling image he sees. It reminds him of another bouncer with dark-circled eyes, whom he once wasted, in a theater a few months ago.

And like that former bouncer, he's become none too popular. His eighty-sixes have racked up scores on the street. He's got a list of enemies two miles long and has to take special routes to and from the bar.

It's an after-hours evening in which only the desperate will surface in wilted costumes on bad drugs. Even Tina's thrown in the towel and left him manning the post. Tracing circles around him is someone whom he knows considers himself to be his mortal enemy. It's the boy Baby Pop. Tina's overdecorated house in Brooklyn, three squares, and proper medication have put some meat back on the boy's bones. The adolescent face has filled out again, and the clothes are clean and new. Not one to waste resources, Tina has given him some light busing duties a few nights a week. And each night he works he does a bitter toreador dance around Perk perched in his chair. Whenever Perk looks up, he finds the boy glowering at him, the eyes miming *cabrón, cabrón.* Which is something he doesn't need.

Nor does he need this feeling that he's in the charnel house again. It was one thing to be part of the zombies on the block trying to hustle a shot. It is another to lurch among the corpses completely straight, like an Igor among snatched bodies. But worst of all is tonight's stranded feeling. Halloween in the rain. At the place nobody wants to be.

One thing Apollo never did was hang around a place where there was no action.

Perk the ghoulish bouncer stalks the interior of the bar with a furrowed brow and a snarl on his lips. Among the stoned, he's like a man who's lost his appetite for sweets and fallen into a vat of taffy. From time to time the thought occurs that the best thing to do would be to open his mouth and suck.

As a matter of fact, business has fallen way off. From time to time, the cops come around and make like they're hassling Tina. She cites this as reason to be more stringent about whom they let in. Little by little, she's whittled away at the available population.

Change is in the air, but Apollo can't figure it. He shuts off. He picks up a bottle or two missed by Baby Pop. At least it's something to do. He frowns at the lowest of the low creeping in for shelter. Angelo with a broken arm, his wet cast dissolving. The woman who lives in the cardboard box making an attempt to enter and Apollo leaping into action to stop her at the door. Real heroics. He watches her tramp back to the wet cardboard. There's too much wind tonight for any protection from the overhang. The cardboard shreds as she pulls it around her.

Later a bewildered German tourist steps in to dry off. The only other client, a hook-nosed drag queen, puts herself in his startled face.

By 8:00 A.M. Apollo decides to shut up shop. Not one tip or bribe to supplement Tina's twenty-five bucks waiting with the bartender in a white envelope. Tomorrow is his day off. He puts the five in his pocket for coffee and an egg sandwich and the twenty in his shoe. Better safe than sorry. Out there are all the people stuck in the rain whom he eighty-sixed at one time or another. He begins sloshing east through the rain toward the subway.

Under the pelting rain he considers strategy. This is the third week of work, and his friend is still throwing shit fits. He's waiting for Apollo to slip back into the old ways. The rent is due tomorrow, but Apollo hasn't been able to put away any money. He's still a freeloader. What will he do when Daddy gets sicker or dies?

His sneakers inhale the freezing water like a sponge. He can feel the cold, slick twenty-dollar bill caressing his heel like an aged trick's clammy hand.

# XV

Love and kisses from your common-
law wife.
If you don't get the chair, I hope you
get life.

—Prison Toast

*L*ook who come out of the woodwork, my one and only, my
first true love, my Casio. Yeah, baby, it's me, Monica,
writing back like you hoped. You'll excuse me, papito, for not
writing sooner. It's just that I'm not about writing to cons up river
anymore. Surprised, chulito? Being that you always thought
I was trash and never would make nothing of myself anyways.

Well I got news for you, Big Man, I'm moving to Fort
Lauderdale! I got me my beautician's license and a cousin of
Pablo's is opening up a salon. I ain't with the jailbird shit
no more. I decided to keep away from anybody tries to pull
me down.

You know I got two kids from Pablo after you moved out and I got rid of Cubby and his crew. I'm going to make damn sure that their life is going to be better than mine by the way. Down there in Florida they got cheap apartments and good weather. I don't know nobody come along knocking on my door which is fine by me.

Listen to me, Mr. Jailbird. Don't run off at the mouth about Baby Pop to me. Didn't I give that boy every chance I could? Well a couple months ago me and Pablo find a big garbage bag of clothes against the door. I put it out back with the trash and went to bed. About three in the morning somebody starts banging on the door. It was Baby Pop out of nowhere saying he come back to move in!

Fine and good, I told him, but I got a life too. I'm living with my husband and two babies and I don't think they would want you here. Well you know what? When we got up the next morning there he was in the hallway on top of his garbage bag. Pablo come out and told him you got to leave and Baby started mouthing off bad. He's a chip off the old block and don't want to know nothing about the laws that get normal people through the day. Living with you was sticky black and finally a ray of light is creeping in. Don't take it personal, but you shouldn't be writing to me no more.

Take it light, my Big Bad Homeboy,

_EX_-wife Monica

P.S. I called up your aunt and said send you the hair. And as for the legs and tits pictures, sorry but my shit ain't available. I put something in with this letter that I know is more your style. I hear she be doing so well that she moved to California.

The sound of lockup in the unit was a pulverizing echo inside Casio's ears. The noise went through him and threatened to grind up his bones. He grasped the corner of the picture that had come with the letter in a shaking hand.

Obviously, it had been ripped out of a porno magazine. And to get it through prison censors, Monica had felt-tipped out certain body parts.

Angelita looked plump and sensuous in some *Dynasty*-style bedroom, her black hair moussed into a stiff mane. Her naked tits were stretched firm and luscious over their new water sacs. At the edge of one of the felt-tip marks he could make out the tip of her hard erection. It looked about to enter the asshole of the spread-eagled blond man lying half on the satin quilt and half on the broadloom rug. He'd stretched his beefy arms back so that his tanned fingers could spread apart his ass cheeks.

Within his world of the perennial tuning fork, the incarcerated man let the picture fall from his white-knuckled fingers. Rather than smash them against the cell wall, he groped as if for a charm under his mattress to find and clasp the lock of wavy hair.


His attacker got home soaked to the bone and gulped the coffee and egg sandwich, then yanked off the drowned kicks to take out the twenty-dollar bill. Half of its printing had been erased by the combination of water, shoe dye, and heel friction. He could barely make out President Jackson's face or the number *20* in two of the corners. The other side of the bill was a web of small paper cracks. Disgustedly, he went to put the bill on the bedroom table, where he found a note. It was scrawled in the margin of half a page hastily ripped from a pad.

*Fever 106. At emergency room on 12th and 7th.*

Without knowing why, Apollo began to panic. Cursing under his breath, he threw his wet kicks back on and smoothed out the bill. He stuck it into his shirt pocket under his parka.

The rain was even thicker now, as he trudged back to the Korean market where he'd bought breakfast. He picked out a box of chocolate donuts and carried them to the counter. But when he held out the bill, the guy pulled a blank face and shook his head. Apollo surmised it was the hostile expression stamped onto his own face that inspired the refusal, yet he could not unlock his muscles. When the pretty blond girl in back of him placed her two carrots on the scale and held out a twenty-dollar bill that was far from crisp, the clerk's face abruptly changed into an indulgent smile.

Apollo tossed the donuts onto the counter and dove back into the rain. The ailing bill had stood no chance because it was part of the short circuit that made up his world. The cash register at Tina's After-hours was full of similar currency that was worn, cellophane-taped, or velvety with grime. The same bills passed from johns to hustlers to dealers to bartenders and back to johns over and over. That was how hermetic his world of users was.

It wasn't the fear of facing two whole days with the two dollars he had left or even the inconvenience of trying to change that twenty that got under Apollo's skin. It was the fact that although dead President Jackson's face worked for everybody else, Apollo was obviously not considered a citizen of the realm. Dead or dying people were all that were available to him, and they were coming through less and less often.

Thoughts of this nature shot a rage through him as

needlelike as the rain under which he hunched as he headed for the bank up the block. Though he had never had an account, the bank had not escaped his notice whenever he passed that corner. Inside it were people who had always elicited the same dumb contempt in him as he did in them. At certain predictable hours, he could see them crunched into a sullen line at the cash machine in their strangely drab outfits, dangling briefcases or pull-out car radios, making money appear from the machines. Or else they were squirreling it away in some system Apollo had never understood. Yet their different sense of time and its rewards was almost palpable to him, who no longer had any pleasures since he had quit dope. He was convinced these camouflaged clones had some long-term way of enjoying themselves that they were hiding from him, who was still trapped in his world of quick tricks and shoddy results.

There was, he knew, a necessary protocol for banks. Those times he'd gone to the bank with his sick friend or skulked near a teller's line while a john withdrew money to pay him had alerted him to the things that caused suspicion. So he rehearsed his plan carefully. It was to wait in line until a number flashed and stroll casually to that number, acting like he knew what he was doing.

Apollo wasn't sure he had chosen the right line, behind two black girls who were sulkily dissing somebody named Tahara who had cheated on her time sheet. But when an officious-looking woman wearing a tweedy skirt yelled out "payroll," his hair stood on end. The woman had bellowed the word just the way commands were barked out in jail. His eyes narrowed in rebellion, and his muscles stiffened as he shifted to another line.

So close to his eyes that he could see the pores on it was the freshly barbered neck of the white man in front of him.

The short-cropped hair gleaming with gel, over shoulders enlarged by calculated exercise in a gym, held a disquieting fascination. He couldn't pull his eyes away from that neck, its white shirt collar and suit. It was as if it held some power to sentence him to slow destruction. He'd never been so close to the feeling. It kept tensing the muscles in his mouth and chin into a grimace, against which he kept fighting. It was also what tuned him in to the man's conversation in a spooky experience of eavesdropping.

He was talking to a similarly suited partner about girls at the office. One of the men had lost a "bundle" taking a girl out to dinner who'd never "given her pussy up." The other ribbed him about "not keeping your cards close to your chest."

Apollo had no control over the astonished feeling the conversation caused. The portrayal of a white office female as "pussy" and the use of the word "bundle"—which in his world meant ten bags of dope—seemed borrowed and false. So this was how they talked—by stealing phrases, expressions, and sensations from his world to portray their own boring lives! What a laugh that they needed to talk like him to talk about pussy! They should know that he hadn't even jerked off or thought once about wanting sex since he stopped getting high. And what was he getting out of their rip-offs? He made up his mind that this time the tables would be turned.

The continuation of their conversation added perplexity as well as a sense of inferiority to his strategy. As if there were some connection between lack of pussy and making a living, the two were suddenly talking about the economy. Something about the middle class having to pay an unfair share of taxes. The hard, flexed tone of their righteous indignation sent Apollo into manic laughter. But when they glanced behind them, he shut up fast. What were taxes, exactly, and how did they affect anybody's life? Did what they were talking about have some bearing on his fate that he was too stupid to understand? No wonder he was stuck where he was if his future had been consigned to their manicured hands.

Suddenly they left the line and shifted into a now-empty line marked "Privileged." Apollo intuitively sensed he was to remain where he was. Finally a number flashed, and he followed a blinking arrow to a teller. But he was unable to escape from the irrational feeling that every eye in the place was on him.

In his world, at times like this, you stiffened your pelvis and strutted, careful to let your arms hang low to swing in an apelike way and brush against your crotch. Automatically he felt himself shifting into his dominant display mode. But the sudden realization that the two men near him wouldn't be caught dead walking that way curtailed it, and he bounced awkwardly to the teller window.

The pale blond man with a crisp collar and stiffened hair seemed obviously gay. One or two types like this wandered into Tina's from time to time. A half-flirtatious, half-intimidating scenario flashed immediately into Apollo's mind. The fag, he felt, wouldn't be able to resist his body if only he could see it without the clothes. He wanted to inform him of this, since it wouldn't be obvious under his shapeless parka. Through the Plexiglas window he wanted to communicate some of the ingrained machismo he was sure the guy wished he himself had. Flex a little even, then ask him to change the ugly twenty.

But the absurdity of this approach in a bank curtailed that thought as well. Without warning he was forced into the unexpected strategy of trying to act polite and unobtrusive. Why hadn't he thought of such an obvious thing before?

Apollo's thoughts went frantically through his meager mental file of polite public behavior. Hotly he realized that it was something that was part acting like a pussy and part speaking like you were entitled to what you wanted. But the two opposing strains twisted into a nervous jumble of intentions. The street was not a place where humility and pushiness combined in that way. He found himself fumbling in his breast pocket for the twenty and holding it up by thumb and forefinger in front of the glass.

"Listen, lemme change this?" he heard himself blurt out. "I put it in my shoe and the face of the president got washed some away."

The teller was unimpressed—in fact, he was embarrassed. If any male animal power was apparent in Apollo at that moment, he did not appear to notice. "Do you have an account here?" he asked with eyebrows arched in doubt and strained patience.

Apollo knew what an account was but not whether he should lie about having one. So he said, "Kind of." And through the corner of one eye he thought he caught the businessmen at the Privileged window eyeing him with amusement.

"Account number?" sighed the teller.

"Listen. My heel rubbed it is all. Gimme another one, would you." Aggressively, he shoved the worn bill through the slot.

The teller withdrew from it as if it stank. Gingerly he pushed it back toward Apollo with the end of a ballpoint. "Go speak to an officer."

The word "officer" was panic through Apollo's stomach, so he fell back into street pride and took the bill from the slot with angry contempt. He hunched up his shoulders and shoved the bill back in his pocket. His eyes spit flames.

"You think I need this fucking business? I don't need your fucking bank!" he said, and now everybody really was staring. Fixing his best glare on his face, he stomped toward the door.

He didn't want to go home to find out if his friend was back or if he'd lost him to the hospital. And now he noticed the bum lying in the corner of the lobby where the cash machines were. Perhaps he hadn't been there when Apollo had entered. But now that they were the only two in this space, the image of the ill man could not be avoided. He smelled the acrid odor of urine coming from the man's clothes and noticed the dirt-caked ankles above the sockless shoes.

It wasn't until Apollo had charged halfway up the block with a destination for the twenty-dollar bill that he realized of whom he was thinking. Through grime and puffiness, the black and stubbled face delivered its overwhelming memory of a father he had not seen for years.

*Back in the cell after the methadone that I got this vision. It was a methadone dream, 'cause though they be lowering my dose, a few minutes after gulping the stuff you get a little bit fucked up. I'm lying in the cell with heat boiling in my armpit about to make me going to come. There's a cat lying in my armpit having her kittens. I got to lie so still, 'cause the babies coming out of that pussy one after the other make a nest of my armpit that they mix up with her belly. Then out come the afterbirth and the cat gulps it down. Abuela walks into the cell and says, You are the father. All of a sudden one of them cats turns into a tiny Baby Pop saying his mother's no good so he wanting for me to come out of the cell.*

*That dream is a sign that I got to start planning my release. To save money they been hurrying up my detox schedule—fourteen* days instead of twenty-one, the bastards. I'd like to tell 'em I shit on the cunt of their mothers. They fill me up with such hate that most of the time I'm thinking about the dope waiting for me soon's I get out. I ain't gonna become a junkie again, but now and then on the weekends I'm gonna find the Big Man and get me some of that brand called D.O.A. Dead on Arrival. I'm gonna do it up but I ain't gonna go overboard this time, being that I got my boy Baby Pop waiting for me and I don't want to look too bad. Fuck Monica and Angelita and all them other lying pussies, they ain't gonna hear from me till hell freezes over.

Now let's see here, what that I got to figure how I'm gonna get through the urine checks which the Parole talking. Oh shit, don't you remember what Sugar Bear did and it worked fine every time? You get yourself an empty nose spray bottle and you go to the subway station to start looking over the people that be waiting for the train. You find somebody you know he needs money but you know he ain't into dope or no drugs. You got to look him over good. Check out the eyes, the arms for marks, the color he got in his skin. The hands. The nails got to be clean.

Excuse me, you says, but you want to make ten bucks by urinating for me in this little bottle here?

Then you got to take the bottle and tie it to your fly with a piece of thread. Wrap the thread right around the neck of the bottle. You put the bottle into your underwears right up under your dick. Now when you fill the cup for the urine test, you take out the bottle under your dick and squeeze that instead. Somebody want to watch you, you say, what's a matter, you gay or something?

I keep thinking about that cat eating up all the afterbirth. You are the father, she kept saying to me.

# XVI

The guy looked familiar, like the ghost of somebody. Whoever it was, he had lost weight and aged. He stood out against the night like a white burn on a negative, but he flickered, as if you could put your hand through him. An old candle in a tired night.

He was part of the landscape ruled by the Big Man, whom Apollo knew would not turn down his fucked-up twenty-dollar bill. The Big Man turned down no one. You didn't have to have a barbered neck and a suit, talk pussy, or wait in the Privileged line to get his attention.

Apollo vacantly wondered whether the dope the Big Man had would be as good as it had been the last time. Though he had been unable to remember what it felt like to be high before, now that he had made the decision to buy a bag, he suddenly remembered the feeling of that last shot bought on 112th Street. The Big Man would charge ten for a bag and works and give a good ten-dollar bill as change. Apollo would do it only this once and be fixed up until he went to work the day after tomorrow.

If everything was figured out, then why was this half-memory flickering on the Big Man's space? Not that Apollo was complaining. The sight of this ghost from some past was an improvement over the disjointed fragments of memory about his father and mother that had been torturing him as he walked up here earlier this afternoon from the bank. But he wondered how he knew this white guy in battered sneakers and too-large jeans who kept haunting the two-block rectangle of Ninth Avenue from one corner to the next and back.

Thinking about who the guy could be lured Apollo into a tunnel that traveled through the thick tar of a night. The night seeped into his nostrils, ears, and eyes, and slowed his bloodstream. Deep within this sluggish blackness he remembered who the person was. It was the crazy trick who had wanted to do dog training. The one who'd watched him shoot up and then gobbled his toes like a dog. *Remember?* Apollo saw the memory from the depths of the tar. *And now look at him.* He'd been swallowed up by the night too.

The guy flickered on the blackness of Ninth Avenue among the other users like a moth caught in tar. His bones showed through his clarified face, and his expression seemed to eat itself. Apollo wondered what he had done to end up here. The question was answered almost immediately, as Big Man's black limousine pulled to the curb. The ghost of the foot gobbler got first in line. Big Man was wearing an enormous tent of pleated black silk as a shirt and numerous bracelets and rings adorning each hand. In one of his arms, he clutched his red-haired Pekingese, who burrowed into the flab of his chest as if it were too sensitive to face the users on this black nocturnal block.

The Big Man sang out his hellos almost jovially as the throng of hungry users encircled him. The moth from the past was first, flickering in and out next to the Big Man's big face and swollen, overfed cheeks. "You got rockets?" he asked anxiously.

So that was it: the researcher/dog or whatever the hell he claimed to be was now just a white crackhead. This was proof that even white guys with dirty sneakers and cash-machine cards could end up stuck in the night, if their timing and patience went all haywire. Apollo imagined the two shaved-neck businessmen at the bank stumbling into the tar. They kicked and flailed in it for a few moments with their attaché cases, complaining shrilly about big taxes or how much gym membership had gone up. Then they too were still, like flies caught in new amber. They were getting all the pussy they could want now, stuck in the big gooey night. *I'm gonna tax you,* Apollo sang grinningly to himself. *Now I'm gonna tax you.*

The Big Man gave him dope and works, and even a little bottle of water, for the ten. But the feel of the glassine bag in his hand had nothing of the magic he'd imagined when he'd finally given in to the urge earlier that afternoon. Maybe because now, he'd been awake for almost twenty-four hours and was too exhausted to get excited. The bag felt so concrete and unevocative that he began to doubt that a small, plastic-covered lump could have any power at all. It was like a charm you bought at some magic place or sacred shrine. At some point later in the trip you unclasped your hand and found a piece of stone or a cheap little bell. But maybe if you continued to hold it, it could transform itself.

He told himself this as he passed the entrance to the tunnel, where Mercedes and six other transvestites frantically hooked in garters, stockings, and heels. Stalking in some stylized dance punctuated by yelps and hisses, they flashed jackets open to bare tits in the crisp post-Halloween air. Cars perked along like a ghoul's parade, spitting catcalls or insults on cue from their windows before disappearing into the tunnel.

Apollo imagined the tunnel as a passage into blackness where a vehicle got stuck and congealed in something it would never get out of. Then the queens would fart into the mouth of the tunnel, and cackles would pass from their big, lipsticked mouths. Suddenly he didn't want to do up the bag. A science-fiction hole in his skin might yawn open and swallow needle and all. It might even chew his hand up to his wrist just because he wanted to do dope this one time.

He was passing a peep show he remembered, which had once let him bring in tricks. He could see Angelo in slurred argument with the Indian manager, who kept waving him out the door. Angelo was stoned enough to see perfect logic in his own point of view, and speeded words spilled from his partly toothless mouth. He boldly insisted on his right to use the booths to hustle tricks in order to make a living. The booths were, Angelo maintained, just like parking meters. So long as a john who was servicing him kept slipping quarters into the slot and the manager kept collecting them, he had no right to fucking complain.

On impulse Apollo slipped by them into a booth and decided he would do the bag. He took two quarters out and dumped them into the slot. He imagined Angelo as a human quarter sinking into a big slot. Suddenly all of Earth was sinking. Apollo went down with it so swiftly that his stomach rose in his throat. The whole fucking world, including his sick friend, his job, and the bank, were being flushed down the toilet. He stood in the light of the sex movie to use its pale colors to tie up and shoot the bag. He realized that he had missed the burial of the needle in flesh as much as he had missed the dope. *It's not the dope that makes the big difference,* he thought as it seeped into his flesh. *It's doing it*. The realization shifted his focus. He was high on heroin for the first time in months and, despite his lack of sleep, could finally see clearly. *Something like getting them to lower taxes or getting office pussy.* Something like a need that sank into the night but re-emerged again and again.

With the withdrawal of the needle, he imagined everything floating backward in slow-motion, not really time reversing, but reversing space: the quarters floating back out of the slot, the cars floating backward out of the tunnel, the moth-man floating clean out of the tar and beating its wings again, dope and blood squirting back out of a vein, crack smoke funneling back out into the black air.

When he got to Tina's Lounge, a couple of blocks from what he thought of as Mrs. Huxton's sex theater, he was shocked to see that the building across the street had been completely leveled. In its place stood murky grayness. Everything on the block had been coated with the demolition's dust. Between the police barriers at each end of the block, every inch of street and sidewalk was inch-thick with the stuff.

On the protrusions and edges and in the cracks of all the building facades, including Tina's Lounge, trails of the powdery stuff clung like snow. It coated the panes of Tina's windows and the accordion folds of her open steel gate. Though Tina hadn't mentioned it, the place was no longer a transvestite-and-hustler bar. Through the filmy windows he caught a glimpse of a sweater or a down coat. Inside, college types were playing pool.

The street looked like a spray-painted set for a play about nuclear fallout, so mysterious, poisonous, and uniform had everything been made by the coat of dust. This part of the neighborhood was changing. It had all happened while he'd been away from it, working at Tina's After-hours. Where were the queens and crooks now? he wondered. Dully, he took up position in the artificial scene, imagining his rumpled parka and hands that felt spidery against the gray-on-gray. Perhaps because people were afraid of asbestos from the demolition, the street was empty except for him. He enjoyed posing in it in an affirmation of the toxic, as if he were its mascot or logo.

Like an image brightening on a black-and-white television screen, a face burned into focus. To his doped astonishment, it bore a strange resemblance to the teller at the bank. The blond, washed-out teller was made luminous against the gray, like a white hospital sheet on the blurred burn of a fever . . . But what was strange was that there were two images, not one.

Neither was the teller, of course. Revenge was never that perfect. But they were teller types. Two thin, blond gay guys with starched shirts, and overly neat hair. In their pale bleached-blue jeans, they stopped and told him they were from Missouri and could not find Tina's Lounge. They'd read about it being a gay bar in the gay guide, but it wasn't there anymore.

This time Apollo did not restrain the calculated movements of male preening that he used for challenge and display. He clasped his hands behind his back and pulled his shoulders down so that the parka was stretched against his chest and upper arms. He revealed their sculpted meatiness and flashed a surly smile.

The tourists responded to the proprietary gleam in Apollo's stoned eyes. Terrified and excited, they stepped aside for a hasty conference, then invited him back to their decent midtown hotel. With edgy delight they snuck him by the desk clerk to the elevator.

*

It was with cynical amusement that he observed their nervous, provincial hospitality. They offered him a chair, while they perched on the neatly made bed. They folded their hands in their laundered laps. With patient courtesy they asked him if he was a native New Yorker and what he did for a living, trying not to glue their eyes to his crotch, which, slumping, he casually stroked through his pants.

They talked about their families, and Apollo told about his "great" relationship with his father. "I'm his sweetheart," he said. The term must have taken the pair by surprise, because suddenly they became awkwardly silent. So Apollo suggested one of them go to the TV and punch in a straight porno film that would be charged to their hotel bill. With the same Midwestern cordiality, one blond walked uncertainly to the TV. Lapsing into plain-folk candidness, the other flatly asked whether that meant Apollo was straight. Apollo boldly answered that he was but considered both of them girls.

The offense colored both faces. Apollo understood. Upstanding and reasonable, they'd worked hard to forge a gay identity clean of ludicrousness, ambiguity, or doubt. For that very reason he enjoyed gauging the proportion of insult-to-arousal he had caused, blowing just enough against their house of cards.

Insolently, he stood up from the chair and dropped onto the bed. Start the movie rolling, he commanded, and slipped off his pants. And with the start of the movie, the movie of the past finally replayed. For although Apollo had already gotten high, he had not really found the old feeling until he found this link. It was a sexual mastery that radiated from contempt. It scoped right into others and played with who they were. It took care of him and took care of others without his having to bother to like them. Within it, he gave everything he had, but lost nothing. It was an affirmation that he had never had anything in the first place. That was the pleasure of being high and selling sex to get higher.

So ecstatic and just was this expenditure that the two blonds seemed mesmerized. Below them on the bed lay all the physical health he had been squirreling away by not getting high, just as those drab ones squirreled away money in the bank. Now he understood what it meant to save and spend, and he hoped that some unknown power in the future would allow him an unexpected accumulation once again. Because his cock was rising in a great arc to fuck the squirming porno actors on television, it fucked the world of banks and fucked the mouths of both men skidding against his tingly, numb skin. It fucked sick friends whom he wished he could save and fathers dying on the floor at cash machines.

They had stripped naked, and their larval bodies showed red marks wherever he had grasped or slapped too hard. It occurred to him that his touch was like a branding iron. It cauterized them into becoming lustier men. Gleefully, he realized how increasing pleasure enlarged them into accepting the role of girls he'd assigned them.

To their reincarnation he offered the blood boiling in his high veins. He gave them what even the best courses in consciousness-raising had denied existed. He showed them the suicidal ecstasy of setting on fire everything that you had saved. He helped them trample their careful masculine gardens and squander their harvests. How wild the blond boys became. How eager they were to relish this real man watching porno and letting them skim off pleasure's overflow. Their admiration for his cock, which had gone stiff all the way to its root near his anus, was not ruined by the thought that they were working on a dope stick. A dope stick

207

was a cock that stayed hard interminably on a high junkie's body. Orgasm was leagues away, and when and if it came, it too would be protracted. But these two were strangers to the junkie world. With eager trust they licked and sucked the magical dick and balls, whose voltage never diminished. All three men hovered and trembled at the same level.

He wanted, most of all, to see the look on the primmer one's face as he pushed his dope stick up his ass. For the night of tar was melting into a rushing ocean. Every tight withdrawal that had marked the last weeks of sobriety loosened and swirled away with it. The white bodies clasping him on either side with suckers fastened to his nipples and cock were like huge sails tugging on his floating body. He gave in to the rushing current that made swollen the huge bladders of silk. He was shooting into this ocean a hot expulsion he couldn't distinguish from peeing or coming. With the help of two white butch queens, Apollo and heroin had finally reached white waters.

In his underpants, the primmer and taller of the two blonds looked piqued. He was standing near the television, which he'd angrily shut off, counting out the sixty dollars Apollo had demanded. Behind him lay the shorter, rosier one, still naked, his forearm shielding his eyes to conceal his embarrassment at having ended up with a hustler.

As Apollo pulled on his wrinkled clothes and worn-out kicks, he studied their leather-trimmed luggage and extra pairs of polished shoes by the bed. He made note of the fancy digital travel clock on the night table. Then he saw the one who was standing shoot a meaningful glance to the one on the bed, who grimaced.

So then. They'd finally figured out who they were.

*

Who was he? Somebody who chipped,* he told himself. It flushed out the system and cut loose hang-ups. Going back to the old desperate ways was out of the question, but right now he had three new twenties from the butch queens in his parka pocket. Whatever he decided to do with the rest of the night would be no problem, even if he hadn't slept in twenty-four hours.

So he hailed a cab. Encased in pleasure, nearly crowing in freedom, he rocked in his seat, as it took him back up to 112th Street, one of the best copping spots in Manhattan, just to see it again.

The new night setting was full immersion into the old world. Memory, which had been nonexistent for the last months, brought back the image of his last trip there, feeling sick, next to his sick friend, to get a bag. His friend had been in much better shape then.

Apollo felt a touch of nostalgia for the old days, when getting high was a freewheeling affair and before his friend was hit so badly by AIDS. The thought put an idiotic half-grin on his face.

The driver caught it through his rear-view mirror.

"You okay?" he asked.

Apollo nodded, mutating the grin into a beatific smile.

Soon the corner floated into view, like a slide of itself taken at night. It was a memory from the past that he could not imagine becoming real again—that school you used to go to whose corridors have shrunk, that town with different neighbors. Two cold whites of eyes floated in the darkness of the block where he had always bought the stuff. He figured they were the eyes of the dealer. They drew him onward like a fish drawn at night by a phosphorescent lure.

---

* shot heroin now and then

But as he got nearer, he noticed that the dealer wore a hat with a glowing *X*. He turned back toward the cab, but it had already crept to the next corner and was continuing through a green light.

The person wearing a matted stocking cap with a big white *X* on it was hurrying toward him as he backed into the street. Now the *X*-cap was raining blows on his head while trying to trip him at the same time.

"You fucking junkie bouncer," it hissed, "where's your queen bodyguard now?"

With great lucidity he recorded the blows hitting him. But his nerve endings resisted them with strange numbness. *What is it like to be high and then beat up?* he queried. *This is happening to another body, not mine nor his.*

"You killed Angelo's cousin," he said as part of the script.

"So what if I did?"

He felt bizarrely monolithic, his body rhythms so slowed down that he would not fall. He took the beating half as punishment deserved and half in resentment, with an eerie sense of irony. It was like when the effect of a Novocain shot at the dentist is tested successfully with a probe for lack of feeling.

When it was over, he copped the best brand, D.O.A., and dragged himself west to a shooting gallery in black Harlem, a repair garage during the day, where he figured he'd be less likely to run into the *X*-cap again. The place was full of old-time junkies, in their forties and fifties, with some old-time ideas. But nobody was fazed by his ripped parka, swollen eye, and bloody lip. Blood was an abundant commodity here—junkies squirted it from their spikes into soiled water glasses or wiped a dribble off a punctured neck. However, few shared needles these days.

He took his place among them and politely shot up a man who was having trouble finding his one remaining good vein, in his armpit. But as he withdrew the needle, the man jerked into convulsions and fell off his chair. Someone came running with salt, and Apollo pried open his mouth and tossed some in. Then he clamped the lips together, hoping that saline in the mouth would hit the bloodstream and prevent the guy from O.D.ing, while another guy mixed a shot of saltwater. Here in the shooting gallery the problems and their solutions were all familiar. Everything fit together fine.

When the guy revived, Apollo took his shot and fell out on a mattress on the floor. The old junkies let their eyes rest on him and began philosophizing between nods.

"Lookit that young punk crashed out on the mattress. Remember just a few months ago, when he was looking so wasted?"

"Come back fine, like he was in Hollywood or something."

"Or jail."

"Yeah, they feed 'em good nowadays."

"They got a warrant for me. Maybe I should turn myself in and get me away from the stuff for two months."

"Might be just as good as going to one of them detoxes."

"Yeah, they take you off in seven 'stead of twenty-one nowadays."

"That way they can put somebody else in your bed."

"It's legal to be greedy."

"Know what cracks me up? Can't smoke in the hospital no more. I went into one of them detoxes and got through the sickness."

"Don't tell me. But you walked a few days later just to get a cigarette?"

"You got it."

"And those methadone motherfuckers lower you instead of increase you if they find opiates in your blood."

"Now that's perverted."

"Downright vengeful if you ask me."

"Lord, take a look at that baby boy's veins. They're so good I can see the valves in 'em."

"What I wouldn't give for pipes like that again. Wouldn't have to hit in the neck no more."

"I bet you gonna be doing that till you're eighty."

"If I live that long."

"When that happens you become a saint or something."

"'Member that seventy-eight-year-old junkie living up here in Harlem we used to call 'Mother'?"

"A real purified glow to her face."

"How'd she go finally?"

"The bone-crusher got her. She was in such a hurry she didn't draw her shit through no cotton or a cigarette filter."

"Oh yeah, them particles can sneak right into the heart!"

"Reminds me of the time the tip of my spike break off in my vein. But I dug the sucker out with a tweezers 'fore it could travel through me."

"Lookit the jeans on that kid falling off his rear! You know, they wear them big clothes like that so they can hide a weapon in 'em."

"You'd think it would be a obvious tip-off to the law."

"Come on, Rupert, how they gonna come down on just a *style*?"

"It's the mentality of the new generation I don't like. When they got a slight advantage, they sport a lot of gold jewelry."

"Just challenging the other no-gots in the neighborhood to make themselves feel big."

"You think anybody falls for that image shit?"

"What they don't know is we all been lyin' to each other from day one, and we'll be lyin' till West Bubba."

"Each and every one, some of us lie better than others, that's all. This one probably lied eight times today."

Apollo's inner alarm system jerked him out of the deepest nod as he felt the force field of shadiness. He hopped to his feet, disoriented.

"Don't bust a nut, junior, we was just statin' an opinion."

"I want to do up half more a bag," he said.

He propped himself on a broken-backed chair and tied up, then cooked some more. He could sense the dried-up bodies of the old junkies getting off on how easily it slid into his young veins.

The shot gave him a strange speed rush, as happened sometimes, so he started to rap about his big plans for the future. The old-time junkies sat back and laughed and slapped their knees.

He felt jerky, like a marionette.

# XVII

What an old maid I am getting to
be, losing the nerve to be in love
with death!

—ARTHUR RIMBAUD,
*A Season in Hell*

They saved me, but for what? No Apollo, and no word from him.
The apartment's abandoned, the undumped-garbage smell over-
powering, a fungus on the dirty dishes in the sink that's worse than
the thrush that had coated my throat in the hospital. The note still
there, right where I'd left it a month and a half ago. Fever 106 . . .
Light bulbs are burned out like they'd been left on for weeks.

He never came once to see me in the hospital. And when I called
home, nobody ever answered. Finally, they said the phone was
disconnected. He's been sucked back into the depths, just as I feared.

I myself have become a human syringe, with a Hickman's catheter sunk into my chest for shooting drugs directly to the heart. A

*way of slowing the spread of the cytomegalovirus that caused the fevers and has spread to my retinas, they told me. The junkie's dream, I suppose. If I ever run into him again, maybe I'll suggest he get one of these implanted.*

*You could dump anything into it, making suicide easy. But for the moment I hook up an intravenous contraption to it twice day. Drip some Ganciclovir through my veins to stave off the threat of blindness.*

Conversely perhaps for Apollo, there was the feeling of something leaking out of his body, so that a part of his self was leaking away. A feeling of shame. He spent some nights in a flophouse in the West Thirties that rented out chicken coops. At least, they looked like them. Each dormitory floor was divided into crude little wooden-partitioned cubicles with padlocks, containing a wooden bunk with a mattress. The roofs were chicken-coop wire, the bathroom communal.

Getting in and out of your padlocked coop wasn't that easy. There were drunks and paranoids in the hall. Across from him was a young girl on welfare. He spent one night padlocked in her room with her, but when she told him she could think herself into becoming Michael Jackson, he got scared and moved back into his coop.

He'd never gone back to the apartment or to Tina's After-hours since that first night of getting high. And when the place got shut down by the cops right after elections, word about the manhunt for Apollo leaked out.

Tina's Lounge remained changed, welcoming no hustlers or drags. Even the sex theater had become a straight porno movie house. Everyone in the crowd was now crammed into another after-hours, over a Portuguese restaurant. They had a video monitor with a wide view of the street so that they could check you out long before you rang the buzzer. The evening began at 3:00 A.M. and was often a desperate waiting game. With Apollo's return to hustling, this was the new place of operations. That or Port Authority in the afternoon. Rumor had it, however, that another club would soon be opening. In Apollo's mind the power behind it had to be Huxton.

He stayed away from the apartment of his sick friend and tried not to think about him. Near the beginning there were tricks on that mother trip, which he knew so well, who fell in love with his skin and lost look and pressed their attentions on him. While it lasted, he took what he could. They bought him little address books so he could come back to see them and "get organized." But just like everybody else out here, he always lost his address book. He remembered telephone numbers and faces, but not names. He could tattoo a telephone number on his mind if the trick allowed him to hear it only once. Then he played the game of calling and saying, "What's up," without announcing who it was. Even if there was perplexed silence on the other end of the line, he bided his time. It saved the embarrassment of the guy not remembering his name and his not remembering the guy's. If the guy recognized his voice immediately, Apollo knew he'd made inroads. Or he got bolder and called collect. If the guy accepted the call, he'd saved a quarter and it probably meant the evening was in the bag. Then there was always the intimidation technique, standing outside the building at two in the morning and howling up at the window like a newborn in the middle of the night.

The routine of addiction and hustling mass-produces looks and personalities. Slowly but surely over the next few months he felt himself falling into one of the several stereo-types. There are those who get skinny and mangy and lose their luster as the street takes hold. With diminishing sexual appeal, they get bitter and violently impatient. Or they go the other way: discovering a sexual part of themselves that is clinging, whiny, and willing to accommodate. But there are others who thicken in a stolid-looking male way with a hint of the blowsy. They wring their appeal out of an increasingly unreasonable pride. Apollo was lucky enough to belong to this last group.

Was it an enlarging liver or the grease and starch he gobbled whenever he had the chance that had begun to develop the slight gut? A filled-out face and extra body weight gave him a more mature look, a broader swagger. Now he attracted johns who were looking for real rough trade instead of son figures. He had to adjust his sexual techniques to incorporate a new surliness, a little casual sadism. Then when he lapsed into dope passivity the tricks got hot at seeing the giant take his tumble.

Flippiness, he knew, was the great sexual tender. To see a burly lard-ass who reminded you of a construction worker moan and grow passive under your mouth or touch turned worlds upside down and set hearts beating. So what if it necessitated a shot of dope? When he got out of bed, he was still just as surly and as uncompromising, just as unattainable. That's what made them keep dropping coins into the slot.

When he caught a case of head lice at the "Chicken Coop Hotel," he shaved his skull. He made jokes about his new hairstyle being called "twenty-five to life." He found himself housing olive fatigues and an army jacket from a willing trick. Then he traded his sneakers in for construction boots. They turned his walk into a new stomp. He developed a seedy bravado, bawdy humor, a new corniness. Such exhibitionism added to the sham "take-control" image and lured more of the same type of trick.

One freezing afternoon in early winter he found himself at a chain pharmacy with a balding-businessman trick. The guy had said they had to stop to get condoms because he'd run out at home. For some reason all the brands were in a glass case. The trick was adamant about the brand he wanted, Trojan Plus, which were tapered and golden in color. But among the native languages and alphabets of the Syrian manager and the Korean and Haitian clerks accumulating at the condoms case, no one could locate the package the customer kept pointing to. When the correct package was produced after several wrong ones, Apollo satirized the laborious process by loudly assuming they now wanted him to try them on for size. There were various titters and embarrassed eyes. So he kept insisting. The trick was humiliated and thrilled by the public display. There he stood in a suit with a briefcase with a skinheaded tough in fatigues drawing raucous attention to them both. Little by little, performance was becoming a larger share of Apollo's hustling skills.

He was also taking on the poignant narcissism of the aging outlaw—the type who spouts testimonials to his own self-worth. One time a drunken trick sent him from the after-hours club to find a slice and two packs of cigarettes, one pack as a tip for Apollo. When he finally found the cigarettes and the pizza at that ungodly hour, he brought them back to the club. But he was so stoned that he never counted the change. The trick accused him of housing some of it and threatened to tell the manager. "Nothing against you," he slurred drunkenly. "I just wouldn't want to put other johns in danger from somebody stole from me, you understand?"

Apollo stood tall and stuck out his chest: "You tell him, and this what he gonna say. 'This individual Perk been coming to my establishment for years and I have confidence in him. Why don't you go to that nowhere bar up the street to see if you can find any dick to suck. Then maybe you come back here and won't complain so much.'" It didn't matter to Apollo that he didn't even know who the manager was.

The man really did complain to the manager, and Apollo was thrown out for the night. His charades of honor were thin protection against winter weather and the fact that without the trick he'd be sleeping in the cardboard village tonight. After the bust of Tina's After-hours, the whole block had been cleaned up. The village had moved to the docks, where the inhabitants surrounded it with a half-circle of trash-can fires for warmth.

In order to get there with the shot he was saving, he had to pass Tina's and the old sex theater. Across from Tina's the big hole of demolition had been filled by an improbable skyscraper with a big banner advertising condos. Midtown had become a patchwork of crumbling deco and new, half-empty towers. A fragmented rhetoric jumped out at you as dying after-theater restaurants tried to speak of old sophistication and showmanship against the new faceless and monstrous facades. None of it fit together, and it was a little like Apollo's mind. As if to contribute to this schizoid display, his thoughts kept up a frantic soliloquy as he moved toward his cardboard home. He added false plans and tired legends to the decrepit buildings collapsing under the weight of the faceless new.

Underpinning it he saw Mrs. Huxton as entrepreneur of a new midtown empire that had savvily adapted to the new rules. She would combine the old tricks of selling fast kicks with fresh mass marketing. In his mind he saw the megaclub she was planning in deco that recalled the old days of Times Square but was bolstered by new neon. Her waiters all wore jackets, and the hustlers and the johns were all top-drawer. With rich tricks coming to the neighborhood, he was sure his fate would change.

When he got to the cardboard village, he saw that one of the plastic garbage-bag tents was empty. Quickly he dived into it and pulled the flap down. Inside it was a small kerosene stove with a little fuel left. He lit it for warmth and used it to cook up his shot. The new shot was good and smoothed out the running monologue in his mind. With a feeling of luxury, he began a new round of legend making.

*My life: a hand of cards played illegally in the trashiest of places, thrown down between shots of the best dope there is. That's why I'm used to the wild cards falling. Being on the edge is the only thing that ever gave me the feeling of being alive. Let's face the truth: if my only friend tried to stop me from doing half the things I done, I would a killed him like that, if only it didn't involve too much trouble or me going out of the way.*

*What gives me my legendary strength is knowing that when I suffer, it ain't no big deal. Come to think of it, I saw my mother suffer at the hands of my father, which was something you are supposed to get used to. When shit happens every day, the eye of the storm is something an old soldier like myself might even seek out. I'm a big bad elephant stomping toward the pit, just like my dad.*

"Dad" was like a pebble dropped accidentally into the hollow well of the soliloquy. It brought everything to an abrupt, echoing standstill. Instead, he imagined the prematurely old father figures at the shooting gallery, slapping their thighs and laughing, shouting, "Right on, baby, right on!"

*

My bourgeois friends formed a reliable support group, now that I was out of the hospital and having trouble being on my own. How happy they were to see me back in the fold after my perplexing detour into the underworld. Now they were willing to run out and fill prescriptions or help me figure my dwindling accounts. A couple of times a week they brought hot meals or came over and cooked.

I'd gone to the hospital in a terrific panic that had knocked all the tongue-in-cheek philosophizing out of me. After they'd brought the fever down and had gotten rid of the thick coating of thrush on my mouth and throat, I became a cooperative patient. I suppose there's no greater brainwasher than the lifesavers who take your fate into their hands no matter how brief the respite they offer becomes. As a matter of fact, it occurs to me that the legendary French Bluebeard Gilles de Rais supposedly heightened his pleasure in torturing children by setting himself up as a fake savior who ran into the room and stopped his henchmen. Then, as the saved child sighed with relief in his arms, he switched and became the torturers' leader. Accordingly, as time passed in the hospital, the medical attitudes that had seemed so plausible gradually led to conclusions that seemed more and more deranged. It was, apparently, their business to keep the cells of my body functioning. But what they in euphemism called "quality of life" was considered an entirely private affair. This lack of concern for the libido once again alienated me, and I began thinking of Apollo and wondering where he was living and how he was getting by. It was obvious to me that he'd gone back to dope, and partly because lengthening his life span was not his top priority.

Thoughts of this nature would torture me as I hooked up to my intravenous gadgets twice a day for my Ganciclovir infusion. Despite, or perhaps partly because of, my friends' good intentions, I was getting more and more sullen and withdrawn. Sometimes I even lapsed into an infantile state in which I berated Apollo in my mind for abandoning me. It didn't matter that he had never learned to show more than inklings of supportiveness, like getting me some orange *juice once. What I unreasonably expected was for him to realize that he represented a world. Without it, I'd come crawling back to who I was supposed to be, despising myself all the way. But, of course, his world was notoriously unhelpful when the chips were down.*

*I was preparing for the evening infusion when a key began to turn in the lock. He walked in as if he hadn't been gone more than a few hours, though the change in his appearance made it seem like years. He was still handsome, almost strikingly so, but his physique showed a new loutishness, and his millimeter-long haircut made his usual saucer eyes look a little slitty. Or perhaps it was the puffiness of his face that had whittled them down.*

*I didn't challenge the sudden visit or question the fairness of his still using his key. Instead, what little heart there was left in me beat with anticipation . . . as if, despite my knowing better, he'd come bringing some new antidote to pain or secret of oblivion.*

*In a strange charade of casualness, we sat on the couch "catching up." Both of us were painfully aware of his new manner, the booming voice, the heavy-handed boasts. He claimed to be proud of his independence and vowing to "make it on my own." Maybe he'd go to school, he said, after he landed a construction job. He said he was living with a buddy who asked for no rent because "he believes in me." But when I kept repeatedly asking him for details, he turned sullen and said, "What you all up in my business for?"*

*"That's something you'd never say if you weren't getting high," I said in the ridiculous pose of the reformer.*

*"So what the fuck!" he answered and picked up a glass as if he were about to fling it against the wall.*

*He was, it turns out, basically homeless. And when he saw the pain in my eyes caused by the avowal, he took advantage of it by asking if he could take a shower. In my pitiful need to fantasize for a few moments that our domestic arrangement remained, I agreed, though I knew I was no longer in any position, physically* or financially, to have somebody in my home who was in constant need of dope.

But for the moment he played house by weaving out of his soldier-of-fortune hand-me-downs into an image of the adolescent I'd known. It was astounding. Aside from being somewhat heavier, the naked image brought back the budding sensual Apollo of a few months ago. But then, how much could he have really changed in such a short time?

He ran to the scale and weighed himself and seemed happy that he'd put on weight. Weight is, I know, a valuable commodity among street people, as it is among us HIV-positives. In an attempt to make the scene even more domestic, I decided to do the infusion usual for that time of day. In his underpants, he helped me set up the paraphernalia. But instead of taking his shower, as I infused, he began to cook some dope in a spoon over his lighter. When I threw him a reproachful glance from my tubed-and-needled installation, he winked and gestured toward the stove. "Remember how I always said I wanted to cook? Well, I ended up doing a lot of it."

So he had his medication, and I had mine. I knew that even if what he took were prescribed by a doctor, it would have been unlikely to be portrayed as an escape from mental anguish in the direction of pleasure—even if that doctor knew Apollo was using it to numb the discomfort of having to sleep in the freezing outdoors. The doctor would have to use the alibi of observable symptoms, such as an improvement in sleep patterns or more manageable behavior or a decrease in negative verbal expression. That was their only lexicon.

Our separate infusions became a perverse duet in which he was getting happier only for the moment and I was killing off germs that were bound in the future to return. In the face of the human condition, is there really such a thing as "medicine"? I was tempted to ask for half a teaspoon of his concoction mixed with mine. But the big-brother memory of the hospital's rescue from my last trauma squelched the impulse with ideological guilt.

*When he finished his shot, he sat and watched me continuing mine, which takes about forty-five minutes. He was fascinated by the catheter implanted in my chest and asked a lot of questions about how it worked and how it was maintained. He was much less interested in the substance and its purpose than in the way it was administered. Junkies can go on forever about needles and penetration, how to locate veins. I now had a passage that was permanently available, so I explained how the Hickman's catheter on my chest allowed fluids to travel directly into my circulatory system by way of the heart and how an internal valve in the device prevented flowback.*

*His growing familiarity with my predicament lowered more defenses and increased the fantasy feeling that he had come home. Sensing this, he lolled in his high on the couch, and our warm and gentle chatter continued. It was the least anguished of my twice-a-day infusions that I had ever experienced. But when his remarks made it clear that he thought he had moved back in, I had to speak up.*

*There was no way, I explained, that I could deal with his problems in my condition. He took the remark as a blunt, blanket rejection and coldly informed me that he didn't need anybody's help, including mine. When I said he'd misinterpreted me and that I'd always care about what happened to him, he cut me off angrily, then burst into tears and renewed his pleas to start living here again.*

*I've got to admit that as thrilled as I was by the short session of playing house, and as radical as I liked to think I was in terms of security and health, the idea of dealing with him brought out the new reactionary in me. Infusion schedules, uninterrupted rest, and pinching pennies had edged out some of the old appetites and squelched my perverse bravado. I wanted to hold on to my shrinking island, so I stuck firm.*

*His breaking down had humiliated him. He dressed quickly and sullenly without bothering with the shower. He put on the fatigues* like a man reinstalling his pitiless shell. Using the boots for empha-sis, he stomped about the apartment. Brazenly he threw open the refrigerator and stuffed his mouth with food. Then he tremblingly marched to the VCR and started to unplug it. The action was accompanied by a stern and nasty monologue about the "need to survive out there," but his voice was shaking.

I was still hooked up to my contraption and couldn't get up in the middle of my infusion. So I challenged him to name how much money he thought I owed him. I'd learned some lessons in life, I said somewhat sarcastically, with him as teacher. But I didn't want to pay a higher rate than I did when he sold me sex. As far as I was concerned, the total education wasn't worth more than about fifty dollars, one sexual experience, and the VCR was worth a hundred and eighty.

Crazily wounded, he tossed the VCR on the couch. Why don't you take that vase, I said. It's worth about fifty dollars. I couldn't sell it for shit on the street, he snapped. So, in black burlesque I suggested more objects in the apartment, purposely choosing those few remaining selections that would fetch little price outside the realm of yuppiedom. Becoming part of the strange comedy routine, he picked up each classical CD, Italian bath brush, StairMaster, Noguchi lamp, or abstract silkscreen I indicated and dropped it in laconic rejection on the floor at my feet. Then, in an explosion of rage, he started tearing all the drawers from the dresser. He threw the contents on the floor and pawed through them for money. He ripped the couple of dollars from my wallet and tossed the wallet in the sink. Then he smashed a wooden chair against the table, split-ting both. He shook the VCR in my face, screaming, You think I need your shit? and smashed it on the floor as well. The neighbors below started pounding on their ceiling. Frantically he stripped some silk shirts from the closet and stuffed them into a shopping bag. He threw my CDs on top, then stalked out the door.

*

*Since that time, my mind has circled the robbery again and again, as if it were some monolith, an incomprehensible edifice of secret motives, secret fear. I've queried each sealed entrance of this horrible structure, which can produce cold violence and betrayal. But I'm locked out of it and half hoping not to get in, to find that self inside I've been avoiding.*

*Now that I know he is gone for good, I feel that old protective veil of excitement receding like an illusion, like someone being deprived of a drug. This must be how death comes, a peeling away.*

*Was I just a naive bourgeois who broke the rules in a depraved context? Was the cure of the leper—through enough daring and sacrifice—just an illusion? I lie in bed with eyes closed, arms spread, and palms turned up, still trying to expel this pain into the atmosphere, where all are forced to breathe its fumes.*

At one moment he wanted to hurt Apollo so much that it would even penetrate the heroin and both could feel the pain. At other times he reasoned that doing time would get the boy off heroin and it was his responsibility to turn him in. Being a full-time medical patient had, he realized, instilled a sense of "civic duty." If Apollo had done this to him, a sick friend, what would he do to others? Finally, he saw his snitching to the cops as a simple cry for contact, the only way left to reach out toward him.

When he called the cops and described the cardboard village and where Apollo had said it was located, they did not react with surprise. If they'd wanted to, they could have taken the time to comb Apollo out of the neighborhood haunts. But going to the trouble of recognizing Apollo's face, which resembled that of thousands of mug shots of people his age in the precinct files, required more motivation. Now they had two charges, the assault of Casio and the robbing of a sick man whose apartment he'd trashed.

\*

Their unmarked car cruised toward the village in the early morning, as the fires were growing paler against the putrid light. Two chubby near-rookies had been sent out to do the dirty work. They were to pick up a youth who'd been wanted for more than seven months, just because somebody had put it on the day's agenda.

Both cops were white. Both would have said that they'd "paid their dues." One had nursed an alcoholic father and had turned the tide of family do-nothings by becoming a cop. The other was the son of an abusive mother with a bitter vengeance for "those who preyed on innocent people."

Like some outlandish antigen attacking an already sick body, their blue-and-white police car pulled up to the squalid cardboard village. With a melancholy disgust, they watched a man crawl out of one of the two plastic tents and take his morning shit into the gray river. He didn't fit the description. Their suspect was much younger and not as dark-skinned. Finally, they saw him, climbing from the tent in his stained fatigues. His head was still nearly hairless, and his sallow face was pinched into withdrawal. He was vomiting thin liquid in the dawn light as shaking passed through his thick torso.

When he was done, he wiped his mouth on his sleeve and walked jerkily to the sidewalk. As he began moving north, the car pulled away from the curb and began tracking him at a crawl. Then they pulled over and called out his name.

"Apollo Nelson?"

"Name's Perk."

"What kind of name's that?"

"Spanish. Perdido. Perdido T. Colón."

"Get over here, we want to see your I.D."

He reluctantly approached the cop car, and the two men

leapt out. They laid him out over the hood and made him stretch his arms over his head. As soon as they began to frisk him, they pulled out his works and a knife. They sat him in the front seat of the car. One climbed back behind the wheel and the other got in back. As his nose ran and his face twitched from withdrawal, they began firing questions.

"Why no I.D., Perdido?"

"I lost it."

"What's your address?"

"I ain't got one."

"Why aren't you working?"

"I can't find a job."

"You know this needle's illegal?"

"I'm waiting to get in a program."

"What's your social security number?"

"Three-five-six, oh-nine, seven-eight-nine-one."

The cops phoned in the name and number and came up with nothing. The stink from the suspect was beginning to fill up the car. They were fairly certain they had the right man but didn't want to make an error. The waste of time and space for bringing in somebody and booking him just because he had works on him didn't win you friends at the precinct. It was primarily because of this that they lapsed into a desperate note of levity. Perhaps the grimness of the sick junkie stinking up the car fueled the need for entertainment. Or maybe they hoped their brand of humor would spur him into an infraction that would make it worth bringing him in.

"Bet there's plenty of free pussy over there in that village."

"Don't know."

"Why not, you a dick junkie or something?"

"Yeah, are you one of those sperm slurpers?"

"You should try a little muff now and then. I bet you'd forget all about being a faggot."

"Sneezing in the suitcase is much more fun than chewing on the stick."

"I guess you two cops would know."

"You calling us faggots, you dumb punk?"

Apollo put his hand on the door, but the cop sped up and pulled so tight to a parked car that he could not open it.

"Don't try to jump on us, punk."

"We're telling you now that you're cased."

"We got a reason to believe that you're Apollo Nelson."

"You better own up now if you are."

"Next time we see you we won't be so friendly."

"Don't lie to us, faggot!"

"What the fuck do you want?"

When they saw the wave move through his stomach and his cheeks balloon out like a squirrel's, they knew he was about to upchuck all over his lap and the car. The cop in back dove forward to roll down the window. He shoved Apollo's head outside but banged it against the window of the other car. The cop at the wheel pulled the vehicle forward so that the suspect could vomit onto the street. He grabbed him by the collar and yanked forward so that the stream of vomit would clear the side of the cop car.

When the heaving subsided, Apollo slumped against the window with his head hanging out. With force out of nowhere, he dove through the opening until he had emerged to his waist. Then, kicking the hands and face of the cops who grabbed for him, he squirmed and crashed onto the pavement. He reared to his feet and shot up the street.

# XVIII

Tina's last performance took place early that following spring. The notice for it read:

TINA SHAUGHNESSY

APPLETON FUNERAL PARLOR

TUESDAY, 5:00-8:00 P.M.

ONE NIGHT ONLY

To the Irish barkeeps of the neighborhood, "One Night Only" meant there would not be an extended wake. But a large majority of the queens saw the notice in theatrical terms. Tina's private war against illness, like Jacqueline Susann's, had been fought silently and alone. Although Baby Pop was still living with her, he had not known that she had AIDS until her first—and only—stay in the hospital with pneumonia and TB.

Now that she had gone so swiftly, the fact that she had taken him in had another level of meaning, which gave his fears and hopes new depth. Well-fed and sensibly medicated at fifteen, he was the only male image at the funeral. Not one of Tina's protégés or any of the queens' boyfriends had bothered to show up.

Baby Pop could also have been considered her widower, since her death had canceled his domestic situation. In a few days he'd have to vacate her house. Bereft and touched, he stood staring down at the heavily made-up face in the coffin, girding himself for his male role in tonight's serious event. A few queens approached and offered their condolences in the need to ritualize him as husband.

Inside him, a rage burned at what he considered Tina's maltreatment at the dreaded hospital—the same one that had housed his father only as a prelude to arrest, that had diagnosed Baby Pop with HIV, and that employed the *cafre* of a rich doctor who tried to trade drugs for ass. Bleeding into his mind was one incident in particular, when a nurse had yanked an intravenous needle out of Tina's arm and hadn't noticed that the puncture in her flesh was spouting. Half the bed sheet had been drenched as the nurse strolled casually out of the room. Baby Pop ran down the hall to get her with the distinct impression that queens and homeboys didn't speak her language. He also remembered the doctor's contemptuous dumping into a wastebasket of the fish dinner Baby Pop had brought, even though Tina had begged for it. As far as the doctor was concerned, his fasting regime in response to her backed-up liver was more important than the fact that she'd said she was famished. At that moment Baby Pop had made a mental note to go to law school and sue that doctor. As far as he was concerned, Tina had died of starvation.

The queens were thick in attendance and on this occasion displayed a rare sense of modesty. Baby Pop had never seen them so subdued or dressed down. He'd also never seen them with so little makeup and this early in the evening, before it was even dark. Their heels were low and their hemlines long. To mourn they had abandoned the exaggeration and parody of dress and gesture with which many tackled situations. Quite a few of them knew they were HIV-positive, or they were dealing with full-blown AIDS. In addition, the death of Tina raised the question of who could ever again open a queen's bar.

In the harsh fluorescent lights of this funeral parlor, which was one of the few that accepted the corpses of queens or people who had died of AIDS, the effect was one of a sorority of pallid sisters squelched by drugs or disease, yet darkly determined to push ahead in sullen dignity. The five-o'clock shadows peeking through the foundation of some were no cause for irony, as no one at this moment was using fantasy to face the grim horizon of the future.

With their innate sense of ritual, they revered Tina's last appearance in a group Ave Maria and farewell kisses to the corpse. Then the hushed room with its tired faces seemed to wilt the air itself. The unfriendly wattage of the fluorescent lights pressed on everybody's spirits. One by one they wandered into the reception room to have a smoke.

They gravitated toward Angelita, who'd flown in from her new affluent life in California after her very recent sex change. Here was a positive image around which they could rally and from whom they could seek advice.

They asked her how the operation could have changed her legs, which now looked so much more feminine and shapely. Angelita kindly told them that they too could improve the texture and silhouette of their legs by wearing several pairs of nylons—as many layers as they could stand. The pressure was kind of isometric and toned them up.

They admired her pineapple-shaped bouffant, and she generously explained how you do it: you freeze the hair around liter-size Coca-Cola bottles with a ton of hair spray, then you pull the bottles out and tie the giant curls together.

Finally, they touched on the operation and asked how long it took to heal. Angelita said she'd been told she had to stop hustling for two months, and that she had another month to go. One queen asked if it was true that the depth of your pussy was based on the size of your dick, which she'd heard kind of got turned inside out during the operation. Did that mean that people with little dicks would end up with shallow pussies? Angelita calmly responded that that was a question the asker should discuss with her doctor. Then another queen piped up and asked whether doctor-made pussies were higher up on the groin instead of right between the legs, since a guy's cock and balls were higher up on the body than a born-woman's pussy. Angelita said that was true but that there were variations in the way that guys were hung. The base of some dicks began quite low, and those would make better pussies.

Then she loosened up completely and told a funny story about her two visits to Leavenworth prison. Her wealthy sponsor had spent six months there for running an escort service. When she'd gone to visit him the first time, the female guards in the women's section had searched her thoroughly, because of the epidemic of drug smuggling. They'd found what she had between her legs but let her go through the women's line anyway. When she came back a month later, they'd searched her again. You can imagine their astonishment when the searchers discovered that the dick had disappeared.

The story of the stymied prison guards livened things up and got the queens chattering. It soon became apparent that life had started up again and would go on. Even the sobbing Mercedes blew her nose and began to gossip. She confided in another queen that Angelita had always said, "Let's see who'll be the first to get my pussy once I've got it made." The two conjectured about how rich or how powerful the lucky man would be.

From his position across the room, Baby Pop gravely watched them reanimate. As the only official man at the proceedings, he had appropriately avoided the girlish rap. Instead, he began wondering if he should bother mentioning to Angelita that his dad was getting out of jail this weekend. But as he watched her, he couldn't match her successful image to the present condition of his dad. Instead, he considered the possibility of living with Casio on his social security. Since his father still had trouble walking, he might need Baby Pop's help. And he himself knew that physical deprivation could cause another early slip back into the complications of AIDS. He was determined to continue his healthy lifestyle, and maybe the release of Casio would give it a chance.

As dwindling as life within his sphere may have seemed, unbeknownst to him another chapter was just taking place. Baby Pop would probably have had trouble remembering the homeless girl he'd met and had sex with during his period of starvation and camping out at Grand Central. The encounter had flowed almost unconsciously from the fatigue and desperation of both. On this very day, the labor from their fleeting union began. The birth was in line with Baby Pop's family, where generations had usually occurred in the slim increments of fifteen or sixteen years. If seventy-eight-year-old Abuela had lived only another eight months, she would have become—probably also unknowingly—the great-great-great-grandmother of the child.

# XIX

It was June, and the construction workers were used to the mangy, outspoken street person who'd made the sidewalk in front of the site his home. He would ask for handouts and relentlessly heckle when anybody shook his head or said no. Sometimes his desperation and black wit were entertaining, but a couple of times the bum got out of hand and a wrench or hammer had to be raised to the insolent face or thrown at his head as he ducked.

By July, he'd become a kind of mascot at the site. The guys began tossing him their lunch leftovers, which he stuffed down before you could blink an eye. Then one of them passed him a cast-off pair of construction boots, which he sported by rolling up the cuffs of his dirty fatigues to show the tops. He stomped around the site all day like some fantasy construction worker or *Playgirl* stallion.

His wisecracks and preposterous charades made the day pass faster. Some of the guys took a liking to him despite his cracked lips, stinking clothing, and sallow-colored skin. He walked and talked like a mature animal who had been down for a thousand years. But little kindnesses brought out the kid in him and brought a grateful gleam to his eyes.

Probably because he thought he was God's gift to manhood, he'd dubbed himself with the unbelievable name "Apollo." When he appeared in his rags and with his matted hair, the guys enjoyed asking him to strike bodybuilding poses to prove he was a Greek god.

By August he started turning up with merchandise suitable for the guys or their girlfriends. He'd fence gold and silver chains, an occasional pocketbook, or a shirt still bearing a price tag. The guys spent part of lunch or their coffee break bargaining for the hot goods, ribbing and baiting the mange-ass, or tossing him loose change. They gave him errands or shit work, which he performed eagerly. Most surprising was his unquenchable interest in the project, a sleek new dance club to be built on the site of this old Irish bar. Improbably, he claimed to be a personal friend of the one ultimately responsible for the contract, whom he named as a certain Mrs. Huxton.

Orders, however, came from the ex-owner of the joint, a cranky eighty-year-old man named O'Hara, who always chased away the mange-ass when he saw him and always complained about how much better the place and the neighborhood had been when the space was a simple Blarney Stone and types like that never came this far downtown.

Each feature that was added to the new interior as it neared completion—the svelte booths, strobe lights, and aluminum bar—seemed to thrill the mange-ass more. He stepped up running errands for the crew and doing odd jobs at the site, talked more and more often about the important role he would play in this business and about opening night. He was sure he'd become a waiter, doubling as bartender some evenings; and he had even designed in his head the sharp vest, white shirt, and crisp bow tie he said was waiting in his size.

Then, near the end of the afternoon, he'd disappear for a while and return in a changed mood. He'd be out of it and vague and lost in his own world. He'd be half-smiling and still and could stare at his boot tip for an hour. Some of the guys said he had to be high, but he became so manageable that nobody pushed the issue. His cranky face would be relaxed into a moonlike glow, and his mouth would look drugged and sensual.

It was at such moments that he'd ask the boss in a sweet and childlike voice if he could crash out at the site for the night. If the boss said no, he'd pout and beg like a practiced whore.

It was unusual to lock a street person up with expensive installations in progress. But sometimes the boss would give in and let the baby-doll mange-ass have his way. They'd pack up for the night and bolt up the tools and other valuables while he climbed onto a shelf or bench. As they locked him in, he'd fall out in a happy delirium, mumbling about his Huxton lady and the details of their joint glorious venture.

*Maybe it is no dream that the veiled woman lunches with slow elegance in the midtown Brazilian restaurant. She wears white gloves. Under the veil her looks have been plucked by tweezers and made up a shade lighter than her own skin. From the way the waiters dog up to her every need or hang at the table to light the cigarette in her old, trembling hand, it's obvious she still has clout. More, anyway, than that wide-eyed but aged blonde in a suburban getup who seems to hang on her every word.*

*At the moment, the blonde is gabbing on about her fabulous middle-aged son, who has grown up to be an investigator but still lives under her nose. She boasts one minute about his glorious* career, then sinks into her fears for his safety, trying to pry information out of the older, higher-class woman about a babe she thought he was dating.

The older one lets her gab on, because she knows the more innocent one has always thought of herself as her sweetheart, her protégée, and can't resist spilling the beans those few times they now come together. She keeps some things she knows of this son close to her chest for fear of upsetting her simple friend, 'cause as a businesswoman she understands facets of him that his mother perhaps could not deal with. Both dames cluck and nod and shake their heads like old harpies, so that anybody peeking from afar would take them for your typical senior citizens lunching.

In the back of the mind of the veiled one, new plans are being hatched. Of these she drops only carefully phrased hints to the dumb blonde. This venture will outrank every sex palace and club the neighborhood has ever known. Ancient as she is, she prides herself on her savvy business sense, which she feels keeps her going. A slew of old haunts have closed in Times Square, but she won't be left behind by the big change. The city may be planning a new convention center, but she's devising ways of entertaining the tired male with the new modern methods. There is no way, she realizes with her sixty-odd years of experience, that mens' needs and tastes will be chased forever by the new tight-ass goody-goodies from Manhattan. And there'll always be those needing work, who'll get stuck in her net.

Those together countries like Holland and Denmark that made a smooth industry of adult entertainment provide the inspiration for this new club. One entire room won't ever have a liquor license. Those between the ages of eighteen and twenty-one would be stuck there, waiting all night for the johns who drink, dance, or dine in pleasanter accommodations above.

Then they'll come down and make their selection. So strict will be the surveillance and so hand-picked the clients and personnel that *the old betrayals and fucked-up behavior won't have a chance. In fact, even intimate encounters will occur in a special wing so there'll never be a complaint from customers that a trick ended up getting mugged or beat up in a hotel room.*

*Now the luncheon takes a turn, as the two begin their grievance session; bitter stories of betrayal are the old girls' bread and butter. In that self-pitying but turned-on tone of old ladies who lunch, the blonde tells the story of her husband's fuck-up, which the veiled one has heard hundreds of times before. Her story is the one of disappointment and loss that some grow to treasure. But when the veiled one launches into her tales of things gone wrong for her, they leave the domestic shit far behind. Though fellatio for money, drugs injected into festering holes, and deadly diseases hovering everywhere are mostly left out by the veiled one, the stories make the blonde's eyes big as saucers.*

*Distant-acting as the veiled one is, she keeps close track of all the individuals who make up her world. She has her favorites and pets who she thinks she nurtures as projects in rehabilitation. One by one they betray her and throw away their own chances for a secure future. Such disappointments have hardened her heart but also make her a wronged mother rather than a purely get-over businesswoman. She can claim that each time she reaches out, it's returned by shit and betrayal. But this time, high technology and brilliant marketing will eliminate all of that. The new business, like clockwork, will be programmed for fabulous success.*

He waited on the corner with the razor blade in his mouth, on the flat of his tongue and pressed gently up against the roof. Maybe the wheelchair would fool them into thinking he was an easy mark. But he could jump up from it using his arms on the rests and get to them with that blade before they knew it.

Ever since Casio had come up here to 112th to cop and been taken off by a laughing teenage junkie, he never showed up without that razor blade. The kid had tipped over the chair and gone through his pockets. But now with the blade, Casio was ready for anybody. Then he'd cop and roll up to a cab, which took him to the SRO hotel room seven blocks away.

This time, however, he had an escort. Right across the street Baby Pop was buying a dozen eggs and two cans of Chunky Chicken soup. He was going to cook up a feast for Casio on their illegal SRO hot plate.

Casio copped just as Baby Pop was heading back. The guy who'd passed him the stuff he recognized as Carlos the hustler. He wondered if the guy remembered he'd been a manager at that theater where Carlos used to turn tricks. Casio hadn't been to the old haunts once since he got out of jail. And Baby Pop had informed him that most of them did not exist anymore.

With his stuff in his pocket, Casio gave Baby Pop a sign. The boy started to wheel him back toward their SRO room.

Baby Pop had told him that the *cabrón* who'd wasted him was doing really bad. He looked like shit, never turned tricks, and God knows where he got the money for drugs these days. But Casio kept planning anyway to get over to the old 'hood with the blade in his mouth and see what kind of trouble he could cause for the *cabrón*. The only problem was, he needed a cab to get around. By the time he'd spent his social security money on the dope, there was only enough left for food.

When he was wheeled into the elevator, he opened his mouth and carefully picked out the razor blade. In his pocket was the new bag, and upstairs a comfortable chair and a TV with cable stations were waiting. Baby Pop was standing in back of him with dinner in the bag. He'd cook it up and also help Casio do his shot if he was having trouble finding a vein. Casio made up his mind that as soon as he himself went back into rehab and got off the dope, he was going to give some serious thought to organizing finances. He really wanted that boy to go to college.

They hit their floor and Baby Pop pulled open the elevator. He wheeled Casio down the hall toward the room, where everything was kept as neat and balanced as Abuela had used to keep it. There was a framed picture of her on the dresser, and Casio had pressed the lock of gray hair inside.

All in all, things were going better than they had in a long time. What more could a man ask for when he had a roof and some food, no trouble from bitches, enough dope, and a son by his side? Whenever Casio laid eyes on his son, he'd think of Monica, whom he resembled, and wonder if Florida was keeping her away from drugs. Then he'd think of Angelita and wonder what she felt like as a real woman now. Spitefully he'd fantasize that her pussy was too shallow for his tool. He'd seen her dick once, and it really hadn't amounted to much.


Apollo hated the whole bunch of them. They belonged together: Huxton, Pargero, Pargero's mother, and maybe even his own white mom. Here he was, standing in front of the new club he'd built with his own hands, and they wouldn't let him in. It was just down the street from a restaurant owned by a fancy nigger who used to be a model. Between the two establishments they kept the block clean, sending out white bouncers with attitude to do hourly sweepings.

He couldn't believe who he saw entering that lounge. No one belonged to the old crowd. Those that were left, like Mercedes and Cubby, were all on Eighth or Ninth Avenue, without any bar to go to. The ones going to this new club were white and collegiate looking, with haircuts that probably cost a lot. It was all part of a plan, he realized in his most lucid moments, to clean up Times Square. But who had devised this plan, and how had he enlisted so many supporters? Part of the plan had obviously been what turned Forty-Second Street, the main drag, into a ghost town. But the joke was on them. Instead of getting rid of the dealers, hookers, and users of the Deuce, they'd scattered them. Now they infiltrated every block of Eighth and Ninth Avenues.

As Apollo watched the couples or groups filing into the club, he noticed that some of them clasped theater programs and not one seemed to be looking for a hustler. Well, maybe they just had that white shyness but were different once they got inside. But when Apollo tried to tell the doorman he was a friend of Mrs. Huxton's, he said they had no idea whom he was talking about. This was a private club and Apollo had better move on.

Cruising outside was worse. The whitebreads traveled in packs. When you waylaid them on Eighth Avenue or threw them some of your strut, they got scared. They started to walk faster and said they'd call the police. These guys didn't like muscles unless they'd been made in a high-tech gym and were packed in the right clothes. Let the sissies suck each other's pussies then. In his day they'd been looking for real men.

He took to coming back to the block with the restaurant and club with shopping bags of boosted merchandise in his grimy hands. If he had the right merchandise, even the yuppie fags stopped for it. A shirt with a Ralph Lauren label or the right watch style caught a greedy eye. He made some sales, but they were cheap bastards and never gave in until they'd got over.

Weeks went by like this, and nothing was easy. He had to sneak onto the block while the bouncers weren't doing their sweep. If they saw him, they'd chase him with their bats and trash his merchandise. Then one day he was nodding a couple doors from the club when what he considered the inevitable happened. A black limousine pulled up. But instead of a bevy of fags on a rented joy ride, a gorgeous woman climbed out who looked a lot like Angelita. With her was a fierce-looking middle-aged dude. He was so craggy-faced that he looked like he'd been carved from granite. He had a pharaoh's jaw with a Kirk Douglas hole in the center of his chin. His head swiveled like a gun turret and his eyes pierced Apollo like lasers. Then he took a black notebook from his tuxedo pocket and his hand moved staccato to jot something down. Giving Apollo a deathlike smile, he took the jeweled arm of the beauty and marched her into the club.

Who would believe the account of a man whose mind was riddled by drugs and months of deprivation? How likely is it that a down-and-out junkie with a year-old crime could even make any cop's list? But in Apollo's mind the man was Pargero. And the fact that he'd seen him going into the club he thought belonged to Mrs. Huxton only clinched the conspiracy theories in his mind.

There was, he thought, some justice in being busted by a cop in a swank tuxedo, especially one with a fierce and foxy transsexual on his arm. And there was, he admitted, no longer any reason to resist him. Jail almost seemed inviting, 'cause the world was mixed up and everything happened upside down.

If junkie queens somehow became real girls and rode in on the arms of the law itself, while cops went after drag queens and rented limousines, why shouldn't he have to pay for a crime he barely remembered the feeling of committing? Apparently, you could never predict how your actions would bear fruit. Maggots grew on yesterday's live meat. Then the creatures sprouted see-through wings that looked classy in some light. Soon they too would be part of the dung heap. So, if Pargero wanted him, he could take his body.

Like a faithful whore waiting for the beating from her pimp, Apollo waited near the club for the evening to end and the cop to resurface. And in the wee hours he did, the babe looking flushed and pressing closer to his arm. But though Apollo stared brazenly and sensually into his eyes as if to say, Come on and get me sucker and make my day, old Rushmore breezed right past him and into their waiting limo. The door slammed shut, locking Apollo out and leaving him where he'd always be.

If Pargero didn't want to take him in this megaworld of cold blank stone, he'd go back to the hotbed of the first mix-up.

He'd go home.

He went to the phone and called 911.

*911? This is Apollo T. Nelson himself, and today's your lucky day. 'Cause my ass is the most wanted one in town. Check your books, and I'll be waiting for you on my mom's roof. I ain't gonna give you no address, and I ain't gonna turn myself in. Send the faggot detective Pargero to get me. He'll tell you I'm wanted for attempted murder, if you don't believe what I'm saying.*

244

*Don't ask where I am—I told you I'll be at my mom's. I can't even get in the club I helped build, so where the fuck else do I have to go? Only cops and sex-changes who hated their own dicks can get in now. Remember to send the faggot Pargero. I'll be waiting for his sweet face to come and take it raw.*

There was no bread on the roof for anybody this time. It had been almost a year since he'd been up here. But even so, he nourished the mad hope that the pigeon would swoop downward out of nowhere. He imagined the touch of its claws on his face as he heard his mother two floors below rising to begin her morning rituals.

Her chanting floated softly in the air. He thought of her standing over him with the sun peeking through her blond hair. *The bird is eating out of your mouth again* ... Although the chanting was saying something different, he imagined it was repeating those words again and again. He lay back and waited for the arrival of the bad detective. In his mind he saw his mother in her Indian cotton blouse and sweatpants go to the door to let him in. He waited and waited for her betraying finger to point up to the roof. The hours were passing but he couldn't keep up with them. They flew right by him like something too high to grasp. Slowly but surely, they lightened the sky, leaving him stuck in the same dark moment like the moth in tar.

He called and called for the bird.